Mice 1961 has notes of Carrington and Oates and Coover. I was captivated by its sibling stars and even more by Levine's syntactical dazzlements. She sculpts every sentence.

—JoAnna Novak

Stacey Levine ignores lyricism as an evolutionary dead end . . . It's not that [she] isn't funny or that she doesn't forge phrases and sentences of throat-clutching beauty. It's just that her effort to dissect humankind's propensity for neuroses, fallacies, and other inanities requires measured drollery and surgical concision.

—Donna Seaman, *Bookforum*

One of the most interesting writers working in America today, startling and idiosyncratic in the best sense.

—Stephen Beachy

Smart and playful, [her] fictions are also deadly serious about the world they reinvent and the realistic style purporting to mirror this world . . . Levine's protagonists reveal the hollowness of contemporary literary realism and the questionable expectations it reflects.

—Pedro Ponce, *Review of Contemporary Fiction*

ALSO BY STACEY LEVINE

The Girl with Brown Fur
Frances Johnson
Dra—
My Horse and Other Stories

Mice 1961

Stacey Levine

VERSE CHORUS PRESS

© 2024 Stacey Levine

All rights reserved. No part of this book may be reproduced, stored in or introduced into a retrieval system, or transmitted in any form or by any means (digital, electronic, mechanical, photocopying, recording, or otherwise), without the prior written permission of the publisher, except by a reviewer, who may quote brief passages in a review.

Published by Verse Chorus Press, Portland, Oregon.
www.versechorus.com

Cover image: Still from Věra Chytilová's film *Strop* (1961).
Used by permission of Národní filmový archiv, Czech Republic.

Copyedited by Allison Dubinsky
Book design by Steve Connell | *steveconnell.net*

Country of manufacture as stated on last page of this book.

Library of Congress Cataloging-in-Publication Data

Names: Levine, Stacey, author.
Title: Mice 1961 / Stacey Levine.
Description: Portland, Oregon : Verse Chorus Press, 2024. | Summary: "MICE 1961 recounts a pivotal day in the fraught relationship of two orphaned sisters through the eyes of their obsessively observant housekeeper. Will Jody be able to cope if her younger sibling Mice, subject to constant harassment in her community for her unusual appearance and habits, leaves home? How will their all-watching companion convey her fierce attachment to them both? When they encounter an unsettling stranger at a neighborhood party, each of them is driven toward momentous changes. Set in southern Florida at the peak of Cold War hysteria, this novel is a powerful meditation on belonging and separateness, conformity and otherness."—Provided by publisher.
Identifiers: LCCN 2023055127 (print) | LCCN 2023055128 (ebook) | ISBN 9781959163015 (trade paperback) | ISBN 9781959163022 (ebook)
Subjects: LCSH: Orphans—Fiction. | Sisters—Fiction. | Housekeepers—Fiction. | LCGFT: Novels.
Classification: LCC PS3562.E912 M53 2024 (print) | LCC PS3562.E912 (ebook) | DDC 813/.54—dc23/eng/20231208
LC record available at https://lccn.loc.gov/2023055127
LC ebook record available at https://lccn.loc.gov/2023055128

I

Jody Marrow turned the corner, moving fast on Reef Way, heading toward the spring party. Her real name was Josephine. She wore a skirt, crisp blouse, and black flats. Passing the Student Prince lunch counter, Keely's Brink drugstore with its torn forest-green awning, and Parrotts Grocery, she glanced back to the store's sand-scattered stoop. A white cat slept inside the screen door, motionless as if pasted there. Jody's footsteps rang the pavement. The cat jolted awake.

Hurricane Donna was long gone. It had wrecked much of Miami the year before. Farther west on the boulevard, Jupiter Gasoline still lay in soft piles of crumbling cinder blocks and rusting rebar. The filling station's old glass-topped pumps jutted from the rubble at angles, curiously undestroyed. Jody, possibly accustomed to the storm's wreckage, sped past unseeingly.

Her marble-brown eyes: heavy with responsibility. At age twenty, Jody never lost sight of the big picture.

Who on Reef Way was more worried than she?

Running tall, full of breath to spare, nerves surely frayed, she maneuvered past onlookers. As the sun downed itself into the soft cakes of clouds, she took the corner at 74th a bit too quickly, hopping to correct her course. Jody must've known it was unbecoming, running that way, but then again, it must've felt a little free.

Her mother had died the year before, somewhat in the middle of things.

Set in a flip: Jody's smooth chestnut-brown hair.

She blurred onto 75th with its sidewalk planters and fan palms. Through sidewalk cracks thin volunteer palms grew—in that context, errant weeds.

What bothered Jody all that year was the future of things.

The sky to the south: burnt sugar and tangerine. The birds were so many in the sky, like poppy seeds flung there. Jody wouldn't've noticed them, though. Surely she was thinking of one thing only: her half sister, her life.

*   *   *

Mice Huberman ran beneath the sun at 4:30 that day too. She wore a plain day skirt and a pink pearl-button blouse. Who in the neighborhood was more nervous than she?

Feet skittering fast despite the heavyish shoes, the girl had first set out for the spring party on a path so well established that it was known only as "The Way," a trail of dried yellow grass alongside the canal at 73rd. Sometimes locals discussed The Way, for it was straight as no other footpath was and bewilderingly short, connecting an open field to the rear parking lot of Richard's department store and the local business district. The Way sloped upward, leaving wayfarers no choice but to climb a rock cleft in order to reach the store.

On that day, Mice scrabbled over the cleft, darting across the parking lot so fast that for moments I lost sight of her.

Today, I can still see her quick-legged gait between the parked cars.

She hurried to the boulevard. I followed.

*   *   *

Each half sister was on the tired side, nerve-riddled and thin. The two lived together with some degree of peace but with profuse discomfort, too—I saw it.

Though Jody required the younger one to stay indoors during the day, it was typical for neighbors to see Mice hurtling down Reef Way or through neighborhood side streets at sunset. Perhaps the girl's racing around in the evenings satisfied a need.

In the small apartment those months, I watched the half sisters near-always, impatient to be part of their to-getherness and clashes both. Soon after moving into the apartment, I acquired the habit of breathing them in, of trying to draw goodness from one sister, then the other. Among family, satiating cuddles, from what I understood, could arise at breakneck speed: I waited.

Each next day, I trained my focus on the sisters all over again and reeled inside their togetherness. Sometimes I focused most acutely on Jody—at other times on Mice. Yet weren't the sisters really the same being? Yes, in my eyes. I tried reminding myself of their individual makeup, but could not hold that idea for long.

Living with them, speaking with them, was nerve-rattling. I sat as if on a high, narrow ledge, gripping some nearby flange so as to keep my spot and not fall—the scenario was long familiar to me.

*   *   *

On that afternoon before the spring party, I concealed myself for some time in the pinkish late-day light beside Gorge Discount's recessed doorway, watching as the sisters on opposite sides of the street ran west, each unaware of the other. My cheek against Gorge's side delivery door, I spoke scant words, enumerating to myself the girls' differences that I knew of. Jody had brown hair and a strong gait, her gaze grim and steady as she ran; Mice, on the other hand, with her froth of white hair, was less physically sure and stumbled with occasional missteps. The younger one's head bobbled a bit, too, as she ran. At particular junctures, beside a lamppost or brick facade, she stopped running altogether to stare at the ground, for infinitesimal things, grain-like, drew Mice in.

Past the shuttered cinema and palm fronds jumping furtively in the wind, the younger sister squinted through her sunglasses. Yes, she must've heard the teenagers gaining on her—it was for this reason that she changed course rather than continue to the bakery.

But Jody, across the street, continued west.

I followed Mice. Hadn't Jody made it clear I must always keep track of her? Stalled by two workers on the sidewalk hauling a large fruit horn on a plank, I struggled to keep the girl in sight. Black frosty grapes dropped from the horn, rolling across the sidewalk.

The group of teenagers advanced. Calling to each other, running faster now, they chased Mice outright. The girl fell, scraped her knee, got up, and ran headlong toward Settler's Bank, outstretched hands slamming into the pockmarked brick wall. As the teens closed in, she dipped behind a telephone booth adjacent to a little cement cavity otherwise known as a window well.

That year, Mice, on her evening explorations, must've mentally mapped every small in-between space and must-ridden aperture in the neighborhood. And since Jody expected me to tail Mice, keeping track—it was necessary—of her whereabouts, I knew many of the recessed, hidden spaces too.

People look past such notches and unnamed nooks, fissures, dusty blind holds, underbushes, and other gaps for which it's difficult to find names. But someday, who knows, when the world changes, then changes again, neighbors in droves might extol such local cavities and seek them out, even the pits and hollows in their own homes, furnishing them with soft, euphemistic names.

Mice moved atop the window well's metal rim, balancing there. Then she leapt below.

* * *

The high schoolers, during those months, knew about the girl's dusk and nighttime expeditions through the streets and began to pursue Mice, whose weakened eyesight put her at a disadvantage. Natively loud, the teens never seemed to have second thoughts about harrying her, the new one to the neighborhood, with their heartless name-calling—and I never heard them call out the sliding syllables of the girl's given name: Ivy. Instead, they vied with each other to throw down insults and invent fresh, rude monikers for Mice, who in their eyes was likely on par with dust.

Yes, a more mature person like an aunt or the city's head librarian might've jumped to action on that day, confronting the tormenters, forming quick spears of words to halt them, but I couldn't. And up until the evening of the spring party, Mice had never spoken or stood up to the teens either.

Face it: people like Mice are shy.

If it was clear to me on that day as to why the girl jumped into the cement depression and why she'd left the apartment so early when the sun was strong, less clear was where the story would go and where it might leave me. And if the story could ever hope to become itself.

*   *   *

I spent a few months with the sisters in the heavily curtained apartment, sleeping behind the lint-colored couch. Even today, I see that if not for the death of their mother, Candy, I might've missed the chance to know the girls. I might never've met them at all.

I found them during a heavy squall. Standing on the roadside with my suitcase, wet vines blowing across my legs, I spied the girls in the rain with their market bags, sheltering beneath a broad silver palm tree. I had never seen anything like their pair of similar, heavy-looking, long faces. A thought squeezed through me: "I have traveled the world to find them and now I have," although I had not traveled the world in the least and never would.

Instinct told me to approach them and extend my open hand to show them my emptiness, my nothing to lose. I told the miraculously strange-looking pair that I could sweep and scrub in exchange for a place to stay—just for a while. Jody diverted her flinty eyes toward Reef Way. I knew that meant *yes*.

* * *

At the beginning of my stay in their apartment, I kept four words in mind: "Be brief, stay back." I hadn't had too many friends before aside from one nice dog. If I started making mistakes with the sisters, I'd need to control myself with dictums tough as clips and pins—otherwise they would toss me out, I knew.

Didn't I take care to learn about them? Didn't I track their course? Upon their mother's death the year before, each had become the sole relative of the other, so Jody wanted to widen their circle. She tried to get them both back to living.

The sisters needed music. So on some evenings that winter after Jody's downtown typing shift, they ventured into The Potato. There, the jukebox's heavy, bulging glass created glares of split rainbows, and as the venue's owner turned the machine off and the evening's musical players stumbled onstage under a wobbly spotlight, Jody and Mice would stare at their glasses of pineapple juice.

The odd sister pair drew excitement and talk: neighbors and a few apparent beatniks glanced at the dark-haired, taciturn older sister and the colorless, awkward younger one who lay her hands face up on the table beside the syrupy drinks. As the rhythms became evident and the music grew louder, so did whispers and snickers. Jody, leaning forward, would tense every muscle. It was all because of Mice.

On other evenings, they tried going to Toddle House for mousse pie and milk cups, consuming mouthful by thick mouthful until closing time at 7:40 p.m. They also went a few times to The Zot on band night, where the two danced morosely, dry palms locked, mouths low seams, clinging to each other. As each sister hid her individual grief over the mother, a second type of grief hovered and developed between them, a snarled tissue of joint grief. This pain, I thought, caused the sisters to take each other for bitter granted.

Standing side by side at The Zot's refreshment table, swallowing free lemonade, skittish Mice would bite the edge of her paper cup; Jody would swat the cup away. "Manners!" she'd hiss while keeping an eye to the club's sidelines where unfamiliar men gathered, curious and therefore hazardous, and likely to prey on Mice. Jody tried to dispel the men with her angry eyes.

But how many times can that work?

Jody's original intention was that they, as orphans, should start to socialize in the neighborhood, yet they never quite managed to. After visiting the nightspots, the two would head home wordlessly in the dark, surely wishing to hold back time and avoid the stale apartment, just as the pages of a delectable book can delay life's movements and undertakings too.

The younger sister would twine her arm around Jody's as they walked, setting her fingers into the crenellations of the sister's knuckles as they dragged up the stairs of the West Horn apartment building with its timeworn and wobbly iron rail.

Didn't I follow, seen or unseen? In the dark behind them, I angled myself, following as the moon's light glanced on them, wishing for a second moon to expand the glow and improve my sight, let me know what was real.

I was decades younger then. The sisters were younger than I. Living with them on that narrow yet warm ledge, trying to hang on to that life, I did not care if I was free to leave or not. I disliked the notion of independence and wanted to shut it away as the sky with its range of blues locks out the infinite every day.

The local palm trees, canals, Jody with her shiny hair, and Mice: all that existed outside of me was indelible. But me? I was merely a faint pencil sketch to myself, a smudged nose and eyes inside an unfinished outline of a face.

*　*　*

If Jody experienced a premonition while she ran toward the party, that day she also seemed to hit her fastest-ever speed. Past the cabbage palms along 77th, she flew with long strides, her body's momentum rattling the dried fronds. Unconcerned by neighbors staring through the shop windows, she continued along the sidewalk to burst the premonition, keep the sister from slipping free.

Premonitions are made to be crushed, aren't they?

At the intersection she collided with a local police detective, grabbing his blue jacket. "Denny," she panted. "My sister is lost. She's simply nowhere."

The detective's face squeezed with humor. "Oh Jody! She's not nowhere."

"This time it's true."

"Baloney now Jody."

"I didn't think it would happen and not like this!" she specified, gazing at him, eyes brimming. "Your job is to *do* something." She pulled at the detective, taking steps forward as if to make him run with her, but he did not.

"My God you two." The man shook his head.

"She is determined to ruin my life."

"Mice? Doubtful." He inched a small notebook from his back pocket. "How is the little girl these days by the way?"

Jody smirked. "You know how she is Denny. That's the point."

"Look. Why don't we read the notes from your previous calls to us regarding Mice? In that way we might see patterns."

"No."

Neither sister had been well trained into ladyishness.

"Aw you two girls've probably tussled and tugged at each other all your lives," the detective assessed, his oil- or dirt-filmed fingers pinching the pages' delicate vellum.

"Don't—"

"Shh. On October fifteenth at noon you called up the station," he read, head bent. "An' you said she vanished. But later that day she turned up at Milam's dairy—gobbling down milk and asking Russ question after question about the cottage cheese. Then in November—"

"Stop it!" Jody plugged her ears with her fingertips, eyes rolling upward, dry halves of peeled eggs.

He pocketed the notebook. "Hey Jody? 'Member that time outside Toddle House?"

"Yes I do. Can't you *listen* to me? I'm talking." Her raucous-looking eyebrows and wild eyes may have prompted neighbors, at times, to think she was as poorly behaved as her younger sister.

"All *right*. What happened today? How'd the little girl get lost?"

"Well not lost—not exactly," she said. "When I came home from work you see she was gone."

Denny White laughed hard. "Lands! After all this you're telling me she's been gone forty-five minutes?"

"But this time she may've run off for good. She warned me of it." Jody swallowed hard and touched her forehead in disbelief. "Don't you see? The worst could happen. God it seems so real."

"Well . . . lotsa things *could* happen. Couldn't my brother Derf disappear into the sea?"

"Has he tried?"

"Nope. I keep Derf close. My point being Jody we just can't let fears come so *alive* . . . y'know . . . on our *sleeve*."

"You so often change the subject of a conversation Denny."

"Look. What's so bad about sis toolin' around town awhile?"

Then Jody's horror was clear. "Mice is just a kid! She gets into scrapes. I think something's going to happen but I don't know *when*. Denny don't you understand what it's like to lose something difficult but precious?"

"Well—I lost Daryl."

"Oh? Your other brother?"

"My goat."

She straightened minutely. The warm wind riled her hair. "The truth is early this morning my sister left the apartment for a long time without telling me. She's never done that before. Later she threatened to leave home entirely. What if she actually ran off? Was her leave-taking this morning a harbinger of my losing her for good?"

The man shook his head slowly, looking at her.

"You know she needs protection. She just doesn't realize it."

"Hey. Do you like puppies? Cute little—"

"Stop it Denny. I need Mice home. Once she's back I promise you I won't let her out of my sight again."

"Jody," he breathed warmly, blinking, still shaking his head. "What's the worst could happen? Say the little girl leaves home. She's nineteen after all."

"She's barely eighteen! Can't you keep anything straight?"

"An' say in the style of today's youth she takes herself a little job. Rents a room to live in—"

"You'll be sorry you said that Denny!"

"—and she could experience life's roses."

The two stared at each other, fast arid breaths between them. What was at stake?

"Look. Your sis'll be at the party tonight. And you know me on this Jody."

"Oh Denny!" Jody burst into a series of dry sobs that the man ignored. "Do you know what it's like being with Mice every day? One thing happened a few days ago. When I got home she was gone—just as she's gone now. And the range was on."

The man squeezed his hips. "Hm. Was it on high?"

"No. Low."

Denny wrote on the pad.

After this, Jody's energy seemed to drain. She stared at a blue-eyed daisy growing from a sidewalk crack. Tall and showy with a blatant purplish center, the flower bobbed. Across the street in Pinkus Park, yellow-and-white daisies swayed in profusion, each one a mute assertion.

It's difficult to imagine anyone ever putting a stop to

comparisons between girls and flowers.

"Whatever your sister does . . . I hope she enjoys herself." He gestured to hummingbirds. "Miami is a paradise that starts with the sun."

Jody's voice sliced. "Is that what you think?"

"Oh go to the party and enjoy yourself Jo. Call me up tomorrow. The three of us'll go to Dressel's." The man's tone shifted, businesslike. "As you know . . . it'll be onion ring day."

"Yechh." She stepped off the curb, looked, and dashed across the boulevard.

"Hey. You like me any Jody?" called Denny weakly from the intersection, but she could not be bothered, and did not answer.

Neither she nor Denny had noticed a lone shadow gliding across the base of a nearby sidewalk planter and along the pavement where passersby walked, laughing and chatting together, likely en route to the party. The shadow retreated behind the planter's glittering stone. The shadow was me.

*   *   *

Many say that life's fable is prearranged. It's a famous feeling, that sensation of fate. Some stories proceed as if fate were real. They try to beguile. Some keep up a frantic pace, and other stories scarcely move: wine pooling in the brain. Many finish in that celebrated, falsely conclusive way, the lacquered finish I both long for and cannot stomach. Some fail to see that a story is far more than a recounting of events. And certain stories stray to a faraway edge that tastes as unreal as saffron: metal crushed with honey.

I don't mind being yanked along with a plot's train: I'm curious. I don't care about clichés, either—I crave that sugar. I love pressing stories' flavors against myself. At some point I found myself inside this story, its earthy furrows and grays surrounding.

I saw how real a story can be, even when untrue. In a world-sized skein of stories and dreams, various threads pull and ride atop each other; some break away while new versions form. This one, drawn from a yarn about two rival sisters, starts and ends on Reef Way, the boulevard that barrels the miles west from Miami into the Everglades.

*   *   *

Immediately, I began to study the siblings. From the moment of Candy's death in the bed the year before, as I understood it, the two girls began to drift, lost but for one another. In the crushed standstill after the death, each seemed to live in fear of losing her sister.

Even so, sometimes I wondered: Which girl's lonesomeness outweighed the other's?

On the night before the party, Mice sat at her hobby table in the front room. Jody, having cooked and cleared away dinner, sat tiredly on the half-upholstered chair, stroking each eyebrow one after the other, removing her wire-thin wristwatch, balancing it on her knee.

Did her faint smile burn discrepantly with anger, or was that me?

Behind the couch I lay in my place, listening as they spoke, my feet tucked under an old yellow sham.

With the day fading, Jody brought mugs of hot milk. The sisters lay side by side, two sore thumbs lashed together, on the hallway's dull striped carpet runner.

"Mother gave speeches while she was alive," she told the younger girl. "In the park. Do you remember?"

"Mother was quiet. She made no speeches."

"The things you don't remember. Mother tried to help people. She hated the Party but she never left it."

So Jody knew something about the mother's political life. But that wasn't anything Mice could understand.

"Party?" she asked.

The older sister reached for a hairbrush on the end table, working it through her sister's rowdy white-yellow hair.

"Ow!"

"This brush sticks," Jody said. "Your hair is hopeless." She retrieved a fork from the table, poring over it before spreading the tines, then applying the utensil to the sister's wiry hair, smoothing the strands.

It's impossible to ignore the gossamer link between girls' hair and freedom.

"That hurts too!" Yet the younger girl's voice was soft, as if originating from a gel inside her.

"Hair has no nerves. It doesn't *hurt*," said Jody.

"Yes it does. Mine does."

Watching this, I told myself that the two sisters were not the same girl. See, I chastised myself. They have different points of view.

Then Jody smartened the girl's hair by stroking the edge of a spoon along her scalp.

"Isn't that better?"

"Yes." The girl relaxed, chafing her head against the metal utensil, eyes closed.

The two smiled wildly different smiles.

Behind the couch, I grew warm with indignation. What prevented Jody from grooming *my* scalp with the spoon? What stopped her from realizing that, but for the absence of color and different texture, Mice's hair could've been mine?

I inhaled what of their closeness I could.

"Oh Mice my sorrow. You look so like Mother sometimes," the older one murmured.

Yes, managing Mice every day strained Jody badly. You could see the exhaustion down to the whites of her eyes.

Suddenly I sat up to check, with alarm: Was my own private coffee spoon still neatly stowed beneath the couch? Yes. Was the coffee jar sealed tight? It was. Coffee was no good for Mice.

If it's possible to measure the universe against the racing of light, then surely it's possible to measure a lifetime—even a blankish one—with an old spoon. I kept an old toe of bluish garlic under the couch, too, for luck.

The older sister reminded the younger: "Tomorrow's the spring party."

"The what?"

"Everyone'll be there. And the new neighbors—the brother and sister who moved onto Bird Road? Them too."

"I don't care. They hate me. All of them."

"No silly. They'll grow to *know* you over time."

"But people in stores don't like me. The kids laugh."

Jody grew stern. "Then there's no better time to start mingling and making friends. In that way we can change how things are."

Though she said these words, I knew the older sister did not like Mice getting close to others. And if the younger girl had any impulse to explore the world on her own, she also wanted Jody Marrow as close as she could be—I knew it.

Once, when Mice and I sat together at the hobby table, the girl quietly informed me that she didn't like her sister's pushing and pulling at her. Reef Way neighbors bothered her too, and, she described, all people were surefire paths to disaster. I leaned in, wanting to tell her that people can often be kind, mild, and benign, yet I said nothing, for no specific examples came to mind.

*　　*　　*

So throbby and overwarm in that rented apartment heaped with its heavy furniture and artifacts of living: pilled sheets, clots of dust and hair, moccasins, and packaged dice never thrown, all of which Jody periodically kicked into corners for me to sweep. And packed inside the hallway closet: tangles of skirts, blouses, and slips, a disused blind cane, cards of rickrack, and an up-ended stool, all forming a domestic avalanche waiting to break.

After the hair brushing and the evening mugs of near-boiled, near-yellow milk, Jody turned on the television. Reclining together upon the hallway carpet runner, the girls sipped the last of their drinks in silence, looking into the living room at the TV.

"What separates two people?" One sackily-suited comedian on a gray stage posed this question to another. The answer came: "Other people."

Jody changed the program to *Playhouse 90*. This show depicted a soldier who carried on with life unfeelingly after a war.

Mice's sudden voice, a silver burr aggravating the air. "Jody! My cup's still so hot!"

Pressure-sensitive girls: such burdens.

"Set it down. You complain more than Boatsmann has fleas."

Boatsmann was a prominent neighborhood dog, one of the leaders.

"Now lie on your side," ordered Jody, though the younger girl had already obeyed. "It's almost time for bed." She switched off the TV.

"Keep it on Jo. I like when there's a story on."

"No. Bedtime."

Outside, the last municipal bus of the evening downshifted.

The sisters' talk returned to Candy, and how she finished living.

"When she got sick . . . Mother didn't even have time to grow weak," said Jody, heavy.

"I know I'm just like Mother," said the other one. "So like her I'll get sick and die."

"You're nothing like Mother. But yes—you'll die someday."

I winced. Couldn't Jody be softer?

Then the older girl nestled against Mice and held her sister's hair in her hands.

"All those pillow fights we had with Mother."

Mice smiled feebly. "I remember. And all her boxes? Mother stored everything."

"All mothers store things."

"But . . . pins? All those *pins*. And the batteries in the icebox. Remember the crocks of thyme soup? I couldn't stand that soup. It stank."

Four lips pulled into simultaneous grins. Saliva pops; it clicks.

"And she froze jars of milk. Guernsey milk."

"Freeze milk she did."

"Why?"

"No questions Mice."

"But they're good questions. Jody why's our freezer so dark?"

"Shh." Jody lay back, rested her eyes, voice sleepy. "And don't go into the freezer."

"But I must—for patties!"

"The messes you make."

"Why's the freezer so *dark*? Are all freezers dark?"

"*Stop asking questions.*"

"But Jody. Some mothers store poison in the house."

"Mother kept no poison."

"She didn't?" Mice stared at the sister.

Each pair of moist, vulnerable eyes seemed to seek and drink in the other. Or was that me?

The elder sister gave a sudden push. The younger girl sat up and returned the shove. Then both lunged, and they grappled, rolling, grunting, each mouth on the other's shoulder. Then Jody pinned the younger girl.

"Get off me!"

I enjoyed the sisters' wrestling.

"Mice," Jody panted. "We spend every day together. Every night. And who does the work around here? The shopping and dinners and cleaning? I can't stand it—I'm tired of this life and besides who keeps you from burning up in the sun? *I* do!" The older one sweated with the passion of her complaint.

It was true—and she forbade the girl to be outside

during the hours of the full sun, not knowing that Mice often flouted the stay-inside rule while she, Jody, was away at work.

Surely it was Candy who'd first taught Mice to bite.

"*Ow!*" Jody hollered, shaking the sister off, standing and rubbing the shoulder, going to the hobby table, breathless, leaning her hand square upon a mound of staples, yelling in pain again. "It's your turn to do something around here! Get up and wash the sink."

"It's not dirty. Besides I can barely see the sink."

"You see it."

"Jo? Did you say 'I can't stand it' because a minute ago I said I couldn't stand the soup? Did my words influence your words?"

"Oh *stop* that Mice!" The elder sister looked ragged.

Sometimes she was able to ignore the girl's questions. Yet Jody's voice had over time grown strident because of Mice—and perhaps Candy too. Often after an argument I would spot Jody lying on her own bed wearing an unmoving frown, unwilling to speak.

"Jody did you say that you can't stand it because—"

"Oh why doesn't the floor just open up and swallow me *whole*?"

The sun went down.

In some faint way at times, Jody resembled Mice. And sometimes she did not.

Did either one of them ever check behind the couch to look at me as I looked at them? Did they even once remember that I was staying there?

* * *

Alarmingly late, far past bedtime, Jody's nightgowned arm finally struck the bedroom's light-switch plate, blotting out the day. As the milk released its heavy, clayey properties in the sisters, they drifted to their beds. Feeling their ache for sleep and my own, glimpsing their side-by-side beds, I stood outside their door, mostly for the sharp pleasure of being excluded.

An unquestioned metal spar protruded from the middle of the sisters' bedroom floor—such a small stake, yet someone tripped over it every day.

Jody's sleep was heavy.

Mice's breathing: shallow, fast.

The sight of Jody's beautifully weighted parallelogram of brown hair on the pillow often lulled me toward my own sleep.

All creatures, even the smallest, produce nectar—stories—during sleep. I wanted the sisters' dreams to be burnished and lovely, but their dreams, in which they often searched fruitlessly for Candy, were difficult, I knew. Often in the mornings they sat in the kitchen trying to recall their disturbed dreams as I listened from my place behind the couch—feeling, as ever, that I could never do enough.

Neither drinks nor pills, drops nor steams have the power to suppress or restrain dreams, as with trees' arms espaliered against walls—no. It takes so much more than that.

Maybe a lifetime, if you have it to spare, can evaporate terrible dreams.

My dreams are usually pallid.

Jody sprang up like a coil. "Girtle!"

"I didn't mean to scare you Jody. I didn't notice that I'd walked into the room."

"Do you often spy on people in their beds?" she demanded in the dark.

"Not really."

"Liar! Go back to your place."

"May I ask you something Jody? I've wanted to all day."

"What is it? Hurry up," she grated.

"This morning you see Jody I took a shower."

"It's about time."

"And you see the crème rinse dripped down my shoulder and back and dried there all gluey and uncomfortable and—"

"Well wipe it off stupid!"

I sought the sour whites of her eyes in the dark. "But I wonder—"

"Can't you see I'm trying to sleep? Go get some tweezers and hot cotton. Wipe it away. Get rid of it! I'm telling you that's what you *do*."

"You mean you'll let me open the cotton box?" I cried happily, bounding to the bathroom, for occasionally my heart soared from Jody's attention and care.

"Just be quick."

But in minutes, I dawdled at her bedside again. "Gosh Jody. D'you suppose all kinds of substances like crème rinse can settle into a girl's skin over time and disintegrate her—"

"Quiet!" Jody struck the bed. Without fail, intricacies and small, undertowing notions repelled her. "Look Girtle—you've been with us more than a month or two. Isn't it time you moved on?"

A clawing movement inside me. "Oh Jody—mayn't I stay longer? I'll wash the chairs' legs I promise. That will save you money."

This idea must have pleased her, for she blinked as if considering it, and in moments she was asleep, shoulders softly atop the blue pillow.

*　　*　　*

Lying behind the lint-colored couch at night during those months, I began to worry about the story's helper, who inevitably would arrive. The thought of him made me miserable. In these types of stories, this requisite helper arrives by way of some long-standing and rote dictum and usually with no personality. The figure is a non-specific blank whose role is to steer the central girl away from her quandaries and into a better future.

The helper may be affixed to the story's walls from the start, having known the central girl for years. Or he might arrive later, latching on to the girl as a friend or lover.

I sensed that the story's helper would be a man, and an oafish enormous deadweight who'd tug and lug the story away from its center. I pictured him oily in manner, always about to sidle onto the warm ledge of my imaginings where I perched with the sisters, who, heads bowed, hair hanging in hanks, lingered with me out of time.

The helper would commandeer the story, I was certain, and jettison me from it. While appearing to ease the girl's problems, he would in fact fix her into the trap of the story's ending—I felt it. The helper wasn't the worst part, though—the story itself with its claws would grub at the central girl, I believed, and I was right. It would indoctrinate her and tamp her down when her pursuits were not on point. The story, possessing the upper hand, would keep her miserably sanitized. Would I have any chance to outmaneuver the helper and the story itself?

*　*　*

Early on the morning of the party, as the sisters argued in the living room, the helper, though I did not yet realize this, likely sat on the edge of a bed in a nearby motor hotel, starting his day. He might've gone for a morning swim or lain beside the pool on a chaise lounge with a coffee or a morning Coke, chatting with the other men from the job who stayed in the motel as well.

Around the time Jody left for work, the helper might've wandered from the motel in search of an egg diner. He may have sat and ordered a grapefruit topped with butter and brown sugar or a full breakfast—either—then scanned the local newspaper. He had time to kill. Later, loafing with the others at the motel, he might've studied a paperback atlas or magazine listings of favored Miami nightclubs.

Late that day, he'd borrow a car. Slow-moving yet responsible, he'd plan for his evening off work. With his purple-bruised fingernails and brush-cut hair, he'd continue his activities, which would come to crush my place in the story, I knew—filling the gas tank, buying a fancy nightclub jacket, and later, as the sun went down, tooling around Miami in the borrowed car. He'd take in the palm-lined neighborhoods and stop at all the lounges and dance clubs. In this way, I learned later, the story's helper finally wormed his way into the Reef Way neighborhood and made himself apparent to the sisters.

I had to eject him from the story or clip him before he arrived—was this possible? Before he arrived and erased me.

*　*　*

Running that day, each girl split the mild wind.

After Mice switched direction and dashed beneath the thick, life-green palms lining Reef Way toward the bank wall, Jody, across the street, ran a half block west, then stopped to check her tiny wristwatch. She whispered a few phrases to herself—I could not hear them all—perhaps seeking the well-known, scant consolation that words can sometimes bring.

It was close to five—the brightest hour of the day, as Jody sometimes observed.

It wouldn't've occurred to her that I was watching.

"She won't run away—no," Jody might've said to herself. "She wouldn't. She's probably hiding near the canal or playing with those stupid radios."

*　*　*

It was not the younger sister's slightly out-of-fashion Peter Pan blouse collar, that afternoon, which caught the high schoolers' attention, and it wasn't her overbite. My own teeth, large as chalk blocks and chipped, too, drove my ongoing admiration of the girl's tidy, peg-sharp teeth. Jody's teeth I never noticed.

It was likely nothing specific but instead everything that drew the teens to Mice. After the mother's death and the move to the new neighborhood, she had begun the inveterate, unfeminine practice of racing around the boulevard, even wandering much farther than that. And if the teens homed in on her, Mice had the ability, at times, to elude them.

It was the girl's own fault that she had no friends, I heard neighbors say and repeat to each other on my very first quiet evening in the neighborhood. As if those words extended a form of permission into the atmosphere, the teens began chasing the girl that very week. It didn't matter if arrays of adult neighbors watched, on those early evenings, from Pinkus Park's wading pool or Parrotts Grocery—the teens still went for Mice. Maybe in the girl's bobbing electrostatic moon of hair, near-complete absence of color, and oddly quick movements, neighbors saw, then grew transfixed by what it was to be the lowest-low.

*　　*　　*

On the afternoon before the party, the teens stood and leaned outside Gorge Discount's delivery door. This whitened nook took the long brunt of the sun late each day. The store, at 76th Avenue, was among many small shops on the block where merchants' green-and-white awnings generated a uniform look.

But does uniformity denote unity?

Mice had just passed the local movie house, which had been shut down that year for reasons linked to yellowish mold. The girl slowed under the blank marquee, and in her characteristic way pressed and rubbed the bricks' rough stone peduncles with her fingertips.

A whoop erupted from behind. They had seen her.

"Look we struck gold!" cried Laurette Scansion, the high schoolers' leader and a senior at the Ed Slaughter High School. In her three-gore red skirt, she beckoned the other teens, who shouted happily as one and followed her.

Likely the girl began to suffer from the moment they noticed her.

Likely the raucous teens saw but did not see Mice's damp-with-sweat hair, the gravity on her face; they did not hear her worried gasps or whispery-quick footfalls. Likely Mice did not see the teenagers clearly, either, and no one saw me, certainly, for I was never the type to be seen.

The teens' trite intentions were integral to human history. The group would zero the girl out, lob taunts, and watch her endure it all. They stumbled over each other in the joy of the chase, laughing, "Hey Milk Face!" and "Lookit Whitey-White!"

Each barb and voice had a distinct flavor in this rite.

Behind Laurette lagged Helen-Dale Martin with high-set auburn hair and Honey McLaren in her peasant blouse, who, just like Helen-Dale, was older than high-school age. These two seemed unrelentingly enamored of high school and all it was supposed to encompass, spending much time in its social folds. At the rear loped poor tag-along Joyce Smock, also older, though it was hard to say by how much.

"Popcorn Head!" Helen-Dale called throatily.

I looked and saw, but couldn't defend Mice. I went blank on afternoons like that and my throat froze.

"Blindee! Whitewalls! Four Eyes!" they continued, scrambling around trash cans at the corner, almost caught up to speeding Mice with the arrow-narrow scared face and upper lip of sweaty down as she careened past rooted gray passersby: sidewalk anemones.

"Hayhead!" they called, running, laughing more.

During those months, as the high schoolers mocked

and pursued the girl, they shaped her, too, for that's what words, neighbors, and maimed overseers do.

*   *   *

The story of the two sisters was minted when the world's air was fresh. Many versions exist. In some, events are barbed and hot, as confused as life really is. The siblings struggle against each other. In one variation, the girls argue beside a mill's cold stream. The older one pushes the younger one in and she drowns, later rising from the water with wings. In another version, the dead one transforms into a harp that sings.

In other versions, the sisters are brothers. In some, the story emphasizes the sisters' beautifully curious, humid faces and young, swaying gaits, casting them as ethereal, elusive creatures. Others portray the girls as tragic, the harmonies of their singing voices so piercing that the notes resonate in stories nearby.

Some stories are dense as pudding with a set skin, no further words possible to add, none to omit.

How, if its front side bulges ahead to a climax, can a story remain itself?

It could start with an immediate culmination in which those in power are held down and stabbed.

The central girl in such stories often resembles other girls featured in nearby stories; for example, the weakish-type movie star: her hair is blonde. She's girdled inside a film's frames or candied for TV. She's nervous: the plot tracks her unrelentingly and she sees herself only through the story's eye. Her appetite is not for herself. She is not permitted an overbite or lisp. She must never wear heavy oxford shoes.

Why, anyway, did Jody force Mice to wear those awful, tan, brad-covered shoes?

A story's best when convincing the listener it could happen no other way.

Perhaps it's best to relay it as a long, clenched series of asides.

Although to describe is to contaminate, I began my try.

*　*　*

Face it, Mice's eyes were simply not right.

Neighbors said her out-of-date blouses and her skin's bottomless absence of color made her a shadow in reverse. They said her eyes were grotesque and weak, that her oaf shoes were horrors. The girl's all-white appearance, the result of a one-in-twenty-thousand chromosomal skip, as everyone told it, had been a years-long disaster for Candy, and the mother had endured the girl's growing-up years so often in bed, filled with shame.

Now Candy was gone and the girl maundered along the sidewalks most evenings, an activity the mother had prohibited, though Jody tolerated it to a small degree. After being cooped up during the days, Mice must've found Reef Way's flower-scented air and tree-laced, dusk-laden streets delicious.

As I pieced it together, few locals, in the weeks after the sisters arrived to the neighborhood, saw Mice. But after a time, neighbors slowly grew to know about the girl and immediately expressed irritation toward her. As Mice began to traverse the neighborhood during the evenings, neighbors blazed as if horrified to see her, overall full of objections to her tender, chapped-looking hands and the outer ears so peel-thin, devoid of the rolled tops that characterize others' ears. A number of neighbors chewed with enjoyment over the girl's weird, abrupt, off-topic speech, too, confirming for each other that wariness, when it came to Mice, was the best approach. To pity the girl was also reasonable, they implied, in light of her hopeless appearance: the all-whiteness, clumsy-exploratory demeanor, and small blue eyes that twitched near-constantly.

After weeks, I noticed, neighbors were still gabbling about Mice's small limbs, thick frost eyebrows, and white, half-airborne hair, all of which turned their stomachs, they said. Typically, at the ends of most days on Parrotts Grocery's porch, neighbors sat lazily in their friend-group to sum up repeatedly that they not only pitied Mice but were aghast over her and had excellent reasons for feeling so. By extension, they concluded, if newcomers or travelers ever encountered such an awful, small, white-pink creature with tiny hands like Mice, they would deserve comfort and shelter and to be embraced on the grocery's porch as insiders.

If the unstyled and disorderly white hair on the girl's head bothered neighbors most of all, they also discussed to death Mice's white down in general, including her jaw's faint layer of fuzz, then the white brows again too, and the colorless head-hair and the way the pink of her scalp showed flagrantly through.

Beyond that, the girl's small, bald-looking, jittering eyes with their cream-orange-tipped white lashes, much like two thin, tidy rows of camel hair—the look was pure Mice—ignited neighbors' ire in a wholly different way.

They told each other that the milkscape of the girl's face, neck, and shoulders, ghastly because lacking color, was responsible for their own human meanness, that the girl's appearance made them more liable than usual to holler insults or shout uncontrolled remarks: it was all because of Mice.

One evening at blazing sunset, I ran along the sidewalk toward Parrotts Grocery, looking for Mice, who'd gotten away from me, sago palms lining the curb one after the next, and as I paused beside a lamppost to rest, I heard the cluster of familiar neighbors murmuring in the usual self-dramatic tones, no doubt watching out for the girl to appear down the block and provide them with entertainment. And in moments she did round the corner near Gorge Discount, unwittingly moving toward Parrotts. As she slipped off her oversized sunglasses to wipe the mess of parachute seeds from the lenses—West Miami's flowers were numberless in those days—neighbors exploded into a vociferous collective rage.

"Jody always lets her out of the house! Why?" they cried, with so many more exhalations of words slipping free: "How?" "Ugh," "Rats!" "Whatta fright!" or "Lout!" A few nearly sobbed. While neighbors' brief near-frenzies like this seemed to contain some kind of underjoke, they also asserted one unified notion from the group: that they hated seeing Mice.

Yet they insinuated other, separate subnotions such as that Mice, unpleasantly wily, surely more blind than not, piteous, too, not to mention puzzling like a problem as opposed to being a true girl or woman, was more or less a joke to play with.

So most neighbors had forgotten, in those days, that physical appearance and normal visual acuity do not actually determine an individual's worth. Certain others clearly felt bad for Mice—even, on occasion, taking the position that the world isn't fair to those who don't measure up. But even those neighbors spent endless time conferring, checking, gesticulating, clicking tongues, and clacking and tutting, "Won't she ever change?"

They did not think to question their own blaring dislike for and enjoyment of the all-white girl who, with her pinched-looking face, raced along the boulevard every evening past storefronts, exploring. Instead, neighbors focused on, for example, Mice's two index fingers, startlingly longer than her fourth and fifth fingers, which seemed to make neighbors believe that she was terrible bad luck for everyone. One evening, they decided collectively and loudly that Mice's constant running up and down the boulevard, which raised a sandy sidewalk dust that filmed her hands, forearms, face, and neck, made the girl the most alone of anyone on Reef Way, while they—neighbors—were never alone at all.

As the final proof of Mice's secludedness and poor future outlook, neighbors pointed out repeatedly how often, late at night—and it was true—Mice sat solitarily on the West Horn's exterior iron staircase without even a handkerchief beneath her, furiously stripping down old radios.

*   *   *

So the story of the half-blind colorless girl with the now-dead mother, an angry, impulsive, unknowable sister, and a blank of a vanished father spread to the most distant neighborhoods, since that is what words and stories do.

"Whelk Face!" "Ghost!" the high schoolers yelled at the girl on the street. This must've frazzled her at the very least.

Admit it: since fear guts everyone, it must've gutted Mice.

*   *   *

I saw Jody's conundrum. She could try to improve her sister's life by working on the girl's appearance. But even if she controlled the spreading puff of hair with a brush, dyed its marled-yellow undertracts, dressed the girl in chiffon, or applied pancake with a stiffened sponge, neighbors would not halt their evening mockings—I knew it. Such efforts might've spurred neighbors to harass the younger sister even more.

So neighbors continued. "I can't stand the sight of her!" any number of them might've cried overdramatically amid others' onslaughts of chafing, jostling evening talk and bouts of angry coughing. Yet some neighbors, I noticed in those months, fault-finding as they were, also deemed Mice industrious because she built radios and frequently mail-ordered electrical parts. Others declared the girl fully lazy.

Sometimes I looked to the edges of scenes where laughers and others formulated their streams of unnecessary comments and complaints—as a newcomer, I strained at first to learn all their untold names—for example, about Mice's eyes. Locals, so sure of themselves, clearly hated her eye and lash color, eyebrows, eye movements, eye expressions, visual weaknesses, and other traits, and feeling their anger in the air, I often felt blank and at fault: a husk. But on those long gossipy evenings, neighbors consistently forgot another crucial fact: that humans lack the visual capacity to perceive at least a thousand colors—a cornucopia, really— along the light spectrum that other animals see freely.

So neighbors had no idea of what they saw versus what they didn't see.

∗   ∗   ∗

A few weeks before the party, I lingered in the alleyway alongside Parrotts while the usual lazing locals sat on the porch, gazing emptily across the alley as flies fastened and unfastened to the screen door. Among them were old Phenice in her rocking chair; the widow Cissy; a local loafer, Twing; Parrott himself; Hildy, the mother of two look-alike grown daughters; and a few others who sat full-on in the sun, faces nevertheless gray in my eyes.

They watched for Mice. I was trying to track her down myself, for Jody wanted her home. Then Twing raised up in his chair, peering over the railing and spotting the girl while rattling his newspaper and releasing between scraping coughs: "There she is. The waffler!"

Cissy argued immediately: "Tom. Mice? That girl's many things but notta waffler. She's busy all the time—because I know about it."

In the widow's lap lay the large leather purse generally known to contain an iron embosser, for Cissy was able and willing to notarize anything, anywhere, while officially offering notary services every Wednesday at Parrotts, stationing herself at a table near the tuna and razors.

Twing grunted.

"Mice can't do anything of note. A *loon*," came a woman's voice from deep within the grocery, though I didn't know whose.

Cissy told Twing and the other porch-sitters, touching her hair lightly with both hands, "That girl is short a father and a mother and never had a bank account—she doesn't have much on earth to waffle *over*."

"Hmphh," blew Twing, raising the newspaper before him.

"Th' teens'll drive her away. No reason why they shouldn't," said heavily freckled Hildy, always so puzzlingly decisive given life's limitless complexities and grays.

"They should," said Parrott.

"They oughtta behave," Phenice murmured.

"The kids move fast," said the local bank security guard Ron Brahms, arms crossed. "They stole candy from Keely's an' I couldn't catch 'em."

I moved along the alleyway, close to a growth of elderberry shrubs, wanting to wave, for I spied Mice's head in the distant breeze-blown grass. But she would not see me. Then as the wind strummed over my ears and I leaned beside the gray planked fence bordering the alley, I saw The Blur for the first time.

He was a small, thin man dressed in recluse brown. I knew from listening to neighbors that he'd lived on Reef Way all his life and routinely roamed and raced the main boulevard as well as dirt routes, canal paths, and a rarely discussed sunken local lane.

The Blur, whose given name I never knew until that day, also underwent a lot of joshing from neighbors. His constant running and sudden, jittery ducks and backtracks through the neighborhood gave residents much to laugh at. But often, as if to put The Blur at ease, neighbors told him that the teasing was intended to distract him from his troubles.

When he was out of sight, they gossiped heavily about The Blur's skin, which was spotted with common acne. Neighbors described The Blur as contradictorily arrogant to some extent, despite being shy. The Blur lived in somebody's basement.

But while the usually sweaty, worked-up, and forty-ish Blur was unquestionably part of the neighborhood, always invited, even if provisionally, to social events, Mice, I compared, was regarded as a categoric outsider, despite being appendaged to Jody, whom they mostly accepted.

The Blur sprinted through the dusty alley past me so smoothly and silently that I believed he was a thrown ball or low hawk. On tiptoes, wearing a plain sweatshirt, he approached Mice, who stood emptily beside the grocery's side stoop in the alley. He pointed, bellowing geyser-like to her face, "AHAHAHA!"

This wasn't surprising, for people often startled when first laying eyes on Mice. The sun-woozy neighbors on the porch looked over the railing as The Blur and the girl, both competitors for some bottommost rank in the neighborhood, eyed each other. Then The Blur spoke slowly, sea wave-style, to Mice, glancing up intermittently at the watchers on the porch, his words tossing and catching on his breath's crests: "Even if some people don't like me . . . everybody knows me. But nobody knows anything about you. So what are *you*?"

Mice rebutted instantly, "What are *you*?"

Neighbors laughed in their chairs.

No doubt Mice had learned to deliver such fast, sharp-toned phrases from her sister and the siblings' long-standing practice of making stakes of words: poles and demarcations.

The Blur preened.

With her compromised eyesight, Mice squinted, then edged toward The Blur, who backed away slightly. From the porch, Twing eyed the two carefully, then coughed a few times as if to say: There's a substantial difference between us up here and you down there. Then he lay back in his stuffed chair, seeming to sleep, the newspaper floating to his face, settling there, scraping his beard's stiff hairs.

The Blur asked the girl: "Do you know that life is temporary?"

"Yes I know it. But I don't mind."

Sometimes I envied Mice's freedom from guile.

"Well how do you fill your days?" continued the outcast-looking Blur, his thick saliva putting corners around his words, shortening them.

"With radios."

Neighbors on the porch chuckled at this too. Now Mice and The Blur moved closer together, forming an enclosure made of their own heads and shoulders, behind which they spoke quietly, possibly to exclude the porch-sitters who nevertheless leaned over the railing further, the better to hear.

"*My* days aren't empty at all. I've always laundry to do," said The Blur. "I wish I had a hobby like you. One year I got a chemistry set with six flasks but I've never used it."

"I like wire," said the girl.

"If I wanted to I could separate hydrogen from water," The Blur crowed, then immediately admitted: "But I'm afraid."

"Of what?"

"Atoms."

Brahms the security guard, easy to recognize with his large mustache, stood smiling on the porch, eyeing the stairs. "You afraid of doin' experiments with science kits Fred?"

Twing suddenly jumped awake, flailing the newspaper, calling to The Blur over the railing: "Did the first chemist in the world procrastinate? No he did not. Fred if you enjoy science experiments why not just do 'em? Stop lollyin' an' get on with your life."

So Fred is The Blur's name, I noted to myself.

The unorthodox Blur merely turned back to the girl, revealing: "The truth is I waste every day and once I did nothing for a whole year but play checkers with myself."

"Why?" asked the girl.

"Because I wanted to frustrate certain people and also get triple kinged."

Mice waited for more, appearing interested.

"But now I don't play checkers. That's because I'm busy. See I'm studying for the big algebra test. I failed it the first time."

"Freddie! I thought you graduated from Slaughter!" old Phenice cried from the porch.

This seemed to incite a form of rage in The Blur, who looked up to the elder on the porch, hollering: "I just *said* I failed it. I failed the class so no I did not *graduate*!"

"Watch it Fred," warned the guard.

But The Blur continued yelling, widening his gesticulations to include not only Phenice, but all porch-sitters. "I'll pass the makeup test easily if I'm just given a chance! And the *only* reason I failed was because on exam morning my shoe got caught in the front staircase railing and—"

"Oh that was so *long* ago," exhaled Brahms, irritated. "Nineteen . . . twenny years back? You can't take the math test now Fred."

The Blur whirled back to the guard. "Not *take* it! I'm going to *retake* it!"

"But how'd y'take it the first time if you got stuck on the steps?"

The Blur grew extremely impatient with Brahms. "I got there late and took the test with one *shoe* but couldn't finish!"

Then in my peripheral vision I saw Mice bob or jump above the high grass. I departed the fence, wading through the papery grass to catch her, but again she was gone.

The Blur continued proudly to neighbors sunning in their chairs: "Miss Kidd said I can take the algebra test in the kindergarten room next month. If I pass I'll get the diploma." He looked at the grocer. "And don't you dare say I'll fail!"

"I didn't say anything," said Parrott.

"I need to learn the four equations," The Blur continued. "I'll be able to remember them don't you think?"

"Nope," said Brahms, lowering himself into a chair.

"I *will*!" The Blur's face suddenly ran with tears. "I hate tests!"

"I wouldn'ta guessed," muttered Twing.

"I remember the year you *should've* graduated Fred," Cissy drawled sleepily from her chair, pushing and wiggling her dry elbow's loose skin. "It was 19—"

Here The Blur plugged his fingers into his ears, exploding, "Don't say the name of that year . . . *don't*! That was a horrible year!"

Neighbors broke out in a hearty round of laughter.

Now The Blur was in a lather. "I've got to study hard! I'm worried—with the world the way it is . . . I can barely find the time to study!"

"Y'mean y'can barely find th' brains," said Brahms.

The Blur cried at the guard's jab, then hiccupped. "Stop it!"

"Yer life's half over Fred. It'll end before y'know it," Twing chimed over the newspaper's edge.

Brahms rolled his thumbs as little logs, gazing at them.

Then Twing concluded in a cough-laced voice, "And Fred—don't get any fatter. 'Cause y'know the old saying: 'Whale' rhymes with 'fail.'"

"That isn't a *saying!*" The Blur, purplish, screamed at him.

Cissy sat up, alert. "Twing . . . you're right. Our life is over fast. Isn't it? It passes fast."

"It *seems* to pass fast. That's 'cause yer mind gets thin. It can't hold all a' life's happenings in th' memory anymore."

"Who said that?"

"I say it," said Twing. "There's too much t'remember and there's less events to look forward to when yer older."

"And life *ends* faster than a dog at a bone," said Cissy with pleasure.

"Nope. Life goes slow," said the guard.

"Fred—just read the math book a few minutes ev'ry day. Study it," Twing said, trailing off, quickly asleep under the newspaper again.

The porch-sitting neighbors then settled back deeply into the chairs, turning faces aside with closed eyes, though Brahms remarked, eyelids compressed tightly against the piercing sun, "Who'll *grade* your test two decades after the fact Fred?"

"Miss Kidd will," came The Blur's voice from below.

"No Miss Kidd can't. She can't teach anymore. She's too old."

"Someone'll grade it!" cried The Blur, everything at stake.

"People always cry when they talk about their old schools," Hildy piped up. "They blubber like crazy."

"Why do they blubber I wonder?" sleepy Phenice asked her, blinking, and watching her, I felt drowsy too.

"That's easy," chimed in a home nurse who had just joined them on the porch, sitting beside Phenice, taking the old woman's pulse with two fingers while simultaneously submerging her thumb into a small cup presumably containing liquid, as if the home nurse were either soaking her nail or gauging the liquid's temperature. "They cry because so much time has passed. They cry because part of their life that was familiar is gone. That's how people are."

"Maybe that's *not* the reason they cry," posited Cissy, lips pursed.

"It *is* the reason," the home nurse concluded, now folding linen.

For a second, Twing emerged from beneath the newspaper, yawning wide, then turned on his side. I never saw him again.

Suddenly Mice appeared, skittering toward an apple tree that grew in the alleyway's dead end. As my job was always to find the girl and bring her home, I sprang past the elderberry shrubs with their toothy-edged leaves so unnervingly similar to hemlock leaves, and worried: Which plant was which? In that moment I vowed to avoid all plants and their roots. But then I remembered that elderberry shrubs bear not only poison leaves but soft, sweet-tasting, edible fruit.

After Candy died, the sisters' purported cousin Harriet helped the sisters find and rent the apartment near Reef Way. Those were difficult times for the sisters, Jody told me. The nights were hard. Both girls, scarcely speaking for weeks, strained for sleep. Months later, after I'd arrived, Jody still shouted in her sleep—I heard it.

But as time went on, the sisters were less alone in the neighborhood. A salty neighbor from the next-door building named Jack Lance, for example, was often on hand, smoking at the curb or leaning on a dull-green relay mailbox, ready to chat with the sisters. Two upstairs roommates, Marge Sand and Sheila Farr, both in their young twenties and engaged to Florida men, often thumped up and down the stairs in good humor to check on the girls, too, bringing the occasional meal plate or a multicolored vitamin or two. Cissy Lax also lived in the West Horn building and kept light tabs on the sisters; once she brought them a watery casserole. In addition, Flora Horn, the building's longtime superintendent and cleaner, often waved jauntily when passing Jody and Mice on the landing.

A few years before, Flora, hair ever-bound inside a ruby scarf, had managed to name the West Horn and another local apartment building after herself without asking permission from the landlord, named Neihard. Flora had even installed steel plates engraved with WEST HORN and EAST HORN on their facades, though the landlord seemed to know nothing of it.

But locals latched on to the buildings' new names, soon referring to the apartments and even that very district as either the West Horn or East Horn. As such, the new names took root and blurred neighbors' perceptions of past nomenclature. It seemed no one could recall the times when the apartment buildings had been nameless.

Sheila's fiancé, Burt Eddleston, a tree salesman, visited the West Horn often, as did Marge's fiancé, Sal Bianchi, owner of the local Crescent Tender Bakery. Once, after I first arrived to the West Horn, Eddleston built a backyard cook-fire so all four intendeds could steam clams—the creatures writhing briefly in advance of the meal while the young adults socialized on taut lawn chairs. I watched this while concealed near the rear of the West Horn's yard, where a gnarled apple tree grew.

Another neighbor, fragile-seeming Minnie Ens, middle-aged, lived with her shut-in elderly mother in the West Horn's basement corner; after Jody and Mice moved into the building, Minnie brought them a gift of a wilted bedsheet. This shy local had, for years, neighbors said, had her heart set on being a full-fledged librarian, but the path to this profession was difficult. Jobs at the nearby public branch library opened rarely. So Minnie worked sporadically as a shelver in the meantime, also washing the branch's windows and emptying its garbage.

These Reef Way neighbors—Lance, Marge, Bianchi, Eddleston, Sheila, and Minnie—must've glimpsed me within the story's warp as I glimpsed them. I learned how certain neighbors carried more weight than others, and in some way, I envied all neighbors even while the soon-to-intrude helper gnawed constantly at my mind, for, likely very quickly, he would wipe out my spot in the story.

*　　*　　*

The teens scrambled, then closed in on Mice just past 76th and Reef Way.

The girl didn't see them hurtling behind her at first, past the Ed Slaughter High School with its flamboyance of plastic flamingos around the flagpole, drawing closer. Surely she heard them as they ran, prodding each other, panting the words "Hurry!" and "Go-go" as Mice beetled ahead. One of the teenagers, I couldn't tell who, reached out from the pack, as if hoping to knock the girl to the ground, and did.

That was the second fall to her knees that afternoon, but instantly Mice was up and moving toward the bank's brick facade.

Did I mangle or misview it, or did I really see?

I tucked myself against the bank's shadowed exit doorway to watch. She stood with a hand on the telephone booth for balance, then stood atop the window well's rim, her sprig-like foot with its hard corrective-style shoe braced against the bank wall.

Such wells in the ground, designed to allow light into low areas of a building, are not deep. Their bottoms are drainage grates or earth.

The teens ran in, surrounding the well, looking inside. "Didja *see* her go down?" It was Laurette, curled shock of blond hair on her forehead: an asp.

Recognizing faces—what skills or tricks are necessary for this?

"Trap her! Keep her down there!" called Helen-Dale, pink high on her cheeks, while one of the other girls shouted, "Remember the time we almost had her trapped near Parrotts an' she lost us the little whitehead?"

Open cracks of laughter, a cataract of excitement over what was to come.

"It was just luck she got away that time," Laurette

made clear. "Mice could never be considered clever."

"She's a cross between Dracula and Helen Keller is what she is!" Helen-Dale yahooed, dreamy with spittle and a giggle, working hard, perhaps, to please Laurette.

Smudged laughter.

"Can Mice hear us right now?" Joyce asked, looking down into the damp space.

"Who cares?" said Laurette.

Helen-Dale leaned over the cavity. "No use hiding! We'll get you."

But what about humility?

Swirling sidewalk dust, tree seeds, newspaper shreds, street grains, and other flotsam must've burned Mice's eyes as she huddled in the well's bottom, I thought, for, standing in the doorway at a distance, my own eyes stung.

Helen-Dale swung her arms with happiness. "Oh I *love* when we cross paths with Mice!"

"Doesn't anyone else think," asked sincere Joyce, "that with hairpins enough plus makeup and dye Mice could be pretty?"

Sometimes neighbors spoke my most atrocious thoughts precisely.

"Come on *Joyce*. She can't be pretty or even attractive which is second-best anyway," established Laurette.

At this point Helen-Dale, tying a lush green sash around her waist, clearly readying herself for the party, checking herself in one of the bank windows, said, "I'd rather be dead than attractive because attractive's not beautiful. It's cheap."

"And oh—Mice's eyes don't function normally— right?" Joyce asked Laurette, as if to focus on Mice in order to raise her own rank a few notches. Periodically,

Joyce touched a gauze bandage on her large, sensitive-looking forehead.

"That is correct. She can't see because her eyes shake," Laurette announced with a display of deep thought, smooth face lovely. "Besides. Her father is a crook."

Joyce and Helen-Dale grinned at this.

From far off, a thin voice cried: "Hey kids!" It was Bertie Solly, a freshman at Slaughter High, running across the street joyfully to join the high schoolers with his well-familiar thin voice, spindly bare legs in shorts, and slightly sideways, spiderlike gait. "Having fun with Milk Girl?" he asked, panting.

"Me—I call her Snowball," Helen-Dale lazed, leaning, waggling a foot, so relaxed and content-seeming that they all laughed.

"Hello Bertie," nodded Laurette.

"Did you hear? Boatsmann's lost."

"Oh no!" they cried, crowding together with worry for the revered local black-and-golden dog.

"Are they looking for him?" asked Joyce.

"How far could he've gone?" Honey said in her cushiony voice.

"If Boatsmann died I'd just do myself in," ground out Helen-Dale.

"Hope y'do," Solly taunted her, and she swatted him.

"Yum-Yum's been gone for a while too," said Joyce nasally, fingers on the forehead bandage again. Yum-Yum was a vague-looking Airedale who at times seemed to belong to Joyce and her mother, though was often seen bounding happily along with other families.

"Yum-Yum could never be as great as Boatsmann," Laurette challenged her.

Uncertain Joyce seemed to gobble out a reply: "But Yum-Yum's smart."

"Oh yeah? Smart enough t'do what?" Solly prodded, hands in pockets.

Joyce grew defiant. "To live."

They all chuckled; then Laurette, businesslike, re-routed the talk. "Bertie. I was just reminding everyone how Milk Girl's father's a thief and lowlife."

"Ooh really? What'd he steal?" asked the boy, peeking down the window well.

"Soap?" tried Joyce.

"It wasn't *soap!*" Laurette hurled at the shorter girl. "How dumb could you be Joyce? He stole *so much more* than soap!"

"Well what was it then? Tell us!" Honey asked, the others waiting.

"He stole um . . ." said Laurette, looking around. "Um . . ."

"Watermelon?" It was Joyce again.

"Will you *stop talking* Joyce?" Laurette burst out again, now gesturing with a gardenia pulled from atop a shrub. "Whatever you say no one understands! Just be quiet."

Joyce shrank back.

But for a few swaps of particles in the cosmos, I could or would be Joyce—or anyone. Tired, Joyce's face in my mind's eye, I went to sit on the hot curb between parked cars, laying my head on my bare arms. Did self-recognition begin and end surprisingly far away—in a field, for example?

I thought of my failure to protect Mice from the high schoolers, a botch for which Jody would be horribly angry if she learned of it. And now I'd also neglected to defend poor Joyce. Yet on that late, hazy afternoon, the window well itself seeming to shudder as if with heat waves, I saw that if I'd stood up for Mice at all, Laurette and Solly would've pared me to nubs.

Helen-Dale returned to the topic most juicy to her. "Joyce are you *fatherless?*"

"No!"

Solly's eyes crinkled with salty intensity.

Helen-Dale completed her point. "Well I say *Mice* is fatherless. Oh absolutely!"

"Child movie stars don't have fathers either. I read that in a magazine," said Honey, more or less disinterested.

Laurette looked at Helen-Dale, who was nearly her equal in the clique. "There's always a father. No—this's about Candy. Mice's mother was unmarried," she stated. "Which is highly questionable and maybe even sick according to *my* mother."

Then a gray shape seemed to materialize on the sidewalk with a blast of spring wind—The Blur. Now the man wore a short-sleeved sweatshirt and sneakers. "Hey lumpa sugar," he called down the window well.

Laurette told him immediately: "We put Mice in the pit."

"Don't I know it." The man's eyes, trapped in lines, appeared much older than the rest of his face.

"Watch it," the leader told him. "We could do the same to you."

Honey leaned over the tense Blur's shoulder. "What's your name anyway?"

It was hard to understand why any member of that small neighborhood would not know The Blur's given name, and as he ignored Honey's question, running off with soft whapping footfalls, I realized that all of us alongside the bank—Mice, me, the high schoolers, and The Blur—had something in common: we ran.

Mice ran for curiosity and avidity's sake, and sometimes from fright. I ran after Mice at Jody's behest, to satisfy the older sister as much as possible. Yet running satisfied me as well. The high schoolers ran, like denizens of the ancient world, for the chase, for the purity of uniformity. The Blur seemed to run for reasons buried within himself.

"Whatta fream," Solly dismissed, shaking his head at the gray-shirted receding Blur.

"What year'd you graduate Slaughter Freddie?" Laurette tried taunting, but The Blur was gone.

Joyce drifted back to the window well. Her forehead bandage had grown looser each time she touched it, so by the time she leaned over the well's lip to peer through the dark below, the gauze dangled from her face.

"Mice-y! Don't you ever *talk*?"

The bandage dropped into the well. "Gaaawf!" Joyce blatted.

Crowding over the well, the high schoolers shouted their laughter, with Helen-Dale shrieking before collapsing into happy wheezes over laughing Laurette's shoulder: "It fell on Mice's head! Aw you look good with a Band-Aid Micey-poo!"

Solly laughed too, mouth a small open rose.

On afternoons either sunny or ashen gray in any neighborhood, sulfurous steam does not rise from street vents; trees do not creak; ghosts don't fly; but common, crass human ill will is everywhere. The teens carried on their acid game with Mice, at the core of it one unspoken question: How can any creature presume to be permittable, inviolable, or real just because she exists?

*   *   *

Today, decades later, past all the clattery jobs and addresses, my diversions, flukes, adversities, ill luck, dumb luck, my single godsend, and now my final slowing, I ruminate over the sisters and where they could be. I sit here facing the window. Blue blanket's on my lap with its bright red threads. I balk at the smallest glance of my own skin. After living so many years past one's assumed life span, does anyone remain the person they once were? And if not, which portions of that person persist? What are the names of those parts, though all names are little and fleeting?

I begin to pull the blanket with its red thread and warmth over myself, reminded that before the sisters, I never had even half a home.

*   *   *

On many evenings that year as spring grew warmer, neighbors appeared thirsty to pore over Mice—perhaps simply wishing to dig into her, pull her to pieces.

One midday, I stood in the dusty alleyway adjacent to Parrotts Grocery, concealed in the high grass, listening. On the store's front porch, I heard the grocer Al Parrott reporting to the gathered neighbors: "Candy'd drive down t'visit us on Reef Way a lot during those years, pullin' her daughters by the hand after her. She used t'stop by here. That's when she told me Mice seemed useless as a daughter. That seemed reasonable to me. I remember that girl was hard. An' born with normal eyes that deteriorated slow-like. Y'know the way oil'll seep in an' ruin good wood? Candy said that's how it was."

The neighbors sitting on the porch nodded slowly. Then Cissy disagreed with the notion that Mice's vision had declined and said the girl's actual defect was laziness. Others weren't sure about this. Old Phenice softly opined that no one could know what Mice could see.

Then the porch-sitting neighbors began expressing gratitude and pride for themselves and for whatever degree of eye vision they possessed. Smiling, laughing, they leaned into each other knowingly, two or three declaring their eyesight good and strong, going on to disclose while laughing in surprise that it had been the same for all of them: after Mice, so weak with problems, arrived to the neighborhood, their own self-confidence had strengthened and they slept better at night too—it was all because of Mice.

Then Brahms recounted slowly that long ago during his cashier years in a Hialeah ribbon-and-magazine store, in had come Candy.

"Her kids were with her," said the guard. "An' she was cryin' awful about her little daughter an' said the child was trouble an' the older one was no good either. But as I saw it her kids were good because they minded her."

"Didn't Candy send Mice to the blind school?" asked Cissy, referring to a local institution called Hodges.

"Sure—she sent that little girl over there sometimes," Brahms confirmed, touching his mustache. "But Candy said Mice wouldn't learn Braille so she took her outta Hodges."

It was puzzling, for Mice had never been retinally blind. Either way, did the girl's school and social difficulties stem from her appearance and behavior, or had these come from Candy? One night as I lay in my place behind the couch, recalling the neighbors' discussion, I realized I was, in truth, free to doubt all neighbors, and this idea gave me some strength. I peeked over the head of the couch and into the girls' room: Jody was asleep. Mice sat at the living room's lamplit hobby table, hand upon a crate of radio parts, the peppery freckles across her nose and cheeks a mask of runes. I wondered: Are patterns, by the fact of their existence, asking to be observed and deciphered, or do they just blindly occur?

What color were Mice's small, flat hands anyway? Strawberry pink.

* * *

A few days before the party, I stood in the same high grass alongside Parrotts' porch, watching Mice, and roughly the same group of neighbors sat in their porch chairs. Jody had collapsed that afternoon into a late-day sleep, but before doing so instructed me to follow the younger girl and not leave her for an instant.

On that day, Mice wedged her way into a cavernous crawl space beneath the porch, where I glimpsed a scrapped tractor hood, pale green. Where was she? Then behind me I heard a brushing in the grass and turned. The grass parted. A neighborhood woman with light, nervous eyes pushed into the dusty alley, the expression on her face seeming to teeter between quick humor and despair. I knew the woman's face, but not her name.

She glanced almost frantically at the porch-sitting neighbors, striding to and fro, a bucket-shaped purse hanging from her forearm. Then with an arch grin she gestured at Mice, who had just peeked from beneath the porch. The woman shook her head and made rubbing motions with quick, intricate gestures and expressions that seemed to indicate that she thought Mice's fingers and knuckles were as distasteful and unattractive as old peanut shells, conveying this by pointing to the girl's sharply contoured knuckles, then to several discarded nut casings littered at the alleyway's edge. Mice returned to the crawl space.

So The Woman Who Didn't Speak apparently agreed with neighbors about Mice.

On the porch, Phenice rocked in her chair grand-parentally, quietly agreeing with The Woman Who Didn't Speak. "Yeah. I see those fingers on that girl. Lookit 'em. Fuzzy n' weird."

The Woman Who Didn't Speak nodded, eyes large, intense, and slowly blinking.

But old Phenice, with her poor eyesight, was wrong: Mice's knuckles were not fuzzed, but unfuzzed.

Then Phenice chimed in on Mice's teeth. "They're plenty sharp an' scare children to death at night. That's why she should stay in."

Face it, details shrink stories and shorten their depth.

"Some of th' kids at Keely's poked her with a stick t'see what she'd do. Made her mad," laughed the guard Brahms from the porch.

It was true that Mice's teeth were slightly gray, and the necks of the teeth awfully narrow—Phenice went on to say that the teeth, being teeth, didn't frighten her at all, for she, Phenice, had already lived nearly eighty years and could see what was what.

On the porch, Al Parrott paced and laid bare for them: "Never mind teeth. Here's the real point. Mice ducks outta work and everyone knows it. Did she ever help her mother haul sacks for th' grapefruit festival? No."

Neighbors on the porch nodded, recognizing a truth here.

"Shiftless," added Twing, known for his habit of describing conundrums and intricacies in single words.

"Aw Twing. She's not *shiftless*," Cissy argued then. "She's a fright yes but she's busy. She fixes those radios an' looks around the alleys at night for coils. She finds clips."

Then Twing explained the real problem: "Nobody around here's like Mice."

Parrott joggled his head, agreeing and summing up with an open hand of disclosure: "I just prefer regular people."

At this, Phenice nodded, enunciating for possibly the half-dozenth time I'd heard: "And she's blind as cotton poor thing!"

But Mice wasn't blind. In any case, can ordinary eye vision really guarantee everything it seems to promise, including astonishment?

Normal eyesight in itself can skew perception.

*   *   *

Face it, neighbors' thoughts were pungent and everywhere.

*   *   *

Early morning in West Miami is swamp-still. A silent pink hesitation predates the world. On the morning of the party, Jody dressed for her weekday shift as a typist at Snyder Construction downtown. Her job, as she described it, was partly typing and partly sweeping dust into floor pans. She mopped too at Snyder.

For all the necessaries such as rent, groceries, the scheduling of their lives—the dentist—Jody was wholly responsible. She tried to maintain the household methodically, but she was tired that year. It was not only because of the evaporated mother, but the sisters' loneliness, too, and even the piled horde of dark family furniture transferred from Candy's nearby Hialeah home into the sisters' living room. Jody had yet to sort through it all. But she'd pulled from it the lint-colored couch, ballast of the story if there was one—I slept behind it each night. Today I can still see the apartment's false mantel and nearby stack of musty chairs—all of them Candy's.

That morning I watched as Mice woke and went to her sister—each morning the same. Her wrinkled nightgown's sleeves floated with patterns of lost flowers. Its bottom hem of ribbon hovered, serrated as a dime.

"Yesterday I lost something Jody," she said.

Now the elder one faced the bathroom mirror dully. "Oh."

"I lost a knob."

It's so hard to get hold of this world, with its onslaughts of implements, voices, and sun.

"A radio-tuning knob. I must've dropped it at the bookmobile. Florence shouldn't've rushed me out!"

"You were pestering her with your questions no doubt. It's her job to keep the bookmobile orderly you know."

Florence Stroke was head of the local branch library, in charge of the bookmobile, employees, and so much more.

"Jo will you go to the bookmobile before work? Get the knob. It'd be easy. Or go there after work. It's a beige knob. You'll see it."

"No."

She was never patient, Jody Marrow.

"But I lost it!"

Beneath the sheet, my limbs depressed into the pallet, I turned to watch the sisters on the other side of the couch.

Still in her slip and slippers, the older sister moved through the rooms, Mice following. The refrigerator's light stabbed through the kitchen dark. Jody slammed a glass onto the counter. In the mornings, she was partial to a few spoonfuls of cold tea mixed with water.

"First of all those radios Mice. They're not real."

"They're real!"

The younger one had built them herself.

"They have no power. They're not connected," she said.

Though I knew very little about the sisters at that time, I understood this: when Mice favored something, Jody usually opposed it. And the inverse did not occur because Jody tended not to favor anything.

"Jo," the girl pleaded. "My radios *work*. They get power from the air."

"Nonsense." The older sister opened a glass bottle of the pastel-colored, pillow-shaped vitamins that the sisters chewed and swallowed through the course of the story. "Take one."

The girl did not. "You don't under*stand*. Please stop by the bookmobile before work? Get the knob."

"Asked and answered. No."

"What about calling Miss Stroke? Ask her if the knob's in the Lost and Found. It'd be so easy for you to call. You could do it lying down."

"Mice. I am *getting ready* for work."

"Will you stop at the bookmobile?"

"You just asked that. Tonight's the spring party—remember? We're very busy tonight. I'm not going to the bookmobile and certainly not for a piece of *plastic*." Jody unwound small wire curlers from her hair and flung them, one after the next, into the sink, blowing an aggravated breath.

"It's not regular plastic. It's *acetal* plastic. Oh by the way—Jody? After work could you kindly stop at the bookmobile to pick up the knob?"

What was wrong with that girl? Everyone asked this.

It was not yet 7:00 a.m.

Jody drank her cold tea.

Yes, the younger one was beyond a pest. There was always something Mice couldn't or wouldn't let go. She'd been born that way, neighbors said. Together, though, the sisters likely derived some comfort from their clashes. Complaining, too, is a luxe activity. Family skirmishes are homey as bed pillows—I believed that for a long time.

Jody swabbed the toe box of her shoe with a napkin. "I'll meet you at the party tonight. Five o'clock. Be there."

"No. I won't go unless you call Miss Stroke about the knob."

"Mice. Do not haggle. It's unattractive."

The younger girl bounded to the watermelon-colored hassock with its folded blanket, a nest she'd made beside the hallway telephone stand, from there calling out, "And Jody one last thing. The knob might've fallen out of the bookmobile! Will you look for it in the parking lot on your way?"

"Quiet!"

The egg timer pealed.

The younger girl sped to the front room, her sticklike

arm sweeping back the window's heavy drape, and looked outside before racing back to the hallway.

Jody held the teacup. "Listen. You are almost *twenty* years old. Keep track of your belongings. *You* call Florence. *You* talk to her."

"But you're the one who makes the calls!" Mice near-sobbed, extending the heavy telephone receiver toward the sister, a straining, mussel-blue vein rising in her neck. "Please call."

"You can't *call* a bookmobile!" Jody exploded.

"Yes you *can*!"

This is how it went with those two—always.

* * *

Just one week prior, while preparing a meal of toast, Jody thrashed through a kitchen drawer and extracted a tine-less fork.

The utensil was useless and she flung it in the sink. I watched from the pantry. The small room's sharp scent arose from damp wood somewhere. Hidden from the girls, strewing my bare feet through spilled cornmeal on the floor, pacing, looking to the ceiling sheeted with webs, I heard the telephone erupt in magnificently throated rings that Jody ignored.

From the hall, a voice: Mice. "Jody? The raspberries you brought last week—they turned white."

"Raspberries don't *turn* white," the sister said into the sink.

"Yes they *do*! Mother *said* so."

"When did Mother say that?"

The phone kept ringing.

"She talks to me. Jody? I talk to Mother sometimes and

it's easy. I would talk to her more if it weren't for the wall."

As often, Jody glared up through her brown bangs. "What wall?"

"Mother's behind a wall. Oh it's not a bad wall Jo. If I climbed it I'd *see* Mother and soon I will—I must tell her that she died. What if she doesn't know?"

"There's no wall! Mice Mother is dead."

The younger girl covered her eyes with her hands.

"What'm I going to do?" Jody said to no one. But I was there with her, on the other side of the doorframe.

Later that night on my pallet behind the couch, sleepless, I decided to walk around the place quietly and do some brief thinking about the sisters, quietly listing for myself the ways in which each girl was starkly different than the other. While Jody was left-handed, Mice favored the right. Jody wore a wristwatch, yet Mice cared nothing for the time of day. Jody was taller, and so on. The girls were not the same, I insisted to myself.

But soon I'd forgotten this catalog and returned to the fact that they were one to me. In fact, two can be one. Three, even four can be one.

But what is *one*?

* * *

Over those short months, the sisters' arguments accrued and stuck inside me as an ensorcelled seed, its first root thread curling, a question mark beginning to grow.

Face it, with all her responsibilities, upsets, and frantic efforts to rein in Mice, Jody was agitated and beyond exhausted, more so on that day of the party, when she left for work so disastrously late. I stood beside the snaggletoothed bookshelf piled with her mother's former belongings such as photo postcards of the desert, hair ribbons, and two framed photos of men neither sister seemed to have met—only Candy.

A lone cactus sat on the shelf. Once Jody had reached for the spine-covered thing, holding its clay pot close to her, tears spilling—I saw it.

Candy had run out of life, but the bulbous cactus lived on. The old books with hard blue covers and paper books, too, packed a single shelf—*Thermonuclear War, Kiss Kiss, The Silk Stocking Boycott, Baking Pies and Tarts.* These titles held no interest for Jody, whom I'd glimpsed at night in bed reading government pamphlets on topics like immunization and civil defense.

It's hard to know what a book is. Inside, a slender span of clock time is stored incognito. The book sits among others on the shelf for decades until its pages grow sclerotic, unable to turn; its relevance fades. Its story might manage to slide into the next book on the shelf and commune with this new book. Life contains many more surprising liberations than this. Out of that mingling, a new story arises, holding more joy than the first. Its afterword glows.

* * *

"The knob is *gone*. You won't even *call*."

Once any story opens its gullet, there's nothing much to do—you're in it.

Jody continued readying herself for work. She bounced around the apartment, and Mice couldn't finish talking about the lost radio knob.

"Jody please may I ask a favor? After work today while you're resting could you call Mrs. Stroke and ask her about the—"

Leaning toward the drainboard, Jody waited; her eyes smoldered. "She's not Mrs. Stroke. She's *Miss* Stroke. In fact she's just Florence. And will you stop asking me to *do* things? Do them yourself."

Mice went to toy with the elder sister's sleeve.

Their profiles: bookends. Sometimes, despite their closeness, each girl appeared startled by the other's existence.

"I'm only asking one thing Jo—just call her. Or call Richard's."

Richard's was the local department store, outside which the bookmobile parked on two Saturdays per month.

Now Jody stood over the kitchen drawer, examining silverware, ignoring the girl. "These spoons are getting darker."

Then she stood at the bathroom mirror, Mice standing nearby in the hallway, a ray of yellow sunlight daubing the girl's bare face. Jody fussed with her blouse collar and slip. Now a safety pin lay pinched in her lips. "About the party," she grumbled. "You must look your best tonight. Wear the gray dirndl." The pin dropped with a ping in the sink. "In addition Mice—speaking of the bookmobile? You need a paying job. I've been meaning to speak to you about this. The fact is? You have more or less caused economic damage around here."

"I have *not*."

"Also. The party's a potluck."

"What'll we bring Jo?"

"Nothing. We'll bring nothing. I want you to talk to Florence about the job. Otherwise you should—"

"*What* job?" It was a sob.

"I've been speaking to Florence about a bookmobile job for you. Didn't you know that?"

"*No!*"

"She *might* hire you . . . *if* you can keep quiet at work and not distract everyone with your questions. So make a good impression tonight. Wear the pearl blouse."

"No."

I hated the thought of Jody away at work and Mice at the library with Florence; I disliked being in the apartment without the sisters. Immediately I planned to give the girl the buff-colored sweater from the closet to wear that night—its sleeves were chewed. The librarian might hold that against her.

Jody blinked. "Once you're hired for the job . . . Florence will train you."

"Train me to do what?" Mice said miserably.

"To put books on shelves next to other books."

Despite herself, Mice tipped her head with interest.

"You see?" Jody said. "You'll earn a wage like I do."

The sister's eyes grew tears that hung, tarns lit by the sun. "But they'll laugh at me."

"Mice. Librarians do not laugh."

"Not the libra*ri*ans. You know. Them."

"Oh. The kids? Ignore them."

"But they threw milk at my shoe."

"Think of *Playhouse 90*. Did the soldier not ignore the enemy with a grenade? You'll do the same."

A rapid clicking arose in Mice's throat: a reflex, self-consolatory.

"Whether you know it or not . . . tonight will be a new start for us."

"*How*? No it will *not* be!"

It was like this so often, the sisters pulling hard at each other, the same strand of taffy.

"Why do you argue Mice? You must get a job. Mother said so."

"Mother never *said* that!" The girl picked at her scalp.

"And—tonight you've got to pin your hair up neatly. And wash your neck. It's gray."

The younger one in her nightgown, eyes shadowed purplish, suddenly lowered herself to a crouch against the baseboard with a look of compacted fury and said as if to herself in a croupy voice: "I'll do it someday."

"Do what Mice? Wash?"

"*No!*" The girl grubbed a hand at the bathroom, the hallway, incomplete gesture. "I'll *leave* this place."

A jumpy laugh from Jody. "Leave?! You can't. You wouldn't survive away from home."

"I could," drawled Mice, strangely aloof now, as if she were already a slightly changed girl for having spoken the word "leave."

Jody's eyes fought a sudden mist. "If Reef Way isn't right for you then no place is. You be*long* here. On your own you'd fall ill."

"I won't fall *ill!*"

In fact, Mice had never vomited that anyone had seen. Sometimes she gave a short, sharp phrase, difficult to hear.

"What did you say?" demanded Jody.

"I said I'd survive. I'm nearly twenty."

There came Jody's clout of a laugh. "You're younger than your age. Listen. You're going to socialize and talk to Florence tonight if I have to cut off my legs. Mice you have to do this. Otherwise what will *happen* to us?"

"But what if life could be flexible Jody? What if we didn't have to think about something a certain way?"

"You *will* think about this in a certain way. Girtle!" she called out. "Will you make sure Mice's at the party tonight on time?"

"Oh yes," I chimed at Jody, for at that moment I passed through the hall carrying several brand-new toilet brushes. I caught a glimpse of flushed Mice and her pencilly neck: this was the first time that I'd heard her challenge Jody so absolutely. What could come of it?

"You see Jody I *can't* go tonight," she said. "Because I'll be building a new radio—knob or no knob."

Abruptly, Jody ran down the hall to the bathroom, pulling off her clothes.

Sometimes the sisters' more acute clashes drove Jody to take a second shower. When she did, Mice often raced to her hobby table with its heaps of wires, cylinders, and nails, sorting through them, hammering nails into planks as the white hair shook—these would become radio-set bases.

On that day, Mice did not run to the hobby table and I was glad. Jody's second shower would allow me a few minutes with the younger girl.

From behind the bathroom door the older one called, "Tonight at the party you're going to march right up to Florence and tell her you want the job. Oh and Mice. If you left this apartment house d'you know what'd happen? I'd wind up blaming Mother and maybe even hate her for giving me a sister who deserts the family and causes grief. Do you want me to hate Mother?"

After a silence, the younger one admitted: "No."

"All right. After work I'll go to the bakery. Meet me there. Five o'clock."

So often, Jody Marrow angled for the last word, and got it.

*   *   *

I set the toilet brushes gently against the wall and approached the living room. Mice stood behind the open door, peering at me through the vertical gap between the hinges, whitish fields encircling her irises' blue.

"Did you hear what she said Girtle?" The younger one's voice rushed up and down, rapidly tearing silk. "I hate her. Don't *you*?"

"Mn. Well—"

"Oh *Girtle* you shuffle around here like an old *woman*. You barely talk. Why not?"

"I talk. I do."

"No you *don't*. Almost never."

I peered at her through the doorway's narrow crack, hearing the shower's spatter down the hall. "Well some have mentioned my shyness."

If my voice shook slightly in those days when I spoke to either sister, it was only because I didn't know from one moment to the next whether I was in with the girls or out.

"My personality isn't good," I said.

"How old are you Girtle? Forty? A grandmother with no grandchildren?"

"Mice I'm not even thirty."

"Old old old," she buzzed. "Your arms are too fat Girtle. Why're you *staring* at me?"

"I'm sorry but it's *you* staring at *me*."

"It only seems that way because you're looking at *me*!"

Mice emerged from behind the door then, grinning shyly and reaching, it seemed, for me. So I extended my arms in kind. But the girl had only wanted to touch my hair, and in my eagerness to grasp her, I fell forward, buffeting her backward against the door.

Mice did not seem to take notice. "How old is this braid Girtle?" she asked, tugging the plait on the back of my head, digging her finger into its thickest crux.

"Not so old." Happy to speak privately with Mice, I glowed inside.

"We'll make you a new braid."

"Oh don't Mice. Ow! That hurts."

"It doesn't hurt." Untwining the braid and sectioning new strands, she asked, "Didn't you hear my sister boss and push me? Did you *see* how my sister *is*? Oh I'm going to leave her."

"But Jody means well. She's setting great store by the spring party you know. And she worries about you so— I'll bring you to the party tonight."

"You'd better not Girtle."

"But you must go Mice or Jody'll be mad at *me*."

She focused on plaiting a fresh braid. I was stunned being so close to Mice, the faultless freckles and fleckish texture of her salty face a shore unlike any I'd seen.

She tied the end. "Look Girtle! Finished."

"Thank you Mice."

"There's a string on your blouse."

"It's nothing."

But the string compelled her. With thin, scratchy nails, she harvested it from my collar, immediately placing it on her lips as I watched, staggered. Then Mice chewed deeply, eyes rolling with enjoyment, her small tongue smacking.

"Why're you eating that? Mice stop!"

She proceeded to the front hallway's table, reaching for her sunglasses.

What was wrong with that girl?

From down the hall came the grind of the shower lever. Jody was nearly finished.

"Don't go outside," I told the girl. "It'll upset Jody. She doesn't know how you sneak out. Mice why'd you *eat* that?"

From the bathroom, the water fell heavily from the bath tap, forming the sounds of discrete words: "Asylum." "Verdun." "Dwell-dwell," the water yabbered. "One-two." I thought if the universe's matchless laws shifted only infinitesimally, the streaming water's voice might be able to tell me what to do in life, what to find.

I tried to block the apartment door. "Mice. Don't run off. Remember the rules."

"Sometimes rules could change Girtle."

"Mice—do you know who ran away . . . some years back?"

"No. Who?"

"I did."

"*You* Girtle? Where from?"

"I ran from a place. Three brick buildings. I hated it."

"Poor Girtle." She petted my head.

"Running away is all right," I said. "But you have to be sure."

"I'm sure."

"But Mice how could you leave your only sister? You're lucky to have her."

"I'm not lucky. The kids aren't peaceful to me. They yell names."

I thought quickly. "Then—what about taking a rest instead? You and I could go away. To a farm or cottage."

"Cottage?" she said dubiously.

"Oh there's scads of 'em these days," I breezed, glancing to the steam-cloaked bathroom door. "There's an old empty cottage at the far side of Stevens cornfield you know. Near Jupiter filling station. We could go tonight after the party. There's a table. Chairs too."

"Are you saying we'll play chess?"

"No we won't play *chess*!" I hissed, hand over my mouth, my irritation surprising me. Yet suddenly the idea of decamping to a moldy cabin with Mice, an activity Jody would oppose, exhilarated me.

I heard a skating sound: the shower curtain pushed back. "There's no time," I whispered. "Come to the cabin tonight Mice. No one'll see us leave the party. We can walk there—go on Alt Road. Or we could take The Way," I added eagerly, remembering the little dried-grass path that seemed to grow longer and wider in my awareness every time I thought of it.

The main road is always broken or wrong, in any case.

"We'll sit in chairs for so long that we'll forget everything. What do you say?"

The girl's blinking hesitation was enough for me to take as a sonorous *yes*.

"I'll pack right away!" I cried, diving behind the couch to swipe up my coffee jar, spoon, and one rolled-up skirt, packing all in a sack, excited for adventure.

Mice ran outside on the landing.

"Come back!" I called, energetic and more myself than ever. "Listen—let's stay at the party for twenty minutes and then leave for the cottage!"

"What cottage?"

"Darn it Mice! The cottage behind Stevens cornfield and close to Jupiter Gas where we're going to sit on chairs in silence!"

I heard the bathroom door scrape across gritty tile: Jody. I whispered to the girl: "If you're going with me then turn on the range—that'll be the signal. If the range is on when I come back from errands then I'll know you're coming. If you're not . . . leave the stove off. Understand?"

She was already down the stairs.

* * *

I did not want the story to engage gears and accelerate. Something about it inveigled me to stay close to where it was.

Living behind the sisters' couch had made me better all over—lighter. Beforehand, I'd lived on the grounds with the three brick buildings, a blurry place and time I wanted to forget.

I'd been under the care of the state. Sharp noises even today stick me like spikes. Not until I left for good and traveled south on a bus did I realize no one was watching me and that I had a freestanding life.

* * *

I closed the apartment door, racing to my pallet. Jody trod through the shower steam—I knew her steps like my own. In my frightened excitement I lay face down. She checked the rooms. "Mice!"

Above me she stood and thumped the lint-colored couch with her palm. "Girtle. I said *Girtle*!"

"G'morning Jody."

"Where is Mice?" Her face damp with shower water.

"Maybe she went out for air?"

"She doesn't go out for air and you know it."

"She may go out more than you think Jo."

"Don't get tricky with me Girtle. Mice follows rules. She keeps away from the sun," the older one established. "Where's she hiding?"

"To be honest . . ." I trailed off.

"Dammit. What?"

"The truth is Mice found a string on my blouse and ate it. Then she—"

"Oh the gibberish! You two are just killing me!" she cried, grabbing a small couch pillow, smashing it onto her leg once, twice.

"But Jody . . . I believe that string gave her strength."

"Excuse me?"

"Well—you know that all the good foods in the world make us strong. Well that's how it was Jody. She ate the string and got stronger. I saw it happen. Then she ran outside."

"*String*? *Strong*? How long will you make me a fool Girtle?"

"It's true. I've read about such things happening."

"Where is my sister? If she's gotten outside you're to go find her." I noticed that Jody's mouth widened as if she were scared, lips parted and downturned.

"Yes Jody but . . . Mice said that someday she wants to leave home."

"Drivel." The sister paled.

I swallowed. "There's one last thing. Tonight Mice and I will go sit in a cottage in silence. I think it's some kind of experiment."

"You are one big joke Girtle. Get up!" She flung the yellow sham aside. Then glancing to the electric wall clock, bit her lip. Had she just seen how late she was that day? Vastly late.

Jody slipped on shoes. As always, her elbow emitted a scraping sound such as the joint of a bisque doll. She looked out the apartment door, shading her eyes. "No one's out there but old Jack Lance."

I sat then, looking through the open door at the neighbor. On most days, the veteran stood for long periods at the curb near the green relay mailbox. Sometimes he paced the sidewalk, seeming to scan the area for irregularities. On that day, Lance inhaled from a small toast-colored cigar.

"Get out of *bed*. Go get her before the sun gets any higher. *Go!*" Jody cried. "She won't resist. Most of last week she did everything I asked. Now *go* Girtle!"

I reached for my thick-cuffed socks, my shoes.

Then the older sister sat on the couch, patting it. "Wait. Come here Girtle." She exhaled a long, salty-warm breath, hands over her forehead. I sat.

"I take care of everything around here. Every day. I do all the work. Don't I?"

"But I help you with the choring Jody don't I?"

"You do nothing."

"Yes Jody."

"And all I have is worry. Isn't that true? Say yes."

"Yes."

"And when she's tired and hungry so am I."

"Yes." Poor Jody.

"I must do as Mother asked me to—so Mice'll never get lost or burned."

I'd never met Candy—I arrived after she died.

"And my life is no life. Do you see that Girtle?" Now Jody looked terrible, eyes glutted with tiny runs of tears.

"But Jo," I encouraged, perhaps more curious and relaxed with the older sister than I'd ever been, "I'm sure you'd rather do other things than think about Mice all the time."

"Hmph," she gnarled characteristically, jaw tight.

"What do you *like* in life Jody?"

"*Me*? Well strawberry soda I suppose."

"Oh that's *nice* Jo! And what else?"

"Well kissing I suppose."

"Ohh *Jo*dy!" Her answer nearly rolled me off the couch as a heating sensation stunned my viscera, and I coughed a long time. "*Kissing*? Kissing who?"

She looked at me severely. "That's enough Girtle."

"But . . . you *have* kissed then? And if so Jody did it make you happy? Well if you *were* happy then I'm happy."

"I see what's going on here Girtle. You wrap me up in a long conversation so you can dodge work."

"That's not it!" I cried, scrambling to my feet, on the go. Once in the sparkling light of the iron stairs' landing, I turned, hanging my forearm over my eyes to shade them, noting Jody in the doorway, hair so shiny-brown that it appeared maroon. Or had the entranced sun simply seen fit to try out a new color on Jody?

"I am leaving for work Girtle. Do your job today as usual. Don't forget to bring Mice to the bakery. I'll be waiting outside. At five."

"Yes Jody."

"And after you drop her at the party . . . you'll return home. I can't see you staying there for the evening Girtle. You don't fit in."

"No Jody."

"And wash the dishes today. Don't touch the range."

"But you like a clean range I thought Jody?"

"Keep away from it Girtle! You ruin things."

"All right."

"And don't knock over the can of Scrubrite."

"The . . . what?"

"You see?" she emphasized. "This is the *problem* Girtle. You have no idea what things *are*. Now go!"

*　　*　　*

I spotted Mice in the trees' shadows, moving toward Lance. The older neighbor and the girl had struck up a distant-style friendship, apparently not long after the sisters moved to Reef Way. Soon the two conversed almost every evening at the street curb, despite Jody's glowering at both of them from the living room window upstairs.

Then he'd shown the girl an ancient crystal radio set and described its workings and capacity to snare radio waves from the air. She'd listened carefully, staring at his shoes. He'd soon coaxed her to make her own listening devices.

When the gruff veteran knocked at the apartment door later to ask how the girl's radio building was going, Jody told him that her sister was sleeping and had no use for neighbors besides. Undeterred, Lance simply waited at the curb for the girl the next day, and soon the two of them stood at the relay mailbox talking easily, Mice asking ranges of questions with no seeming fear or shyness of the carbuncular man.

He told her more of what he knew about electrical waves in the cosmos, magnetism, and other energies. I listened to the neighbor, too, usually from behind a tree.

Mice fixated on this information. The elder man soon told her that sound waves derive from stars. The night skies bend such waves to Earth, strengthening them, he said once at dusk. Humans, unfit for any whereabouts but Earth, will never see airwaves, nor feel them, let alone recognize the scale of the universe, since humans are bush-league, the man said. Another day as I listened, he told her that a radio never stops receiving. Its inner coil may be fashioned from any object at all, even a sock, but in order to function, this coil must be wrapped forty times with wire.

After that, Mice went to the bookmobile and found books on electromagnetism. She collected radio parts, and her first homemade radio was a raw plank hammered with several nails and strung with wire. The object failed to capture a wave band. Setting it on the floor, the girl destroyed it with a little gimlet — I saw this.

She built a new receiver from a piece of a chopping block along with nails, copper wire, clips, and a mail-ordered cylinder. This effort captured transmissions at night from a powerful music station in Texas.

Through this I stood by, watching Mice but also looking out for her — wasn't that what Jody wanted? Many nights I stole to the hobby table in the dark while Mice slept and found the small radio earpiece, sliding it past my hair and into my ear, eager to hear what Mice heard. Usually profusions of fuzz arose with music in between — corridas, western songs, and spates of furious talk about Communist enemies and grim, necessary battles to come.

*   *   *

As the girl walked up to Lance on that morning of the party, I stopped on the grass strip to hide behind a skinny lemon tree.

I heard her ask, "How long have people called you 'Old Man Lance'?"

"Since I was extremely young. What'd ya hear on th' crystal yesterday night?" he asked.

"Prizefight."

"Ah. Who fought?"

"A parrot."

"You mean Kid Paret," he nodded. "He win?"

"Dunno." She pushed the sunglasses up her nose.

"Paret's from Cuba. We needa watch that island—it's gone bad. You gonna build another radio set girl?"

She shrugged.

"Lazy won't get y'anywhere. We need t'listen for warnings at night. Keep at it!"

"I ran out of capacitors. I lost my new tuning knob and Jody won't help me find it."

"You lissen t'me," said the elder, shaking his thin arm with abrupt intensity. "You build yerself *more* radios— it's important. Getcha an ol' soda bottle—you hear? Wrap it with copper wire an' that'll make a fine capacitor. You know the rest—" The man jumbled in his pocket, extracting another cigar as well as a very short cigarette. "You gonna do that?"

"I guess."

"Don't say 'guess.' Say 'yes.'"

"Yes."

He struck a match. "Now: 'member I tol' ya 'bout th' midgets?"

"The smallest radios."

"Exceedingly small!" Lance's lips spread in a smile behind the curtain of smoke. "Feats of invention. They don't even need tunin' knobs. Think a' all that information. We'll bring it in nightly with receivers." He reached into his pocket and removed what looked like a coin purse looped with wire, topped by a protruding antenna.

"Take a look at this. We can build more midgets. Wanna?"

Mice examined the small device, holding it close to her dark glasses, pocketing it. "No thank you. I build radios alone."

"Then why doncha build one tonight?"

"Tonight's the spring party Mr. Lance. Jody wants me there. Are *you* going?"

"To a party? Buncha nonsense. Women's rot. Listen: you stay home tonight an' build yer set for our *country*. We needa keep track of all Reds—Russian *and* Cuban. Both infiltrate," he stressed heavily, then grinned. "Like diggin' up spuds—we need t'root out th' dictaters."

"That's not very funny Mr. Lance."

"Ah," he waved her off. "There's somethin' you don't know girl. Russia's been storin' their weapons on th' back side a' the moon."

Behind Lance's speech, an occasional whistle issued, lavish-sounding.

"But Mr. Lance. People're always talking about the moon. They're known for it."

"Don't get cheeky. Listen. Russians could be crawlin' all over Miami. Spies. We know they're buildin' weather towers. This is troublesome. We need t'start contributing to th' Red Watch. Locate th' Soviet wave bands," the man yattered. "Now. What else didja hear on the airwaves last night?"

"Music on the middle wave."

"What kinda music?"

"Horn."

"You like that?"

"I dunno."

"You hear talk 'bout an invasion?"

"No."

Against the lemon tree I began to drowse while watching hundreds of glossy ants moving up and down the creviced gray bark past my face—surely in search of valuable sugars or oils.

Mice's voice was high and clear: "Mr. Lance? Did you say 'crawling' a minute ago because—"

He cut her off. "Stop those questions Mice. It's irritatin'. Now—nothin' more last night on th' airwaves?"

"There was a lady saying numbers."

He struck his leg emphatically. "Ha! See? That's spies. They send codes. Radio's a simple technology but that's its strength see? Untraceable. Russians're crafty." The veteran tapped his temple with a canny expression, nodding.

"Mr. Lance is there such a thing as a Communist child?"

The man chewed on a stick. "Good question."

"A child was reading numbers on the radio."

"Hm. Russians prob'ly hypatize their kids an' set 'em on th' air to read code."

"What do the numbers mean sir?"

"Do I look like a cryptographer?"

"The little girl on the radio said 'five' a lot."

"Well that's th' fifth letter. Could correspond to *e*," he muttered, daubing his face with a rag.

"So when they say 'five-five-five-five' it means 'Eeee'?"

"Ah go on," he waved her away, wiping his nose.

She returned to what interested her. "Mr. Lance—a minute ago you said 'crawling.' Did you say that because there's a beetle crawling right there?" She pointed to the ground, where a large copper-colored roach worried along the curb. "Sir the human mind works by association. People say what they see. Did you say 'crawling' because—"

"Go on home Missy. You pick at things."

"Don't you have questions in your mind Mr. Lance?"

"No."

"But sir did you say 'crawling' because—"

"That's enough!" the older neighbor told her sharply, then crossed the yard to one of his apple trees. "Mice!" he suddenly hollered, for the girl had wandered toward a puddle in the street. She returned.

"People around here think I'm a fool fer growin' apples in Florida," he chuckled. "Well isn't that stupid. They don't realize you just gotta trick th' trees. Cover 'em with blankets so they don't sprout too many leaves."

"Why?"

"Because blankets block sunlight kid! Make the trees think they're up north in the autumn. See?" The elder rummaged through the branches, grabbing handfuls of the small fruits, stuffing them in a sack, handing it to her. "Eat these apples girl."

"Why?"

" 'Cause. They grew right outside yer door."

She took the sack and left the neighbor, who watched as she moved down to the puddled end of 28th Terrace and duly sat on the curb. When Lance disappeared into his shed, I ran toward the girl and sat on the curb too.

She ate the little apples one after the next, thirstily,

rooting for sweetness, I knew, tossing the cores. I grew parched to smell the fruits' cold slopes of water and sugar, the tangs of hay, grape must, and almond traces—yes, apple seeds contain some form of cyanide. Why?

Seeds, apples, and string constituted nodes on the story, in which I saw legend.

With the warm breeze, daily people passed down the block, employees and others starting their day, glimpsing Mice and her sack of apples, looking away, polite smiles fast as upside-down lids tightening away their unknowable lives.

"Come *on*!" I whispered, face near my knees.

"What do you *want*?" said the girl.

I sat upright; a silver tern spun overhead in the sky. From the tern's point of view, how small did Mice appear? Was she the same as me? How large was I?

"Aren't you going to the cottage with me? Haven't you thought about it Mice?"

No answer.

The daytime moon was high: a peeled bulb. Could Mice see it?

*　　*　　*

The story's helper with the purple-bruised fingernails, the one bound to barge into the story, had never been to Miami before—I learned about him after the spring party. He must've borrowed the Chevrolet Nomad that he drove south through the city's neighborhoods, then west, tourist-style, goggling at Miami's tropical flowers, colors, and scents through the rolled-down window. He would've passed nightspots like The Pineapple Club and Tangier Room, then, closer to Reef Way, The Nit-Pick

Club, too, scanning the packed doorways.

No matter how much I disliked knowing the story's helper was en route, he came to mind intermittently, if not constantly. On the afternoon before the party I loathed the idea of him most intensely—his sheeny blue jacket, baubly intrusion to the story, and the arrogance I was sure would permeate him.

He'd deaden the story and cause it to change. Yes, helpers are supposed to improve the central girl's life, but they fail. The words "He is so dull" coursed through my mind like a nonstop chyron, and just as dull, while I went about the days unable to do much but wait for the helper to arrive and make his mess by remolding the story. Yes, he was parochial and would ruin everything.

He probably kept a bottle of aftershave in the Nomad's glove compartment, I thought. A spare clip-on bow tie. His face would be eager, more callow than hungry. He'd turn west on Reef Way at 77th and drive past The Crescent Tender, glimpsing the knots of locals in doorways, then circle back for a second look at the bakery's entrance, listening for the music, airborne intoxicant of a kind he'd never heard before.

I'd never heard such music, either, until the beatnik played his records that night.

The helper would park the Nomad and walk into the bakery through the heavy, green-glassed door.

Why couldn't the helper have been *me*?

*   *   *

In time, the younger sister at last edged through the doorway into the living room where Jody stood alone, holding a plastic comb. She was often late for work, but on that day her lateness had turned out so extreme it was nonsensical.

"Where *were* you?" she cried, running to Mice, grabbing the girl's narrow face, hugging her once, twice.

Mice peered closely at the sister. "Jody. I ate apples and their seeds."

The older one had the girl by the shoulders and shook her in a slow-motion, exhausted manner. "What's *wrong* with you? You can't go out in the morning. Do you understand? I didn't know where you were. What if you'd gotten burned?"

"The sun doesn't hurt me."

"The hell it doesn't!" Jody shoved her sister back, flouncing into the kitchen. "Does the sun not cook slugs who can't remember to go home at sunup?"

I bounded atop the kitchen's high stool and settled there, the better to listen.

"*Mice*," the older one suddenly sighed, going to the sister, wadding the meringue of white hair in her palm. "It will help me if you don't go wandering."

I raised my hand immediately. "Oh Jody? I followed her like you said and I saw everything. She wasn't in danger. She talked to Mr. Lance. He said spies are everywhere and showed her how to trick the trees."

"Girtle be quiet," said the older one.

"There was a gray tern—" I began.

"Tern?" Mice asked.

"I said *quiet*—both of you! Did I tell you to jibber-jab?"

Even if I disliked Jody's barbs, how could I not smile at the sound of her sandpapery voice with the little angry scald on top? Surely she had charmed many, I reflected. Well muscled, she was like the vine that wraps a fence post with an ongoing, slow pressure, bracing it, in fact, providing strength for free.

"Mice go wash your face," she said. "Why do you need reminding? And before I forget: when you both arrive to the party I want you to look around you and see how everything is. Mice you're to find Florence immediately and ask her about the job. In a few days we might even drop by her house on Bird Road to remind her." Jody took the sister's small, damp-looking hand. "Mice. Who cares for you?"

"You do Jo. You."

"And who keeps you safe?"

"You."

"And what about them?" Jody gestured to the window. "They hate me."

"And who never hates you?" She waited.

I jumped from the high stool. "Oh!" I gushed. "*I* hate *neither* of you! It's quite the opposite. And I only want—"

"Girtle *shut up*!" the sisters said in loud unison, their four eyes upon me, identical in shape, but not color. They turned back to each other.

"Jo were you really worried when I left?"

"Oh I hated it Mice!" The eldest squeezed Mice. They smiled together. The enjoyment was strong.

Words broiled within me. I thought: "What about the cottage Mice? Will you go with me?" Instead I said: "Can *I* hug both of you too?"

"Go *do* something Girtle. Go away!" they said, shooing me off.

"Remember: we have to stay together," Jody told her sister. "For Mother."

"She's dead," said Mice, after which, inexplicably, the girls laughed intensely together, eyes squeezing tears, the younger girl adding, a wobble-like thrill in her voice: "When will *we* die?"

"Oh. When we're old," Jody breezed.

Mice: "But how old? Older than Harriet?"

The small dark-haired woman whom the girls called their cousin, and whom I didn't quite think was a cousin, was at least thirty-five. Harriet lived far south in Kendall and had the same luxuriant brown hair as Jody, though styled in a bulb.

"We'll die at night," the older one decided firmly.

"May we be buried together?"

Jody smiled. "There's a question I love."

Their four hands clasped together so the flesh and knuckles formed a mollusk-like mass, which the sisters swung.

"Jo every day when you're away I pretend I'm *you*," singsang the girl, teasing, swinging her arms.

"I know you do," Jody bantered, laughing, head back, arms swaying, enjoying herself. "But what do I pretend?"

The knotted hands swung higher. As I leaned against the kitchen counter, watching, I remembered it like a bolt.

It was the yard of the state children's home in Kendall, site of quick slaps from the matron for picking berries before supper. In through the door and up the stairs, the wardens marked infractions on a paper chart on the wall. The penalty was a stick, a strap, a radiator cover. I took the punishments well. All the child-inmates planned imaginary escapes.

Awaking from the memory, I retreated to the pantry and found a bag of carrots. Through the doorway, I continued to watch the sisters laugh and play while I ate in distracted, hard, covetous bites.

*　　*　　*

Why keep running back and forth over the tale?

*　　*　　*

With Mice cornered, the high schoolers leaned over the window well's metal lip, looking into the dark concavity for some time. Soon their conversation trailed off. The afternoon was winding down. I kneeled beside the well again to keep watch on Mice and the teens too, while busying myself in pulling a label from a discarded jar. A mild neighborhood man called Mel Seeke passed on the sidewalk then, a tidy pack of cloths beneath his arm. He glanced at the teens, then the well. "You kids after Mice again?" he asked.

Solly spun around. "What's it to you Bigface?"

Seeke's frown deepened as he rounded the corner, shaking his head minutely.

Joyce whispered: "*That* one has the brains of a dart."

The high schoolers laughed as Laurette remarked, "Why Joyce! That's the first intelligent and hilarious thing I've heard you say."

Joyce's smile expanded slowly as dough. She asked, "Why should Ghostface be allowed outdoors anyway where she scares people out of their minds?"

While their meanness I could have lived without, the sparkling, high-pitched words emanating suddenly from deep in the well were the most wonderful I'd heard in my life that far.

"All of you," the girl clamored below, along with the clinking sound of a kicked can. "What is your *quarrel* with me? Why are you mean?"

The group looked at each other in silence. Perhaps

they'd never heard Mice talk before this.

"Aw . . . *gee*," Laurette finally called into the well face-tiously. "We *wanna* be your friend Micey. We just don't know what you *are*."

Chuckles from the group.

"Oh that's easy," the girl chirped from the well, earnest. "Nobody knows what they are."

Silence.

"Actually. Personally?" Helen-Dale said then with a single bark-like laugh before her face went slack, serious: "I honestly believe any living thing that's completely and all-over white is a sad error. And I feel sorry for it."

After a pause among them, perky Solly added: "Remember during assembly when Principal said we must be tolerant of the less-fortunate kids and then the bleachers collapsed?" The boy laughed into his sleeve.

"I remember!" chimed Joyce.

Helen-Dale went on: "What Principal *did not* mention is that the lesser ones try to get all the attention. They sneak. They go where they shouldn't be."

Laurette whirled to Helen-Dale, pointing. "*Exactly*. Creeps infiltrate. Because that is the nature of *the creep*."

"Creep?" breathed Joyce, worried-looking again.

Laurette fed herself a pink square of chewing gum, nodding, then stepped to the curb and faced me, surveyed me all over, my spine's nerves rising consecutively as quills. "Know what Girtle? I think Mice has something in common with the deformed boy on Biscayne."

I did not understand if I was to reply to the leader or not. My legs shook. "What boy?"

"The boy outside the carpet store with all his many legs. Six of them? Eight? I thought he was your best friend."

"I don't know him."

"Legs?" Joyce wondered.

"Maybe they're tails." Laurette chewed.

Helen-Dale jumped with recognition. "Oh *him*! On the rug by the sidewalk? I saw that little handicapped boy last week and felt *so sorry* for him."

Amid the talk, Laurette turned away and forgot about me, so I moved down the curb and sat between two parked cars, concealed and sweating with relief.

"First of all," the leader ticked off on a finger to her friends, "has anyone ever *done* anything about that awful boy? First of all he's a beggar and bothers people. He sits on the carpet samples all day and has the nerve to smile and beg. First of all—"

"Hey! Why doesn't that little boy get a job downtown at Burdine's as a greeter?" It was Joyce. "He could get tips."

"He can't do that dummy," Solly told her, face serious. "He's crippled so shut up."

"Oh who can tell the future?" said Honey, tidying her bangs with a little mirror and quick fingers. "Laurette? Helen-Dale? Maybe someday *you'll* be lame. Any of us could be. My father says we live lavished with grace but watch out."

"Cork it *Honey*," Solly shot back.

"Poor li'l chap," Honey smoothed in.

Silence all around for moments.

Then Helen-Dale held on to a lamppost, swinging around it, recounting dreamily, "*My* father told me a story of ancient times when some fellas had a hundred hands. They got jobs as guards. They swatted enemies like fleas."

"Flies," Solly emended.

"Pishposh," Laurette waved it away, looking at Honey. "I *do* feel bad for the boy on Biscayne. I really do—all those legs and he can't go *any*where."

"Well *my* father says when people suffer God suffers," Honey rejoined.

"*My* father says God's too bright to sit around feeling sorry for himself." It was Helen-Dale.

"Who can help that little boy?" Laurette asked.

"Gosh and him being a Newfoundlander and all," said Joyce.

"He is not a *Newfoundlander*! Don't you get *anything* right Joyce?" the leader thundered.

Joyce covered her eyes with her hand. "I'm sorry."

"If no one helps him the little boy will keep suffering," Helen-Dale seemed to realize suddenly and stopped her swinging around the post.

Solly skipped around. "Not me. I feel great!"

"And my father said our hormones stir as we get older and make us very different creatures than we were before," Helen-Dale decided to add, smoothing her skirt.

Laurette rolled her eyes. "Dis*gust*ing."

Honey laughed. "That's part of life."

"Bzzz-bzzz," whispered Helen-Dale to herself, back around the lamppost, whirling faster into her cushiony thoughts.

Joyce looked to Laurette. "We'll teach this brat Mice a lesson. Won't we?"

"Yeah," breathed someone, or was it the breeze wheeling over the phone booth and trees, the air that Helen-Dale had stirred up with her twirling?

"You'd better believe we will," the leader vowed.

Suddenly I remembered my promise to Jody: bring

Mice to the party at five. We were late. I dashed to the window well, worried the teenagers would harass me. "Mice!" I whispered into the pit, crouching.

The girl's improbably thin voice shot upward from the dank space. "Girtle?"

"Shh. Come out of there! We're late and Jody's waiting."

"Oh Girtle—? Please get Joyce. I want to ask her something. Tell her to come here."

"Mice there's no time for questions!" I whispered furiously, yet suddenly Joyce was beside me, leaning over the opening, dropping onto her knees. "Mice?"

"Joyce—a minute ago you called me a brat. Did you call me a brat Joyce because your brother called *you* a brat the other day at Parrotts?" the girl asked, breathless, each such question as absolutely fresh to her as the very first question of her life.

"Come up here!" I cried quietly.

"You see Joyce," she said, "I was under the porch at the time and heard Shane Smock calling you a brat so did you call me a—"

"*Huh*?" Joyce blurted.

In fact, Joyce's antagonistic older brother Shane was frequently seen pacing westward and eastward along Reef Way, alone and toting a pole and sack before him.

"Joyce? The human mind works by association," Mice's voice continued from the well, the rest of the teens drawing closer to its perimeter. "One person says a word. That makes another person say the same word later on and so forth. Is that why you called me a brat Joyce? Because Shane called *you*—"

"You *asked* me that already!" Joyce cried, hands over her ears, running off some distance, bending to wipe seeping blood from her knees.

"Stop it Mice," I begged into the well. "It's so late and Jody must be furious. It's five o'clock!"

"Girtle," came the girl's disembodied voice again from the dark. "Is it exactly the same time down here in the well as it is in the bakery?"

*　*　*

A week before the spring party, the phone rang, and Jody went down the apartment's hallway to lift the heavy, weakly functioning receiver that amplified voices to a buzzing fault. She sat in the hall chair for the call, and I was on my usual stool, thirsty as a sink, hearing the putative cousin Harriet's voice squeak from the earpiece. I drank down the conversation.

"There's a cake sale tomorrow at the beach. Near the band shell," the woman told Jody. "Some of our gang'll be there. Come with us! Bring Mice."

"No thank you."

"Oh please dear! You like cake sales."

Harriet often drove her husband's car the many miles to Reef Way in order to check on the girls. If her husband was in the car too, it was difficult to know or otherwise to remember him; when his name came up, I saw gray slippers in my mind's eye.

To catch the cousin's every syllable, I leaned forward deeply, my face against the kitchen cabinet, catching the wood's sharp fragrance so close to licorice and rye.

"Harriet," Jody said. "This cake sale—is that the reason you called me?"

"I just want to include you girls when we socialize! And you know . . . your sister's so . . . well first of all she's on the thin side. Naturally God looks out for her but I want to help as I can."

"My sister's problems have nothing to do with her puniness Harriet."

"Don't they?" Then the cousin moved on. "Oh Jody by the way! Last Sunday Frederick and I discovered a new method to make our beach bathing so wonderful and satisfying. It all has to do with robes."

"Is that right."

Harriet's mood picked up steam. "Yes! I figured a way to avoid carrying my drippy suit back to the car. So now I just take the suit off in the cabana then hang it on a fence. While it dries I put on my new white robe and sit in the sun. Oh Jody it feels so good!"

"Harriet," breathed the elder sister. "Please."

"What is it dear?"

"I just don't want to hear about Sundays or beaches. I tell you I *can't*."

"Oh . . . but you love Miami Beach to pieces. You always have Jody."

"That was before. Now—"

"I'm not finished. See Frederick's going to start wearing a robe too! And for the next picnic I'll bring new robes for both you girls. What do you think? Pink or white?"

"We don't want robes Harriet."

"Why do you use that tone Jody?" She sounded hurt. Jody was wearing the cousin down. "Goodness I thought both of you would enjoy an outing."

"Try to understand that I can't bring Mice to that humongous park full of people. She'll ask all kinds of questions. And that dumb band shell . . . oh it's exhausting even to think about."

"Why?"

"God Harriet. Don't you know what it's like to live with Mice? She does anything she wants and annoys everyone." Jody seemed to struggle for a way to phrase her frustrations. "And then there's the sun."

"Oh we can work around the sun easy," the cousin promised, forward-sounding again. "You girls'll take a taxicab to the highway. Then I'll pick you up by the fruit stand. Lots of bushes there and fair shade. But to be safe I'll loan you both scarves for the day."

"Scarves perplex Mice."

"The point is you girls need to do healthier things with yourselves. Gee you make it sound a torment Jody but in truth it's just a cake sale!" Harriet laughed. "Won't you come along?"

"I don't want to."

"And to think you were so active as a child," the cousin stewed. "Listen to you now. What do you girls do with yourselves anyway over there on Reef Way?"

I slid from the stool and moved through the dim hall to the telephone table, the closer to hear.

"Well . . . last week I took her to The Potato. You know. And we walked to Dezertland."

"Phooey Jody. Those rooms are flush with beatniks." The cousin sounded let down. "Do you fraternize with them?"

"Not really."

"Not really or not at all? Oh with the recent news of young people attending riots this worries me. Look. Let's grab some blankets this weekend and bring a few friends to the beach for malteds!"

"Harriet God."

"Don't you 'God' me. I want the best for you and your sister."

Suddenly I clenched. It couldn't be, I thought, that Harriet was in fact the story's helper? If so, it would be a nasty surprise.

"Harriet," Jody answered. "Why all this business about blankets and robes? Scarves? You maybe want to roll us up in the national flag?"

"Oh stop it. Look—I know you girls've been through a lot. Don't think for a moment that I don't understand."

"Then please understand I don't want to haul off to a beach on Sunday. Or any Sunday."

"I know Candy's passing has been—"

"I take refuge in it."

"In the—what was that dear?"

"In death's absoluteness. It's a force we should admire."

A silence fell on Harriet's end of the telephone, interspersed with the sounds of static and a rash of giggling that likely came from neighbors listening in on the party line. I worried that the cousin would hang up in frustration or else push forward and take on the role of the helper. If the latter came to pass, I would be thrown out of the whole scenario in no time.

Harriet continued, "The way you *think* Jody. It's just too out of the mainstream. Can these thoughts be healthy dear? And wandering around all night to Dezertland? Smart girls don't do that."

"We went in the *afternoon* Harriet."

"Still!" The cousin seemed to sob this lone word, though in a possible attempt to conceal the crying, burst into either a cough or metallic sneeze. "I've tried to do right by Candy Jody! Oh she had troubles but she was good—Candy was. She was a bit lost. But she certainly tried. And now you two girls're going out into the ether like she was!"

"Did Mother try all that hard? I don't think so," the older sister remarked dispassionately, yet she was all emotions—I knew it. "Candy took me down notch by notch with her insults. Every year a little more. And did it to Mice too."

"Well dear that may be true but you don't really see what it takes to mother children."

"Do *you* Harriet?"

"I do have a name picked out for my baby daughter and plan for her to be born in about two years. In the meantime Jody I've been thinking—maybe I should bring Mice to Kendall to live with Frederick and me."

"Wouldn't that be marvelous for you? Try it."

"Sarcasm is not necessary Jody. Well in any case. I thought the cake and beach idea would be a help to you but I guess I was wrong."

"Oh don't feel bad Harriet."

"Look dear. Consider the cake sale an open invitation."

"You mean to tell me there's a cake sale at that nonsense park every *week*?"

By that point, Mice and I were both on the floor in the dim hallway beside the hassock watching Jody pace and strain against the coiled leash of the phone cord. The younger girl asked: "Jody! Are you talking about *me*?"

Jody pushed the telephone receiver against her midriff, glaring. "What conversation *isn't* about you? Morning and noon and night it's Mice Mice *Mice*."

"Don't send me away Jo!"

"I should."

I heard Harriet's voice needling in from the receiver. "What's going on there?"

After the phone call, the sisters, still so irritated and entangled, continued lobbing insults and weak ultimata at each other, strikes that gave rise to the indistinct gashes at the top and sides of the story.

*   *   *

On the street curb alongside Settler's Bank, Laurette suddenly squeezed between the parked cars, beside me. "What're *you* doing?"

I tried to appear casual. "Nothing. What're you doing?"

"Whaddaya *think* I'm doing— *Miss No-name*?"

"I'm Girtle."

"*Girtle*?" Smoothing her hair, laughing, she made a lance of my name; it stung. "I know your stinking name. Don't look down there at the bugs *Girtle*. Look at *me*. You *live* with those sisters of hydra don't you? So you know two or three things about Mice at least. Tell me. Can she hear us from inside the well?"

"She's not deaf Laurette."

"Watch it weird one," Solly warned, edging behind us, looking on. "What *are* you anyway? Their aunt?"

"No. I'm just . . ."

"Whatever she is it's not good," said the leader, her face close to mine, along with her cologne's scent like heated scrap metal, so unpleasant to me. "Listen Miss Poorhouse Girtle. You better tell what you know. Now: Whadda those sisters do at night?"

"Nothing," I answered.

"Tell the truth or else."

"They drink milk."

"Liar. What've they said about me?"

"Nothing."

"You tell Ghostface to stay off my street an' all the other streets too. Mice shouldn't be underfoot. Be *sure* and tell her. Understand?"

Sometimes in those days, so short on words, I leaned on others' ways of speaking rather than speak on my own. So with the repetitive chime of Mice's endless questions always close at hand, I replied, Mice-like, from the dusty curb, "But Laurette. It's you kids that bother *her*. You-all keep going on about her face and hair. *Why*?"

"Because dummy. That's what we *see*."

* * *

Then I heard scuffling—Mice was climbing to the top of the window well. During this, she addressed the high schoolers, something I'd never seen her do.

"I admit I have problems," she called upward to all, voice growing louder as she scaled the well's sides, now almost to the top. "The worst thing about me is my eyes and hair."

The teens gaped.

"Of course the sunglasses help on that count," the girl continued, white hair now crisscrossed with cobwebs and bobbing at the window well's metal rim. "When your eyes shake you want to cover them up so that's what I do. But Laurette? Solly? Can't you see how my character's different from the lame boy's on Biscayne?"

"That's assuming you even *have* any character!" Solly yelled earthily.

"At least the crippled boy on Biscayne's a boy." It was Helen-Dale.

Mice's pink wisp-like hands grasped the rim, and she tried looking toward the light. But the sunglasses dropped from her face, hitting the well's bottom. Now her raw, chafed-looking eyelids were exposed to the late sun's glow. She blinked.

The high schoolers stepped back.

"You keep away from us!" warned Laurette. "We don't wanna see you."

"Don't you see I'm no different than *any* of you?" the girl tried again, ashen skin around her eyes quivering.

"Yeah maybe on Mars," said Solly.

"But what about Eskimos?" she puled back at Solly, looking over the rim. "Eskimos're more different than you and I are different and you never make fun of them. Why don't you?"

Grasping to divert tormenters into mocking somebody else—who hasn't tried it?

"Weirdo," Helen-Dale addressed Mice with distaste as Joyce peeked over her shoulder. Honey peered into a pocket mirror, picking milkweed seeds from her hair.

How is it done, exactly, anyway—determining who is who?

"Eskimos have snow dances. They dance," Laurette proclaimed.

"Mice—let's go!" I whispered.

But the girl jumped back to the bottom of the well. She called from the bottom, sounding more focused than ever, "Laurette! I'm different than *you*. And *you're* different than the other kids. And everybody's different from each *other*."

The teens laughed riotously, with Laurette mimicking, "The worst part is my eyes and hair!"

I felt proud of Mice though, and wondered: Why hadn't *I* eaten the string and seeds too?

Helen-Dale gasped. "Gracious! I'm late for the party. We all are!" Running off, she called back to them, "Must press my dress!"

"Kids let's blow," called Solly, galloping loosely away. In his shirt's luxuriant cotton and tidy pleated shorts rested the boy's utter comfort with himself, the calm of his family's home. I imagined his prosperous father and mother and all possible advantages that he owned as one.

"And I—I forgot my potluck container! I have to fetch it," cried Joyce, running down the sidewalk behind Helen-Dale, both disappearing around the corner of 28th Terrace.

That left Honey and Laurette who looked at each other awkwardly before running in opposite directions.

The high schoolers had forgotten to follow through with Joyce's vow to teach Mice a lesson.

*　*　*

As the boulevard traffic streamed past, I sat beside the window well, miserable for the girl's hardships and begging, "Please come out of there Mice! We have to go. Don't you want to meet Jody?"

No response. I lay flat on the cement, cheek on the sidewalk, detecting a cool, sulfurous waft from below. "Mice the kids're gone! If they bother you at the party I'll do something about it—well I promise to try."

This was a lie or rosy prediction, for I wasn't fit to oppose Laurette or any of them. I hated my failure to protect the girl and wondered: Do small amounts of unseen sustenance lie scattered on the ground or in the bottoms of wells?

Then Mice climbed up, grime on her face. And inside her characteristic grimace, I saw the small teeth.

"You're covered in soot." I wiped grit or rheum from her eyes.

Her voice was quiet. "I'm going to stay down there a while longer yet. Goodbye."

"No—you can't!"

"It's good for me down there Girtle. It's dark."

"But Mice. What about Jody?"

"I hate her."

I was out of patience but did not let it show. "Then I'll meet you at the party," I said simply, standing, adding casually, as if suddenly remembering, "Oh and Mice—what about the kitchen range? It wasn't turned on. You know—the signal?"

She looked up at me. "What signal?"

"Oh Mice!" I hissed. "You were supposed to leave the range on so I'd know if you were going to the cottage with me. And you like the dark? Well the cottage is dark. Why not go there with me? Come on!"

"Why?"

"So we can sit in chairs for so long that maybe we'll go out somehow and not be what we are. Don't you want to try?"

As she stood there, my thoughts jolted back to Jody. Unable to bear the thought that she stood alone, waiting for us, I got up and ran to the party, leaving the girl in the shelter of the well.

II

All the neighborhood seemed to have gathered, laughing and chatting on the sidewalk in front of The Crescent Tender's striped awning, many carrying their covered potluck plates; the crowd, in my eyes, formed the beginning of a colorful gyre that would spin until the end.

Passing them all, I pushed against The Crescent's heavy glass door, so concerned about finding Jody. I rounded the pastry case and lit down the uneven concrete hallway stacked with disused café furniture, upside-down bicycles, sacks of sugar, piled newspapers, and bric-a-brac. At the end of the hall, I stopped to listen through the screen door: the patio was quiet and mostly empty. Tiny blue-and-yellow lamps festooned the overhead trellis, and the tiki poles' flames wagged near the center garden with its core of palms, jade fronds exhaling tree steam.

On the empty dance floor, the bakery's owner, Sal

Bianchi, stooped behind a hi-fi console, unwinding a braid of electrical cords. Behind him, a pair of sawhorses with raw boards formed a fruit juice bar where a local handyman, Mike Vinnegar, set out tumblers and pitchers and pressed orange halves onto a glass reamer's nose in advance of thirsty guests. Juice ran down Vinnegar's inner wrists.

Marge in her hostess dress stood at the patio's rear wall, quietly hanging construction paper lanterns and cutouts of pineapples and hula girls. The strips of yellow crepe paper dangling and sagging from trellis posts must've been her way, too, to try and evoke effervescence or mirth.

Now the baker crossed the patio with handfuls of plastic putty eggs and bamboo finger traps, scattering these onto the potluck table. "These'll be for anybody," he said to himself. He smelled like sugar.

At odds with the idea of the party's hosts seeing me, I crept into the patio's center tree garden and sat amid the palms.

Soon Larry Moates, a middle-aged umbrella importer and neighbor, arrived, eyeing Vinnegar. He swiped up a small glass, the shadow of his meaty torso moving beneath his pastel-lime shirt. "Mike," he asked the handyman-barkeeper. "Where's everybody?"

But Vinnegar never answered questions.

Bianchi dragged a small table toward the hi-fi, gray-white flour billowing from his trousers. "My guests're never on time Larry an' I wouldn't have it any other way. Hey. You want chicken legs?"

"Nah." The importer sat on a high stool; Vinnegar regarded him.

"Toast or soft roll?" the baker asked his friend, reaching for a bread plate on the bar.

"Roll."

"Sure you don't want the legs?"

Moates shook his head, batting crumbs from his lips. "Sal?"

"Yeah."

"Hate to tell ya chump but The Butterflake's rolls're better than yours."

The baker finger-plinked Moates on the head. "Screw The Butterflake. Now listen. Th' beatnik's gonna spin records 'til eight-nine. Then we'll have a poetry recital an' after that comes th' peanut-pushing contest. I hope there's time! Then the combo'll play. Sound good? Help me carry th' chairs from the cellar."

Moates wiped his mouth. "A live band?"

"Th' Jarouse Four." From the baker's back pocket protruded a shoehorn.

"Never heard of 'em."

"Who?" It was Jack Lance rambling across the patio, cigar in his mouth—he had come to the party after all.

"Jack hello. They useta be Hep House Trio," called the baker. "Before that they were The Three Men. Now they're a quartet." Bianchi's face went serious. "Merv Jarouse has a flute."

"So?" said Moates.

"Larry. Y'don't argue with a flute. Merv's a big deal. They just played Memphis. They're tired. Get the chairs."

"Okay but Sal. I've a terrible thirst." Moates extended the glass. "Fruit juice?"

Bianchi nodded deeply, reaching for the pitcher on the bar, pouring glowing marigold-hued juice for his friend. "Vitamins. Drink," he prodded gruffly.

Wasn't he a type?

*   *   *

Not finding Jody on the patio, I returned down the long hallway and out to the crowded sidewalk, dodging neighbors and avoiding being seen altogether by slipping behind a large planter of eucalyptus, the coin-like leaves rattling as they concealed me.

The sisters' neighbor Sheila, wearing a brown jumper with a square neckline, stood on the sidewalk with a distracted half smile, seeming to stare at Harriet in the crowd, who was alone. Sheila moved fast, grabbing Harriet's shoulders; the cousin yelped in surprise.

"Here's what's funny," Sheila told the woman, laughing a little. "I saw you just now and I thought you were Marge! I was looking for her."

"Why would I be Marge?" snipped Harriet, displeased-looking, straightening her dress, dark eyebrows drawn together.

"You'd never *be* Marge silly but isn't it funny I *thought* you were Marge?"

"Not particularly," said Harriet. "It was probably a trick of the sun."

"But I swear I saw Marge in you!"

"Sheila calm down. You're beside yourself."

"No. I'm beside *you*." The younger woman tickled Harriet's arm, then both women laughed over the differences in their points of view.

Then the real Marge appeared in the bakery's doorway, calling out, squares of sunlight playing over her face. "Why's everyone standing around? Come on in for potluck!"

Sheila ran to her energetically. "Marge listen to this! I saw Harriet through the window and I was positive she was *you*. It was so funny!"

"'Bout as funny as a dump truck," Lance muttered, passing, palm cupping his cigar's ash bulb.

Marge crossed her eyes at Lance's back, and Sheila laughed helplessly, throwing her arms over her friend, kissing the hostess on both cheeks, little beads of kisses. "Look! There's some milkweed in your hair."

"I'll pull it out in a minute."

Today in my chair, holding my blue blanket, I can see Sheila's face framed by her short, set hair and her collegiate jumper's square neckline on her plump skin, as if memories were not oozes of fat and syrup in the brain, but pictures to carry, or maps, tooled and touchable as leather.

The two friends caught their hands together. "You look different Sheila. What's come over you?" asked the hostess, smiling.

"I can barely explain. I feel floatsy Marge. Everybody I love is here tonight. I don't want anything to change."

"Everything changes."

"Don't spoil it! I'm happy and don't want to think of the end."

"The end of *what*?"

When Sheila shrugged, I trembled unaccountably. "I *won't* be fine at the end Marge. I'll be dying."

"Sheila. *What* are you talking about?"

"I fainted twice. Burt took me to Palms Hospital for a blood test."

The hostess suddenly appeared cross and somewhat damp. "That's nonsense. You're not ill! You're a healthy young hypochondriac and always have been so stop trying to scare me."

"I'm not trying to. Marge—have you noticed how *clear-cut* death is compared to life? Just look at Stevens cornfield." Sheila seemed breathless with feelings. "The stalks're so tall. They're magnificent. But the fallen ones're *so* white and *so* dry that it leaves no *doubt*."

"There's a clear difference between alive and dead? Why I've never noticed that."

The younger woman screeched with laughter. "But it's true Marge! The stalk gives itself away to the corn. It *has* to. Oh dear. So often life is unclear—death isn't."

"But people aren't like corn," Marge whined. "Look. If the blood tests show something you call me up right away. Okay? And for what it's worth? Maybe dying is much simpler and easier than we think. Now. Can we put a sock in this conversation? I refuse to think of endings."

Then it seemed Sheila's turn to whine. She reached for Marge's richly fatted arm, squeezing it with both hands. "*But Marge*. Whether or not death is easy depends on *how we die!*"

"Oh Sheila."

"Now me? I want to go slowly and be aware of my death."

The hostess's face now appeared to be plastered with a shell-like, bright expression. "Goodness—will you *look* at us? All whipped up about death and neither of us is even married yet!"

Both friends laughed, sets of teeth showing widely.

"You and Burt'll marry soon," Marge reminded her friend.

"Yes. Oh who'd ever have me besides skinny old Burt?"

"Somebody would—probably," the friend assured.

"No. I think I'm doomed to Burt. Oh Marge he's like

a child. Did you know he owns four yo-yos?"

"Good boyfriends are scarce on Reef Way aren't they?" Marge nodded. "Everybody knows it."

"Sometimes I wonder if I should try to reel in Joe Slaby. He's not too bad," Sheila mused.

"Oh don't take up with Joe Sheila!" cried Marge. "Why do that? First of all there's that big thing on his neck. Besides that . . . is Joe much different than Burt with his model airplane collection?"

"Right," said Sheila dully.

"Anyway you're quite a bit taller than Joe so you two *couldn't* be a couple."

"Oh. That's true too."

"I suggest focusing on Burt since he's already your fiancé."

"All right."

Both young women seemed to look down the sidewalk at Eddleston, who leaned against the bakery's facade, scrutinizing a matchbook.

"No more gruesome talk Sheila. Blood . . . death . . . Burt . . . my goodness." The hostess shook her head and stepped off as if about to depart. But Sheila grabbed her hand.

"Marge—did you fall in love with Sal in school just as soon as you met him?"

"Sal and I never fell in love. We just *were*. It's no matter. More than that . . . I've got to be married by the time I'm twenty-four. Otherwise—"

"Yes?"

"Oh I just *have* to marry by then else I'll gut myself. Will you do that too Sheila?"

"Of *course* I'll gut myself if you do."

They laughed again, Marge's face full of warmth and indulgence for her friend. "Your blood test will be fine. I know it."

Sheila smiled, her glossy eyes tender for her friend.

I saw their brief talk as a paean to life.

*   *   *

At last I saw Jody. She stood at the street curb alongside the crowd, searching up and down the boulevard for Mice, looking more fatigued than ever. I stopped myself from calling out to her, horridly uneasy to bring attention to myself among so many neighbors. Yet I needed badly to speak to the elder sister—so, sweating, I dashed to the far west edge of the building and behind a downspout to watch, for, by a hair's breadth, watching is similar to and can stand in for communication.

I hoped the sister would wend her way toward the downspout and me. But Marge stepped in, going to Jody and ministering in her cheerful voice, "Don't worry. Sis'll be here in a split!"

Jody wheeled with sudden intensity toward the hostess, gripping the woman's hands and wrists as Sheila had done earlier. "Oh Marge I hope so! But can you really know Mice'll be here? If so . . . how? You can't see the future can you Marge? Oh the speculating's killing me. I tell you I'm not well. Marge honestly—what's going to happen?"

As Marge, speechless for a moment, tried to soothe Jody with a calming hand upon the sister's forehead, the widow-notary Cissy passed, shoulder weighed down by the large, fragrant purse as she listened to Jody's pained statements, then announced to nearby partygoers: "See how the sky falls when Mice goes away? Jody goes by her feelings. That's how she *lives*."

"How would you prefer her to live Cissy?" asked weary-sounding Marge.

Jody did not seem interested in any of it. She stared uselessly through the bakery's front window, repeating, "I want my sister."

"Has the party begun?" the widow-notary asked everyone brightly.

"This is it," snorted Lance.

I took a step away from the drainpipe, as if I would go to Jody, yet unable to tolerate the bystanding neighbors looking at me, I ducked back.

"Do you understand that it's after five o'clock?" continued the sister to Marge, Sheila, and distracted Cissy. "She was supposed to be here. Something's wrong—and why should I stand around like a dog waiting to learn what the future holds?" She dived back in between the hostess's strong arms, head on Marge's shoulder, and simply waited there, eyes hidden, motionless but for her breathing.

Marge looked over to Sheila, who returned the hostess's glance with widening eyes.

"I said don't you understand?" went Jody's teary, muffled voice into Marge's dress collar, now wet.

"Well I *think* I do but . . ." said Marge, her own voice muffled somewhat, for her mouth, as it happened, was smothered under Jody's hair's thick sprawl. "I *mean*," she coughed, trying to extract, then swipe, the brown strands from her face, "of course I don't absolutely *know* the future if that's what you meant Jo. I am no clairvoyant. Still—"

"The fact is we *can* predict some future occurrences

based on knowledge of past patterns," Sheila supplied, large-knuckled hands clasped. At this Jody raised her head, nodding, perhaps calmed, though stray tears remained on her face.

"Now Sheil," Marge warned, "you can't say that just by knowing the past we're saved from present troubles," as Jody began crying again.

"But listen," Sheila went on as if now tuned into something else altogether, "I think Jody's really hit on something here because every person every day talks about the future like it's an airtight-sure thing! Marge?"

"All right," the hostess sighed, eyes closed for a moment. "I'll go along with that. But we need strength." She no longer patted Jody's head. "Hard to accept that no one *knows* the future *ever*. I mean even *Houdini* didn't know it . . . before he died but if he had—"

Then the remainder of Jody's calm disintegrated as she put her face back into the hostess's dress and honked, "I can't stand this! Where is she? Mice's trying to run away from me for good—I just know it and I can't have that!"

Marge rubbed Jody's shoulder and back, meanwhile leaning to Sheila and whispering noisily, "I think giving her comfort is best," as Sheila stepped around to face Jody. "What-on-earth-*else* would Mice do tonight but join us here at The Crescent? The child *must eat*. So she'll be here. I—"

"Don't talk *down* to me Sheila."

The young woman looked stunned, glancing at Jody and Marge who stood close together enough that the fabric colors of each woman's blouse and dress appeared to have fused, and she stepped back. "I *didn't* talk down to you Jo!"

"Mice's no *child* anyway. She's nearly *nineteen*," the sister fumed into the hostess's collar.

"Oh really?" Marge said. "But I thought she was in the sixth grade or so?"

"Oh Marge I could lose my *mind* talking to you!"

The hostess's face changed. She grabbed Jody's arm roughly, forcing Sheila to jump away, and through some unknown machinations, exciting to me, glowered and became crisply terse. "All right Miss Jody Marrow. You will *stop* this frenzy. There's no evidence your sister's other than *fine* and I don't want to hear you speak of it again. I tell you I am *finished*. Now you come onto the patio with me and enjoy meeting people."

"No Marge."

Laughter arose at a distance with the arrival, on the sidewalk, of more guests holding potluck dishes and greeting others in the swell of the crowd, with a few dealing out a forward-looking chant of welcome I did not understand, all of this noise overpowering the sounds of Jody's distress, without which I felt lost.

Finally Jody stood upright, having grown quiet again and observant, noticing soberly of her neighbors: "Marge's calm. Sheila's calm. But I'm not. Why not?"

Sheila explained it. "Marge can soothe herself *from within* if need be no matter where she is or what she's doing. Wouldn't you like to do that? You could try."

Jody looked at them.

"Go on and try it! It's not too bad!" said the hostess.

"But *how*? Tell me the steps."

Intermittent neighbors passed the three of them, many smiling charitably, for it was understood that despite the neighborhood razzings, Jody Marrow suffered a continuous, hard-to-comprehend burden, just as the younger sister did. But no one on Reef Way seemed matched to articulate those burdens, which were difficult to see and therefore name.

＊　＊　＊

Then from within the bakery came the sound of Sal Bianchi vomiting loudly.

Marge glanced to the kitchen, fluffing the yoke of her blouse. "Oh dear. I wish he'd stop snacking on guava pulp—he knows it makes him sick," she grinned lightly to Sheila.

I looked through the front window. The baker was hunched over a garbage can.

"Jody don't go anywhere. I'll be back." Marge dashed inside. Through the kitchen's pass-through, I saw her alternately scolding the baker and laughing before pulling a tray from a pan rack and carting it outside, circulating among guests, offering snips of bread.

Again Bianchi gagged into the can. Presently he went to prop open the bakery's green-glass front door, holding the towel, breathing fresh air. He surveyed the sidewalk crowd. "Hi," he said to Jody.

"Mr. Bianchi there's no controlling Mice these days," she said, still far inside her self-generated spell, eyes prismatic with tears. "She could leave for good and even hinted at it broadly this morning. What'll I do?"

The baker wiped his face and paused as if coping with another sick wave. "Simmer down," he told her, vague-faced.

Marge returned with the tray. "I've been telling Jody that *hands down* Sis's out there enjoying life on the boulevard and having a marvelous time!"

"You're insincere!" Jody near-screamed at the hostess.

Marge replied, "I *told* you to control yourself Jody. Now come *on*. This is your last chance. I'm taking you to the patio. Russ van Chaps is back there."

Jody's mood plunged. Behind the downspout, I felt it. "I don't want to meet him," she whimpered to the hostess, trying to twist away as Marge held her arm.

"You'll *like* Russ once you speak to him," Marge made plain, looking tired again. "I'll ease the way socially and introduce you."

She was referring to the owner of Dressel's, not only a neighborhood milk shop but a dairy farm, too, so far north of Reef Way that locals considered it nearly unreachable either by foot or the meandering municipal bus, so generally they found their milk and cream at a nearby rival dairy, Mick's, run by a turmoiled-looking, wiry man. Mick conveyed a consistent concern that his dairy was second-string compared to the larger Van Chaps operation.

"I *mean*," said Marge. "You must know Russ. He's interesting don't y'think? He's ethical."

"No he's *not*!"

"But Jody why don't you like him?"

"Because of his *personality*!"

Neighbors beneath the awning, tumblers of icy juice in their hands, turned to listen.

With passion or imagined passion, I pictured myself rushing, inspired, from behind the downspout and to Jody, separating her from the hostess with a shove to Marge—Jody who was nearly my own sister even though I didn't know or understand her very well and had not yet managed to make myself known to her at the party—but what business did Marge have pushing Jody to meet the dairy owner?

As if hearing my thoughts, Marge nodded reflectively, driving the tray's edge again into the crux of her waist, admitting, "Well it's true that Russ pretty much lives and breathes that dairy."

"*See*?" Jody glared.

"On the other hand Jo," Marge went on, reminiscing with enjoyment, "did you know that Russ recently guided the cows all by himself into a new milking parlor which became a logistical nightmare I heard?"

"*Marge*. Do I care? I need to concentrate on Mice. Don't you *see* that she . . ."

"But he needs to finish the parlor soon because June is Dairy Month!"

At this point, the slight library-clerk hopeful Minnie approached them, leaning somewhat forward over her hard, small shoes as she went, and I saw that she, like me, had been listening to everything. Minnie commented faintly: "Russ does tend to cling—doesn't he? Especially to his brother."

"*Exactly*!" Jody swung toward Minnie, pointing, vehemently agreeing. "Russ sticks like syrup and won't let go."

"But how can you say he's like syrup if you don't *know* him? I tell you Jody I've had enough," Marge said, departing as Jody hollered after her, "See Marge? Minnie thinks Russ lacks strength!"

"I didn't *quite* say that," quavered Minnie.

Then Bianchi, seemingly recovered from his sick stomach, stood at the street curb, laughing, waving the towel at passing cars, and advertising the party. "C'mon folks!" he cried, tipping his head, beckoning. "Party tonight! Live musical quartet!"

Locals in a tan convertible slowed, waving at the baker. "Can we come back later?" the friendly driver asked.

"Anytime!"

The car with its load rolled away.

Eddleston joined the baker at the curb. "I wouldn't mind having a slick brown car like that Sal. Drive my friends around."

"What friends?"

Eddleston laughed, swatting Bianchi on the head while the baker continued flagging the cars, touting his party. "We'll have poetry," he called out. "An' a peanut-pushing contest!"

This time, no cars stopped.

Then on the boulevard I saw a slow-driving harbor-blue station wagon—a Chevrolet Nomad, the driver's head a dark smudge but for aviator sunglasses squarely facing the bakery's door.

That was the story's helper, I knew.

At the curb, Eddleston tapped Bianchi. "Sal I'm hungry."

"Go get some fruit," the baker directed.

The Nomad rolled west. Maybe, I thought, the helper had gone to park the car. From my place behind the downspout, I tried to see—was he about to float himself into the bakery, down the hall, and do something awful, unforeseen? But the Nomad drove out of sight.

Sometimes before the helper arrives to the story, there's a little ping, then a long rest note.

I was convinced he'd circle back, park, push the heavy glass door, and enter. He'd start his oily machinations and efface whatever I was, vanishing me from the story.

I had to leave the downspout and stand on the sidewalk then, unnervingly close to all neighbors and hoping not to be noticed. If I were going to stave off the helper in some way, I needed a clear view of him when he finally arrived. So I inched along the bakery's facade and leaned against the bricks, arms crossed, and no one, not even Jody, noticed me; for this I was glad. Occasionally a neighbor glanced my way—and the fact that they did not recognize or know me at all, though I'd been living on Reef Way for some time? It was me. Something wrong with *me*.

Then a small man with glasses, brown clothing, and hair of no specific color joined Minnie, Eddleston, and others on the sidewalk, a covered bowl in his hands: The Blur. His eyeglasses' heavy frames held no lenses. "Here's my potluck dish. Gelatin," he disclosed, handing the bowl to Minnie, who took it readily, then staggered.

"It's flavorless," boasted The Blur. "Remember: if your throat is sore with bugs or spores . . . try flavorless gelatin!" In his more social moods, The Blur was given to lackluster maxims.

Cissy came to look at the dish as The Blur told her: "See? This dessert is gray."

"Gray? You horrible thing!" let out the notary.

The Blur might've grinned, but it was hard to tell, for, all nerves, he danced around, then sped off, stopping short for a moment, as if unable to decide where to go.

The branch library head Florence soon appeared on the scene, mildly interested in the gelatin, rubbing her injured arm in the beige sling as I watched from my place along the brick facade. Minnie and the assistant librarian, Millie Versh, with her own potluck dish, went to greet her.

Florence was tall. Both Minnie and Millie seemed to regard her as an authority, and with reason. Months before, Florence had gained local notoriety for solving an imposing problem at the downtown library—how to store twenty thousand old noncirculating books, some of them from the previous century. The branch head asserted herself, arranging for the library administration to rent a cave on a nearby landowner's property, where cool, porous limestone vaults would preserve the books perfectly, the owner promised.

Yet only a few weeks after the library trucked the books into the rock vault, spores overcame their pages. The ruin was an embarrassment for the entire library system. As the story of the virulent book mold spread through the city's neighborhoods, Florence, who lived with her old mother off Bird Road near the branch library, was not ashamed of her mistake or even unsettled. Instead, she seemed to enjoy the public attention and even blossom. Much to neighbors' disapproval, she refused to take the blame for the molding books, and in a letter to the newspaper, stated that no one was to blame. Formerly stern and stolid, Florence had grown exuberant, outspoken, and eloquent about other civic issues too, such as the city's plan to demolish homes for the north-south expressway. After the book-mold incident, discomfited neighbors noticed her gait became faster and bouncier, and as the library made arrangements to incinerate the thousands of ruined books, officially warning Florence to be more careful in future decisions, Florence took a vacation, busily acquiring a new wardrobe of brightly colorful dirndls, blouses with swinging pompons, and hats. Once, while shopping at

Parrotts, she even wore a fruit headdress, as neighbors told it.

It was hard to believe that the librarian's character had changed so much. Yet the change seemed permanent, and she continued enjoying life to the fullest, laughing, engaging, and participating almost out of bounds, even after she fell down the central library's front steps one evening and chipped her elbow bone. On the night of the party, the branch head wore a panel dress printed with large yam-colored blossoms, her arm sling somehow working to enhance the ensemble.

* * *

The two librarians and Minnie stood outside the bakery's open doorway. "I hate all these young people," Millie told her colleagues, leaning to them. Her small head, capped with light brown hair, made her resemble an acorn.

"Hate? Why?" asked Minnie.

"They'll have to grope and grasp through life like I did."

"They may have wonderful lives yet," Florence said, eyes shining. "Oh we won't be around to see their lives play out."

"*I* will," swelled up Millie. "I'll live a long time because I eat fruit."

The groups of partygoers chatted avidly on the sidewalk, pressing toward the bakery's door.

"The party's starting," noted Millie.

"Not quite," Florence countered.

"When I hear loud voices my heart beats hard," said Minnie.

"*My* heart beats hard when I see a dead dog," said Millie.

"Why bring it up?" Florence asked.

In fact, two dogs had lost their lives on Reef Way the week before.

Marge appeared in the doorway. "Florence! Is your arm healing quickly?"

"No," said the branch head, eyes merry.

"Miss Stroke! You had an accident?" It was Moates the umbrella importer passing by, holding a juice glass.

"I tripped down the stairs and fell on a coil. Steel," the branch head said.

"Still. You look lovely," offered Moates, toasting alongside the woman's sling.

Marge cut in to announce: "Everybody! Let the party start! Come to the patio. Bring your dishes," as the baker appeared and whooped beside her.

A few went through the doorway, heading down the long, dim hallway toward the garden patio, though most neighbors ignored Marge and continued chatting. I stood against the brick facade, watching, listening to voices. Words formed, then fled.

Two local beatniks, Larry Smolt and his friend Harry Kulp, a poet, hauled cases of record albums across the sidewalk and into the bakery. Others arrived: the smiling young marrieds Mike and Nina Remnick, who walked while swinging their little daughter Phyllis on a seat formed of their four gripped hands, and the dental secretary Cindy Shirley House, who held, as usual, the arm of the dentist, Dr. Ken Warm. Then came the neighborhood sisters Trudie and Sherrie Gagel, in their twenties, both with yellowish hair, their green eyes so similar that even locals mistook them for twins. Behind them was Hildy, their mother, more carelessly confident, to all appearances, than her daughters would ever be. Also arriving through the crowd: The Artist with the Scarf, a loner; the high schoolers, dashing together toward the storefront like a single laughing entity; and gangly Eddleston, heaving a steel dolly piled with salt sacks and a large drum of yeast through the crowd, levering it through the doorway. Bianchi rushed out, helping pull the supplies indoors. Meanwhile, old Phenice rocked in her chair outside the store's front windowpane embossed with gold lettering.

Beatnik Larry returned to the sidewalk, then tugged another box of record albums from a parked car's backseat.

"Whatcha doin' Larry?" Laurette called to him scoffily, her friends behind her.

The beatnik shrugged, smiled. "Nothin'. Sal just wants me t'spin some records before the combo starts."

"Well you must be special as *pie* then," teased Laurette. "Aren't you?"

"Uh," the beatnik tried answering.

Cissy smiled. "Aw. Lookit our little Larry. So *serious!*"

Solly pressed through the crowd. "I heard you listen to devil music Larry Smolt."

"Shuddup," he told the boy.

"You shuddup."

Gripping the records, the beatnik disappeared inside.

Solly turned to the high schoolers. "I saw Larry at the dime store an' he was readin' a *crime* magazine. An' another one about stuff as weird as yoga an' worse."

"Beatniks're unpredictable. It's been researched," Helen-Dale reported, prinking to her reflection in the window.

"Obviously," said Laurette.

"Poor Laurette's stuck on Larry Smolt. Aren't ya?"

Solly grinned.

"I am *not*," Laurette told him. "Honey is."

"You think I give a curd about Larry Smolt?" said Honey airily. The teens laughed.

On a bench beneath the bakery's awning sat the Remnicks with their little daughter. Mike Remnick was a low-rung architect; his project for a new firehouse had been rejected by the local council.

"I'm sure Larry's *mother* loves him," Remnick offered the high school girls.

"You kids are terrible," Nina Remnick told the high schoolers. "You pick on people. It's lousy."

"It's a free country Mrs. Remnick," Helen-Dale whipped back at her. "We say what we want."

"Can't you be civil?" Nina asked her.

"Mommy." The sleepy child raised her head and blurred the word, her foundation.

All of it swimming together.

Then the librarians converged upon Nina and the child as Remnick slipped away.

"Your baby has grown so sturdy over time!" Florence exclaimed, smiling softly.

"She's pink and healthy!" affirmed Millie. "Is she hungry?"

"How old is Phyllis?" spouted Minnie.

"How old *are you* Phyllis?" Millie asked, leaning to the child.

"She's six," Nina said.

"Oh she's just very young then," deduced Minnie.

"Ladies if I could just go back in time," Nina said, eyes tearing a little. "She is growing up quickly. Phyllis was a darling baby. But I had the catarrh and slept the whole time. I had a nurse in. I didn't get enough of the baby."

"But," said Florence, smoothing her dress, "an older child is much better than a baby. My own mother taught me that."

Boggled, Phyllis stared at the women.

By then Nina seemed in a reverie. "Isn't it strange," she smiled faintly, "that after being alive only three-four-five years a child actually has his own thoughts? Oh the things Phyllis says!"

"How long are you and Mike married now?" Millie asked her.

"Forever. God," said Nina, turning with the heavy child on her lap, seeming unable to decide if to stand from the bench and heft the girl's weight. Then she turned and pressed her palm against the bakery's big windowpane as if it were a craved way of life.

Harriet emerged from the sidewalk crowd. "Nina! Are you godding?"

Little Phyllis looked up. "Momma. Remember when I was a small child an' I had a disease an' all I could do was go-bathroom?"

The high schoolers laughed.

"Shh," Nina said, shifting the child on her lap.

"I was sick an' I slept on the toilet bowl all night. Didn't I Momma?"

"Did I tell you to be quiet?" Nina, red-faced, smacked the little girl's head lightly with her fingers. Phyllis bawled, wiping her nose, then slid from Nina's lap as the mother watched her go into the bakery.

Through the open door, I saw the child approach a large stand-up ashtray, glancing to check if her mother was looking. Then she sank both hands to the wrists in the ashtray's sooty sand, fingers wriggling; the sand furrowed and fell away.

"What a wonderful game," Florence seemed to say to herself.

Phyllis's delicious-looking activity drew me off the sidewalk into the storefront where, angling myself behind the bakery counter, I watched up close as the child churned the sand with her small hands.

Phyllis looked at me all over. "Who are you?"

"Nobody."

"Are you from Florida too?"

"Yes. I'm from south of here."

"Why are you from south of here?"

"I just am. I came here to live."

"Why?"

"I ran away."

The child stared gravely. "It's wrong to run away. Why did you?"

"Shush," I told her. "It's nothing big. I lived in a bad place. I wanted to leave."

"Did you go to school?"

"Yes."

"Did it have dirty bathrooms?"

"Lots."

"It's against the rules to run away," said Phyllis. "I'm telling my dad."

"Don't!" I pleaded.

The child ran outside to the bench, where her mother swept her immediately onto her lap, the two of them watching the animated swarm of guests on the sidewalk, their faces in profile indescribable pictures divorced from their names.

I went into the bakery, observing. Beyond the counter, a honey-colored staircase led up to the office. Beneath the stairs lay a small curtained-off storage area. Into this space, cool and dim, I went, breathing the delicious scent of raw, sawn Florida maple, enjoying the pleasant stacks of dry-goods boxes that formed an enclosure around me. The curtain's gauzy fiber allowed me to see through, and I viewed Bianchi sailing from the kitchen with a tray of steamy, fragrant bread, then leaning out the front door, calling again for neighbors to enter.

If bread's scent, to me, meant comfort, respite, and even a type of freedom—not civic freedom, but freedom from the past—could bread and its steam, in neighbors' eyes, mean anything different?

From my place behind the curtain I looked down the hallway past the salt sacks and the drum of yeast, all the way out the store's big windowpane and onto the street.

I wondered if Bianchi had forgotten about the yeast barrel. Why wasn't it in an icebox or cooler?

Jody was still on the front sidewalk, looking up and down the dusky street, a lonely silhouette. Did she blame me for Mice's absence? Afraid of her, I waited, limbs dense and still as butter sticks, so enjoying the dim quiet of the storage room with its blank-faced boxes that I couldn't move at all.

Suddenly Jody shouted from the sidewalk: "Marge!" then ran into the bakery.

I sat up to watch and moved closer to the curtain. The hostess emerged from behind the counter, setting down the tray.

"Marge I saw three people on the sidewalk—two men and a woman I think. I don't know them and—"

"Bring 'em in here! We'll *get* to know 'em!" laughed Bianchi at a distance in the kitchen.

"Goodness Jody. Are you upset?" asked Marge, going closer, the two of them now holding each others' forearms. "Don't tell me you're scared of strangers?"

"It's not that," said Jody, brown hair messy. "The three of them were young and had the same eyes and hair color. You should've seen it Marge—kind of eerie. You see all of them had *exactly* the same face!"

Marge's arm went around Jody's shoulder comfortably. "Sounds like you saw a family!"

This statement seemed to land on Jody with a jolt. Then growing tearful, she told Marge: "You're wonderful. You listen to me and never laugh."

"Goodness. Who'd ever laugh at you? You're wonderful yourself. So what about this family?"

"Nothing I guess. It was just strange."

From somewhere on the sidewalk I heard Hildy tell another partygoer: "*Jody*? Oh she's been tied in knots over her sister since day one.*"

"Feel better now?" asked Marge.

"A little," Jody admitted as the hostess pulled another full tray from the rack.

Then the baker was kneeling at the pastry counter, examining a stain or mar on its side, saying, "Marge! Rags! Where are they?"

"Under the sink Sal," hollered the fiancée, already down the hall with the tray. "I washed 'em in Ajax!"

Suddenly the baker was beside her. "You're lovely," he said. Marge beamed.

Watching through the gauze curtain, I inhaled deeply as if to siphon their warm current for myself.

Then Moates, with his fringe of brownish-gray hair, went to the counter, calling, "Sal! There's no hot salami on the potluck table. Why not?"

The baker turned. "Really Lar? You *are* hot salami."

Marge laughed and went off with the tray.

Bianchi went and cupped his friend's head. "Larry dummy: I love you. Don't get picky on me. Hey. I heard you had a snarl with your mother."

"No Sal. My *sis*ter. I grounded her. She wears on me. Does wrong things."

"Poor kid."

"Poor me."

"What's so bad about li'l Brenda?" asked the baker.

"She's messy! Leaves wads a' chewing gum everywhere. An' now she wants a bracelet?"

"Lock her up," Bianchi told him.

From the sidewalk, neighbors had begun streaming indoors past the case and down the hallway, voices layered atop other voices, too many to track.

"Ah Brenda's a good girl basically," the chubby importer went on. "And how can I not love her name? Brenda Jo Moates. Such a *soft* name."

The Blur sped by, a taupe streak in white tennis shoes. "Love the name—love the sister," he seemed to quote, then was gone.

Passing nearby, the widow-notary Cissy sipped pale juice thoughtfully. "What do you mean by 'soft name' Larry?"

Others, passing, drew near, echoing this: "Soft name? What's that?" And Lance moved inside too, placing a hand on Moates's shoulder. "Who's soft?" he grinned. More neighbors surrounded Moates with curious, bright eyes, including Eddleston, who hopped briefly on a foot, saying, "Here's a soft name for you: Phil Rizzuto."

A few laughed. Moates shook his head. "Sorry Burt—that's not *quite* a soft name. But here's an example: Josh Brausch."

"Who's that?" asked Millie.

"Doesn't matter," Moates clipped. "Some names are soft. You must hear them to know them."

"I'll listen to your nonsense Larry long as there's pot-luck nearby!" cried Eddleston, and Lance chortled.

Below Eddleston's swept, reddish hair: his large bony forehead, longish teeth, and his long legs, all bone. Each part of him was congruous with the whole. I wondered: Where in a body does integrity begin? Looking at neighbors congregated throughout the hallway, storefront, and sidewalk, I saw the answer. Integrity begins everywhere, yet its source is not findable.

* * *

Soon from the Pink Room—a sitting den off the long hallway that Marge had designed with rose-toned wallpaper, pink chairs, and a salmon-hued sofa—drifted a loud, pained groan: Jody and her turmoils again.

Highly attuned Sheila recognized the voice and sprinted down the hall, calling out, "Easy Jo. Sis'll be here soon!"

Marge emerged from a forest of pan racks in the kitchen, running with an empty tray held before her as a Thracian shield. "Tell her don't panic and that I'll make lemonade!"

With my face against the gauzy curtain, I spotted the elder sister just inside the Pink Room's doorway, arms folded around herself, appearing smaller than I thought Jody was. As Sheila and Marge rushed to her in the doorway, Jody flung out skittery questions as if the topic had never before been discussed.

"But Marge how can you *truly know* if Mice'll be here? Is it a hunch or did you get a message or sign or—?"

Sheila looked at the younger woman. "Please Jo—try to remember your sister's at a sensitive age."

"So am *I*!"

In such moments, Jody's intensity, severity, and down-turning mouth made me believe that she might, in her mind's eye, be foreseeing her own death.

The baker emerged from the kitchen with a pan. "Chicken flips anyone?"

"I mean," Marge tried yet again, "remember in October Jody when Mice jumped into the canal and how upset you were? But she was fine. Wet of course—and remember how we found her in the grass listening to that little radio? That's how it'll be today."

"Marge that makes no *sense*!" the sister went on. "Is October the same as *now*? No it is not."

"But in one way all days and times *are* the same," Sheila reflected.

"Jody we know you feel blue and uncomfortable," Marge said, these words nearly a musical lament. "But I want you to listen to me. You are *not* going to let this night wreck you."

Teary Jody nodded.

Nearby, holding a tumbler of bright yellow juice, Moates remarked, turning to look at the three of them,

"Welp! I guess somebody's in hell again."

"Don't razz her," Sheila snapped at him. "She's in hell and hell is agony. Don't you know how things can go wrong in life Mr. Moates?"

The businessman's glad expression deflated and he trudged off, juice sloshing.

Jody then spoke to the situation somewhat differently than before. "This morning might've been the last time I'll ever be in my sister's presence. This could be the end of knowing her and if that's true I'm wrecked and'll never be the same!"

Now Marge and Sheila appeared fully sapped. Coming past again with the towel, carrying an empty ice tub, Bianchi glanced at the women, tipping in with a smile, "Who in the United States worries about a kid sister like this? I've never seen anything like it."

"Me neither!" called Minnie down the hall brightly, having just entered the storefront with jovial Millie behind her, so she couldn't have known what they were talking about.

Jody reached a shaky hand to the baker. "Mr. Bianchi forget the ice for drinks. And tell Mr. Moates to forget soft names because names and words are *nothing*."

Minnie edged up to her. "But Jody? Words aren't *nothing*—not exactly. What about a grocery list?"

"Will you leave me alone?" cried the elder sister as the library-clerk hopeful leapt back, timorous-looking.

"Names?" hummed The Blur, speeding past.

"Mr. Bianchi can't we stop the party and go outside to search for Mice?"

"Cripes," came the umbrella importer's voice from down the hallway. Then Bianchi, departing for the kitchen,

131

called behind him, "Are you kidding? I've got a flute player on th' way. The party goes on!"

"Mr. Moates!" Marge suddenly hollered down the hallway. "Keep talking about the soft names—might take Jody's mind off Mice!"

Moates turned, nodding to this, lifting his hands, palms open and extended, to beckon neighbors from all sides. As they gathered, the umbrella importer announced in a stagy manner, very much in his element, "Let me continue. Some names're just soft. How do I describe it?" He put his hand to his chin.

Remnick, now standing beside his friend, also set his hand to his chin.

"Stop that Mike," Moates brushed off Remnick, irritated. "Now listen everybody. A name has qualities. The name carries the individual and the individual must rise to it. Understand?"

"No," sassed Minnie, and neighbors laughed.

Jody raised her head, listening with some interest.

"You mean a man's name can shape his fate Larry?" Remnick said, all irony. Next to him stood Nina, telling her husband softly: "What drivel."

Smiling Eddleston executed some agile Charleston dance steps, then skipped away.

Moates persisted: "Here's my point. Some names are hard and some soft."

"Larry no one knows what that means," offered practical Millie.

New arrivals entering from the packed sidewalk pulled in close, trying to read what was happening. Moates took Remnick's arm fraternally. "Okay. Here's a hard name. Matt Parker."

"Ahh," said neighbors together, some turning and nodding, faces open, and Remnick laughed outright.

"See?" Moates smiled.

"Larry—what about 'Gerry Sage'? Is that a soft name?" It was Cissy.

Moates gestured graciously. "There you have it," he smiled. "That's a soft name indeed."

Neighbors chuckled lightly together.

"You mean Gerry Sage the high school janitor?" asked Millie.

"Of course," quipped Cissy. "What other Gerry do we know?"

Moates laughed generally, red-faced, enjoying it all. "Oh Gerry has a wonderfully soft name!"

"Just a moment," Marge said behind them all in a warning voice, carting a tray of cold boiled shrimp. "Are you making fun of Gerry Larry? Because don't do that. Gerry's one of the best."

"Making fun? No," said Moates. "Gerry has a nice name and it's soft. Aside from that? It's no fault of mine that Gerry's such a—"

"Yeep!" It was Solly, standing behind his high school friends, his hands upon their shoulders as he jumped once, twice, then hoisted himself high upon them, as if to gain attention or weigh in: "Gerry's all right!"

Cissy went to Marge. "Some of us have our opinions about Gerry Sage and what's wrong with that? You see I feel sorry for Gerry and can I really *help it* if I feel sorry for him? No I can't. It's a shame that he's still a janitor."

Marge appeared speechless for a moment, during which Cissy strode down the hallway with a ballerina's measured gait, raising her arm aloft, her leg suddenly catching on the storage curtain, pulling it back, exposing me for moments to everyone in the hallway before the curtain dropped back into place.

Sweat sprang to my skin as I crouched in the dim cupboard, side of my face to the boxes as I breathed in their musty flavor. What if Cissy continued her impromptu ballerina practice and danced past to pull the curtain back again? I scrambled for cover among the boxes as she skimmed back through the hallway in jeté-like prances; this time, however, the curtain remained undisturbed. My sweat fell. Now the performance appeared finished and she stood before all neighbors, one arm raised as if for a curtain call.

Marge approached her, eyes angry above the shrimp. "What did I just tell you? Don't you *dare* pity Gerry! He's my cousin and a good person."

Looking away, the notary did not reply, her hands and fingers at her sides still engaged in the dance, fluttering expressively.

Eddleston broke in, "I've always felt a little sorry for Gerry too. He's a kinda sad sack isn't he? Could grow out of it though."

Marge grew loud and icy. "Did you not hear me Burt? I said peel back . . . both of you!"

Eddleston and Cissy stood silent. Marge looked around, asking neighbors, "Where's Gerry anyway?"

"Could be cleaning classrooms at the school yet," offered Millie.

Bianchi returned, the ice bucket full. "Gerry's not off work? Ridiculous. He should be here with us. Hey," he turned to the high schoolers. "Go fetch Gerry Solly."

"Right!" the boy in shorts scampered off.

Suddenly, Cissy walked heavily to the curtain and yanked it back, poking her head into the storage area. I felt cool air invade the small space; my blood reversed as I looked up to see the array of neighbors' sharp, strange faces staring at me. Cissy proceeded into my lair with an amused, arch expression, bending forward, the numbing scent of her cologne all over me. She piped loudly as if delighted by a miniature toy, "Goodness! You're hiding back here in your own little world aren't you?"

While the notary was well familiar to me, she had probably never noticed me at all. Stricken by this unveiling, I nodded compliantly, the faster to disengage her. But Cissy remained over me, panting lightly, taking in the storage area before smiling warmly, open-mouthed, blinking. "What do you do back here all by yourself?"

The question could be answered in several ways, but before I could answer, the older woman lost interest and returned to the hallway, releasing the curtain, calling, "Marge! You should really straighten up the clutter under those stairs. You could turn it into a nice little place!"

Returning to watch through the curtain, I noticed Florence nearby, leaning on a stool, flicking and rolling a toothpick between her lips. "Oh leave it Cissy and stop acting. No one's going to redecorate here. This old bakery will eventually go the way of the great auk."

All of it running together.

*　*　*

On the floor of the storage area I found a straight pin with a pearl head and jabbed it through the curtain and into the wall, sealing off the compartment to make it mine. But it was not mine. In moments I heard a huge commotion from down the long, dim hallway, where a thin, right-veering passage led past the bathroom. Then Bianchi boomed: "Marge! Get that monster out a' the tub!"

I ran from the storage area to see what was going on and instantly got caught in the shard-like passage jammed with high-spirited joking neighbors. All moved as one through the hallway, and soon, when we stopped, I peered through the gaps between their long bodies and apertures of bent elbows, trying, like all of them, to see into the small bathroom.

The place was mobbed. Angling stiffly as an outsized penny through the doorway, knowing no one noticed me, I squeezed past neighbors one by one, finally lodging myself between the bathroom's sink and a damp hamper.

"Aw Sal. He's cute!" It was Eddleston.

I caught sight of a claw-footed bathtub.

Florence called out strongly from the doorway, "What's everybody looking at?" Like I had, she was attempting to squeeze into the bathroom, but was unable to. The pack of neighbors in the doorway grew tight. Moates, Eddleston, Cissy, Millie, Minnie, and Moose Riley, a local surfer who'd brought his board to the party, holding it upright, all swayed and tipped together with the weight of the crowd, some raising their faces toward the ceiling, laughing amid their small struggle to stay upright. The guests deep in the bathroom, though, peered with smiles toward the bathtub with its few inches of water and a baby alligator clambering inside.

Marge stood near me beside the sink, which was filled with soap-water and combs. "Oh that's just *Khrush*chev," she told everyone, gesturing loosely as if to make the creature seem more part of things.

The librarian Millie kneeled beside the tub, appearing much smaller and shrunken in the crowd's midst than she really was, crying out, "Oh the darling!" while staring into the tub, face tender.

Eddleston explained to all, "Yep! I got him for seventy cents at The Pet Ranch in Allapattah. He was a present for Sheila."

"I'm a cheap date," Sheila admitted, stumbling sideways with the crowd, grinning.

"Allapattah? That's all Spanish now," side-remarked Riley with the surfboard, turning such that it shied several neighbors off-balance at once. "It's really too bad."

"Spanish? Terrible!" Cissy called. She stumbled and grasped at the towel bar on the wall, keeping herself from falling as all shuffled and swayed as one. She told the surfer: "Neighborhoods always change for the worse. Isn't that always the way Moose?"

"They used to have big lunches at Spatt's," Minnie reminisced, holding on to a neighbor's arm.

"No more," said Cissy. "It was torn down. And now this change in Allapattah."

"Horrible changes," nodded Hildy, swaying nearby.

Then Bianchi hollered from the hallway: "Let's make it clear Cissy and all-a-you. First of all th' Spanish can come into my bakery anytime. But that Khrushchev?" He jerked his thumb. "Get him out."

The bathroom vibrated with neighbors' laughter.

Marge turned, calling out to her fiancé, "Aw Sal! Let Khrushchev stay an' swim in the tub awhile! He likes it."

The baker leaned on the wall, looking worried. "But what if somebody needs the toilet?"

"Let him stay," Eddleston called. "A gator could grow on you Sal. Cute isn't he—Khrushchev? He eats grapes."

Moates pushed eagerly through the tight crowd to the bathtub, managing to hold his square tumbler level. "Let *me* see this thing," he said, the pale juice suddenly canting against the glass, wetting his fingers.

The alligator chafed his lime-green feet against the tub wall.

"Ah look at funny little Khrushchev! Lotsa energy he has," the importer smiled.

Laughter rushed around the bathroom again. The creature's lemonade-yellow eyes rested just above the water's surface, his elastic sides puffing in and out with breath.

Who could see what he saw?

Then a voice strained in distantly from the hallway—it was The Woman Who Didn't Speak, squeezing through the crowd. "I agree with Mr. Bianchi. Don't put an animal in the bathroom. It's unappetizing I tell you."

"Oh *her*," whispered Cissy among the bathroom group, and Millie put her finger to her lips: "Shh."

Then Remnick jammed through the crowd, pulling his sleepy-looking daughter Phyllis by the hand. "Make way for us!" he said, smoothing his tie, stooping beside the tub.

"There's the little gator. See?" he told his daughter. "They don't live long like we do."

The child gazed at the reptile, her hand on the tub wall. She looked just like her mother. But neighbors seemed to love Phyllis more than they did Nina.

Behind them all, The Woman Who Didn't Speak repeated, "I said is anyone going to remove that animal? That thing belongs in The Serpentarium." Before that evening, I'd never heard her voice and had understood her communications solely through her frequent wry, rough hand gestures. But there in the bathroom, hearing the voice that she modulated as if imitating a TV announcer-man, I tried, without success, to comprehend who she was.

From the center of the pack of guests came a small melty voice: Honey. "I just love little Khrushchev's face. Look at him!"

"Yer nuts," said Riley. "That lizard'd murder you for lunch first thing he gets hungry."

"Keep your fingers away everyone," Florence warned all. "It's an *animal*. There's *teeth*."

In a moment The Woman stood beside me, sniffing in an impatient manner, the bucket-like purse on her forearm as usual, expensive-looking: calf. She repeated in her disc jockey-style voice: "Quit yakking and remove the lizard."

"All right ma'am," said Eddleston. He picked up a towel, stepping to the tub, making ready to trap the baby alligator. But quickly he seemed to forget about the capture and nudged Moates beside him. "Hey Larry. Betcha fifty cents this lizard'll be dead in a week."

The umbrella importer's eyes crinkled. "Sure—why not? Maybe I could make a few coins." He glanced behind him in the tightly crowded space. "Say. Where's this monster's wife? Where's Mrs. Alligator?"

Eyes slitted, the alligator appeared to doze atop the water.

"Alligators don't have wives," said little Phyllis beside the tub in her flat speech, and the adults' laughter filled the bathroom again.

"Oh little Phyllis. Look at her everyone! What a beautiful child!" Minnie spilled over about the child again, eyes glassy with tears.

Laughing, red-faced Moates pointed to the child. "This kid's on t'something! You all wanna know why Khrushchev's got no lizard girlfriend? I'll tell you. 'Cause he's a conniving SOB!"

Neighbors laughed again, though less robustly than before, and The Woman Who Didn't Speak appeared increasingly angry, looking at the tub water in disgust. With a salty-type humor on the one hand, yet pent-up intensity too, she implored through her teeth, her voice softening and losing the announcer-man resonance: "For the last time will somebody do as Mr. Bianchi asked and get that miserable animal outside? This is a *party*. Not a *barn*. And I tell you that *sonovabitch with scales* doesn't belong here."

Remnick placed his hands over Phyllis's ears, and silence dropped over the bathroom.

Marge and Sheila exchanged glances. The Woman saw all of it.

"Oh I know. You two'll gossip about me later won't you?" she told them. "When I'm out of earshot." She laughed once, hard, without smiling, in a gust.

"Please don't think that," Marge told her. "We wouldn't discuss you."

"Why should I believe what you say?" asked The Woman. "And as for that animal in the tub—look at its nose and face. Tell me how could God make such a chump? I call this thing 'yoo-gly.' When something's terribly ugly I say 'yoo-gly.' Doesn't 'yoo-gly' make this little monster even uglier?"

Sheila told her fiancé, "C'mon Burt. Take Khrushchev outside."

Eddleston picked up the towel.

The Woman, now leaning as if fatigued against the hamper beside me, blew out a breath of a harsh, endless scent like dust and loss.

Eddleston bent over the tub.

"Take him round the neck Burt," urged the surfer.

The alligator's curved mouth in the water appeared to smile.

"Look! Khrushchev knows we're talking about him!" cried Phyllis. "Daddy I love Khrushchev."

"Listen little girl," The Woman Who Didn't Speak told the child, who instantly looked afraid. "Do you see that sonovabitch's teeth? They'll grow as he grows. They'll turn into weapons he'll use."

"Ma'am please—your language," said Remnick, squeezing his daughter's shoulder. "For Phyllis's sake."

Eddleston bent over the tub quickly and snatched the alligator with a towel. As Khrushchev tried to wriggle away, the man lost his footing and stumbled into the crowd, squeezing the animal's head or neck—it was too much. Then he stood still.

The room went silent, neighbors' mouths flat and straight. I heard a gasp, and Florence stepped close, looking inside the towel. "Oh poor Khrushchev! He was just a *baby*," she said with a wobbling softness in her throat: her heart.

*　　*　　*

Not long after, I wandered out to the patio, glimpsing Jody at a distance as she strode around glaring into corners, still searching for Mice. I knew I must go to her and dreaded it. Neighbors pressed past with water-dripping tumblers of juice in fierce colors—deep orange, naphtha yellow, candy pink.

Then Harriet's warm voice interposed as she moved through the bakery's hallway. "*There* you are dear Josephine! Are you well?"

"I'm the same Harriet," said Jody. "This day has been a hall of mirrors."

"Come with me." The cousin pivoted Jody by the elbow past the screen door and through the hallway. I followed. She steered Jody toward the Pink Room, now so full of noisy, laughing partygoers, many filing in near a sideboard, serving themselves water from a heavy glass pitcher.

In the doorway Jody turned, looking incredulous. "Harriet. I will not *follow* your every command. Where are you taking me?"

"Well where do you *want* to talk dear? I thought we'd speak in here. I admit it's a bit noisy."

In her unique way, Harriet was stately. She nodded and raised her eyebrows in a greeting for Florence, who passed by with a glass of juice. Then she refocused on Jody.

"What did you bring for potluck dear Jo?"

"Nothing."

"Didn't you—"

"About the teenagers Harriet. I'm fed up with them. Obviously I am. They go in a pack and torment Mice. I reported it all to Denny but he does nothing. He was supposed to find her today."

"Truly Jody. Some people really need the police. So don't call them every time you start feeling—"

"I *do* need Denny—or rather his services Harriet. But

he's making no effort here. Should I go over his head and call the chief?"

"Certainly not. Let the kids work it out themselves. Mice will mature dear," Harriet predicted effortlessly. "Subsequently your life will get easier. In the first place your responsibilities will ease. With Mice growing, you'll have time for your own little fancies and plans."

"God Harriet. Whyn't you dictate my entire life for me?"

"There's your godding again!" said the cousin, small, frustrated tears filling the sides of her eyes, sparkling there. "I say it's insolent!"

"Look Harriet. Can we address this? God supposedly looks like a man and makes it all happen," Jody persisted dully. "Therefore if I speak his name . . . that's not *my* doing. It's *his*. So I can promise you the words *I* speak won't give him a coronary."

"God is not physical!" cried Harriet, gently aghast.

"How would *you* know?"

The putative cousins, older and younger, faced each other with anger, wiping their noses one after the other. Another wave of partygoers pushed through the hallway, crowding the two women closer together until finally Jody seemed to fall into the Pink Room.

Once there, standing by the salmon-colored sofa, she gave a groan of discomfort, as if remembering her troubles, then leaned, dropping her head, saying, "Please someone . . . what am I? Help my sister." She must've glimpsed Sheila who sat on the sofa as if resting, a glass of golden juice beside her. Jody went to her and sat as Sheila petted Jody's head once again, perhaps with an intent to bring her back to earth with warmth.

But could warmth work on Jody?

I squeezed myself near the wall against the Pink Room's rose bookshelf, largely packed with red-spined books, their titles indecipherable to me.

Then Marge sailed wordlessly into the room, wiping the backs and fronts of her hands on her smock, and sat on Jody's other side, taking her hand. Jody startled.

"Hands cold?" Marge giggled, and Jody nodded weepily, turning fully into the hostess's embrace while Sheila rubbed her arm. At the wall and behind the rose-colored sofa, I strained to hear the hostess's warm voice as she spoke a long run of breathy words against Jody's hair and shoulder—but amid the Pink Room guests' noise, I couldn't hear.

So I had to admit: not every word in the story was mine to know.

*   *   *

From the couch with its nearby coffee table, Sheila waved at Eddleston, who played near the lamp with a wooden cup and ball, jollying with Remnick and others. He leaned toward her.

"What is it Sheil?"

"Bring Larry in here and keep talking about the soft names!" the fiancée instructed him.

Eddleston ran into the hall, soon ushering Moates and a few others toward the couch.

"Larry?" Eddleston asked the importer. "Is 'Paul Mees' a soft name by the way? I work with Paul at the garden shop. Wouldn't it be a hoot t'surprise him with the news that he has a soft name? Oh I can just see his face when that happened."

More neighbors squeezed in near the couch, listening with interest, as did Jody between the women.

The umbrella importer squinted over his smile. "Burt please. You know full well that 'Paul' is a contaminated sample. Is there any Paul on this earth who's not full of trouble and mess? I disqualify the name."

Eddleston grew a frown. Then Millie asked: "What about Stu Groth who cooks at The Sea Gull? And his cousin Melindy Groth? Are theirs soft names Larry?"

"Oh Groths! They live so far north!" a voice in the group complained.

At some distance, Cissy, arms crossed, head bent, had begun to doze in a coral-hued armchair.

Harriet told Millie: "I don't care if Melindy's name is hard or soft or scrambled. She crushed her husband's foot at Lake Okeechobee and personally I believe that's terrible."

"Crushed his *foot*? Oh! Could that be true?" breathed Sheila from the sofa.

"Couldn't anything be?" said Marge, chewing cake and bread.

Harriet shook her head. "Poor old guy with his crushed foot."

"He must've done something awful to Melindy," Marge ventured.

"Don't talk to me like that," Harriet told the hostess. "It's *Melindy* that did wrong."

Now Florence joined them. "We should understand *why* Melindy smashed Mal Groth's foot. And the reason is that Mal Groth is a dog."

Cissy woke from her doze. "Yes that's it!"

The gnarl of the conversation made me restless. Then The Blur dashed through the room, sweaty, emitting breathily, "Groths? Savages. *All* of them. The worst of the worst."

"Now Fred that's unkind!" cried Harriet after him.

Lance stepped in to speak too, wettish cigar in his mouth, less concerned about Melindy or other Groths than the soft names. "Larry—some say a person's name has a sense of flav'r to it. On th' other hand it's prob'ly the person with th' flavor an' they pass that into the name."

From the rocking chair in the corner, Phenice spoke up: "Not true Jack." Then, head bent, she returned to reading a paperback book.

Brahms told them all: "I heard a bit of news. Melindy's no Groth—not anymore. Didn't you know? She married outta Groths an' into Blitzes. It was fast-like."

"Melindy changed!" cheered Florence. "She's a Blitz?"

"She should've quit the marriage earlier. Wedlock's tough," said Remnick.

"Mike!" Nina warned him, eyes upset.

Florence looked at Moates. "Well what is it Larry? Is Melindy a hard name or soft name?"

But Moates seemed to have lost the spirit or conceit of the name-essence guessing game and shrugged, sullen-faced.

Jody reclined into the crook of Marge's bare arm, jiggling a bit when Marge shook her, asking, "You like hearing about the soft names Jody?"

The sister's mouth gathered into a small, uncharacteristic smile. "Maybe," she said.

I hated Marge's coddling. I hated Jody's ugly clinging to Marge.

Sitting down on a footrest against the bookcase, I then watched Minnie appear outside the Pink Room, her partly silver hair lit by a low bar of sun leveling through the hall. "Lands," she sighed broadly, entering the Pink Room as if bewildered but amused in general by life's slipstream. "Jody," she called, looking at the group on the couch, "d'you remember last year's winter party and how you and your sister sang an' danced practically all night? Oh what a pretty picture that was."

Jody stood from Marge's lap and stomped toward the elfin older woman. "We didn't *sing* or *dance* Minnie! That must've been some *other* pair of jinxed sisters."

Fragile Minnie's hand fled to her neck self-protectively, and now Jody walked away to the banister of the newly built, honey-colored staircase. Fresh lumber curls lay underfoot. She leaned, hanks of her hair hanging as she said in a desolate voice: "Oh I tell you I'm not myself!"

Slowly, Sheila and Marge rose from the sofa in tandem, making their way to the sister, and Minnie whispered uselessly, "Well *try* to be yourself Jody."

But I wondered: How important is it to be oneself, given that all beings are provenly temporary and slide away sooner than can be believed?

Bianchi lugged a steel milk canister down the hallway en route to the kitchen, and its clanging seemed to catch Jody's attention. She raised her face, now featurelessly calm, saying, "I just remembered I had a dream this morning as I slept."

"You dreamed you were *asleep*?" Minnie asked, moving closer as if on tiptoes while I, too, left the Pink Room, working my way nearer to Jody and hoping not to draw others' attention, even while knowing I had to speak up to the sister and reveal myself at some point.

"No! I was *asleep* and had a dream," Jody returned, not looking at Minnie.

Marge and Sheila surrounded the sister, their supportive hands upon her shoulders, waiting for the details.

Purple-green crescents ringed Jody's eyes. "In my dream the moon was too close to Earth. Only a few miles off. It filled the sky and it was horrible."

Her dream unnerved me terribly because I had no idea why it was disturbing.

"Sheila?" Jody asked. "Could my dream've been a premonition?"

It occurred to me that Jody might not need so much if Marge and Sheila needed her to need less.

"Hm," Sheila mused loosely, leaning near the sister along the side of the staircase. "A premonition of *what*? That the moon will fly to Earth? I *doubt* it. Dreams don't predict our futures though they may give that impression. Forewarnings would be nice but there are none."

"Can we have a séance?" cried Minnie, excited.

Lance strode past, heading to the patio. "Dreams. Bunk. Women's rot," he muttered.

A slew of neighbors just off the boulevard entered the hallway then, eyes relaxed and expectant before they noticed the staircase group's uneasy, concerned dream discussion. Suddenly strong-bodied Hildy from the new group went to the staircase, reaching for Jody's wrists, squeezing them, enunciating slowly: "I think your younger sister — whatever disadvantages she has in life — is doing *very well*."

"Is that what you think? Well *stuff* it Hildy," Jody flared with derision as Marge pulled at her, trying to plant a quick, consoling kiss on the elder sister's hairline; meanwhile, Sheila implored her: "Shh."

"You're crushing me Marge!" Jody shouted from beneath the hostess.

"What atrocious manners," said Hildy.

Near the kitchen door, on the hallway telephone, Florence spoke mysteriously into the dumbbell-shaped receiver: "You don't say."

At last I was in the hallway, yet still hadn't made myself known to Jody. Instead I moved away from her to the storefront, where I stooped to retrieve a filthy tennis ball from the floor, squeezing it in my hands. I needed to gain focus, I implored myself, before telling Jody a few facts about the evening. And I needed to know if Mice would accompany me to the cabin to sit in silence, but where was Mice? I looked out the window to the tin-and-gold boulevard painted by sun.

At that point The Artist with the Scarf, standing among the hallway's newcomers, raised a juice glass to toast, "I think life is *silly*," with a punctuative nod.

*   *   *

Long after the party was over, I reviewed the probable course of the newcomer's day—I did so many times. Surely he was rangy and restless as many young men, antsy to see what the day might bring. That morning as Jack Lance stood conversing with Mice in the yard and I hid behind the lemon tree, the story's helper might've been lowering himself into the motel's aluminum-blue pool. After a swim, hoisting himself out, water glittering down his body in runnels onto the pool's coping, he might've lain on a poolside lounger, face tightening in the sun.

The ten or so men stayed in Miami for a few weeks. The stranger would've boarded in the motel room with a roommate. But the whole group of them likely sat together every day, discussing the plan, drinking beer, waiting for instructions. When the group went for practice runs at the old airfield, one of them always stayed behind in case of a phone call.

On the stranger's days off, he borrowed a Chevrolet Nomad to find all the beach and local music spots. I learned later that he'd go dancing at the clubs all night, so tired the next day that the other men let him take long catnaps during the dawn practice shift.

The day of the party must've been his day off. Late that afternoon, he pulled the satiny blue jacket from a hanger in the motel closet and dressed carefully, choosing a tie, shining his shoes. Perhaps he'd found friends at the local nightclubs and was going to meet them. He was likely hungry for further friends too. Why else would he have roamed around in the Nomad that night? When he passed The Crescent Tender Bakery, he circled the block once or twice, then parked. I believed the helper kept the driver's window rolled down as if listening for something new while Miami's creamy, near-tropical air filled his mouth. I craved that delicious air then even as I breathed it. I miss that air today.

*　*　*

Most neighbors remained on the sidewalk, socializing, and did not go inside as the hosts wished them to. I sat on a solitary chair beside the store's front window, leaning my head on the glass, reading the gold-enameled reversed letters that formed the bakery's name.

Bianchi slid steel trays of guava pastels from the pastry case, his big forearms doused with flour, his apron powdered. Marge came for the trays. I felt the synchrony of their bodies' work rhythms behind the bakery counter, part of me leaping to the movements, ready to store the hosts' cadences inside me.

"Merv Jarouse telephoned," the baker told his fiancée. "Band'll be late."

"Aw gee. *Why?*"

"Horn got wet."

"How?"

"Do I know?"

"Hey. It's not a horn," corrected the barkeep Vinnegar, standing in the hallway, holding a jar. "It's a cornet."

"Cornet's a horn," the baker argued.

"Depends Sal." Vinnegar's hand appeared vegetal and distorted through the jar, a beige orchid. He walked back through the hall toward the patio. "Cornets sound better'n other horns."

"Oh yeah?"

"Sweeter."

Holding her tray, Marge looked piqued. "Sal quit yakking!"

The big baker turned to her. "Kiss me," he said. Marge did.

"Work now Marge. Go. Party needs t'start."

The fiancée flew through the hall, falsettoing: "Horn players! Always ruining my life!"

I envied Marge's apparent ease in most circumstances, and her light way of being at the center of things.

Then I saw Minnie struggle through the hallway with a heavy bucket of ice, asking the baker, "Who're the

Jarouses anyway Sal?"

"Brothers. Put that bucket down Minnie," Bianchi prickled. "From Smyrna. Musicians."

"They sing," Moates offered, suddenly there, smoking.

Thin Eddleston pushed through the swinging kitchen door, spinning a wooden yo-yo off his finger, pale ankles near-glowing above his tan loafers. "Their voices harmonize perfectly Minnie," he said. "Know why? 'Cause they're brothers. Same vocal cord structure. Nature makes 'em sound good together. Don't ask me more—I failed genetics in high school."

Minnie laughed shyly, turning to look at the bucket Bianchi now hauled to the patio, as if she wanted it back.

Millie joined them, asking, "Sal! Will Jarouses play that song they sing?"

The baker asked: "You mean 'Go to the Store' Mil? Oh you bet they'll play it." To her, Minnie, and Eddleston standing nearby he opined, "Jarouses've played some extremely ambitious songs in their time . . . and none more so than 'Go to the Store.'"

Millie's face grew plummy; she clapped. "I can't wait!" Brahms the guard stepped in solemnly, daubing his mustache with a handkerchief, opining, "Sal instead a' music I'd rather talk at a party. Talk to people. For music I listen to the radio in my home."

Bianchi ignored it. Relaxed and earnest, he told the guard: "Jarouses're great players. We have our beatnik friend Larry Smolt t'thank for invitin' 'em. Smolt's settin' up th' hi-fi now. He'll play a few records before the band comes."

"Time to show our potluck dishes!" called Marge, beckoning, and a tremendous hubbub began. All neighbors apparently knew the drill. Many ran through the hallway and toward the patio, where they would fetch their dishes and show off their cooking.

Listening to it all, resting my head against the window, now sleepy, I glimpsed Vinnegar through the screen door, high-pouring juices of brilliant colors: deep pink, pastel yellow, apricot, ruby. Rows of iced tumblers glinted in the diminishing sun. Near the empty dance floor sat a desiccated player piano. With a minuscule jolt, I remembered that one day I would disappear, becoming part of everything.

The party was so long ago. But even on that night, the wait for the end didn't seem it would be extraordinarily long. And now the wait is all but over.

Of course, I could not know then how very old I would become or how wrecking age can be. I couldn't know that it is the strangest thing of all that can happen to a young girl.

*　　*　　*

Neighbors brought their potluck dishes from the patio and back to the front sidewalk. Why were they so hesitant to go inside? I waited, still sleepy beside the plate-glass window, watching them re-emerge from the bakery and move into the sun, heavy plates and bowls in hand. New partygoers arrived from the boulevard, cheering. Amid this jangle, Marge stood at the bakery's entrance, one flat green shoe turned and fretting the sidewalk, a few tawny guava pastels remaining on her tray. She made a cone of her left hand. "It's time!" she bellowed through it. "What'd everyone bring for potluck?" Heads turned toward the bakery.

Overtaken by the sensation of exposure and not wanting to be seen, I left the storefront and moved along the building's facade into a narrow passageway between the bakery and the barbershop next door. A sky vine hung over this aperture, its blue flowers tangled amid lusciously green spade-shaped leaves. Fitted behind this vine, I had a clear view of the sidewalk and array of neighbors.

"I brought steak and lamb! Milk too." It was the surfer Riley, grinning, now holding tied-together shoeboxes under one arm, with the surfboard under the other.

"Me I brought potato boats," said Millie in a clogged voice.

"Wonderful!" said a voice from the group: Hildy.

"And you?" Marge asked the yellow-haired Gagel sisters' mother.

Hildy raised a sack. "A black cherry pie. It's in this bag. And you know what? The crust split into two big ugly pieces."

"Will you hush?" Cissy advised.

"Let me finish!" Hildy told her with excitement. "I could've given up on this pie but did I? No sir. I pulled off that broken crust and rolled out a new crust. Smart huh?"

"Sure," said someone.

"I baked that crust separately," the woman went on, "and put it on top of the fruit and it looked perfect but the new crust broke too. Not as badly though."

"How incredibly detailed Hildy," said Harriet as other neighbors looked on. Hildy pulled out a pan, removing its cover to reveal a solid-looking, reddish-brown disk. "It's not really a pie anymore."

"I'll say it's not," said Lance, tapping the cigar.

"It's changed!" strained Hildy loudly. "Now it's more of a cherry Betty!"

"Destruction. Renewal," said The Artist with the Scarf.

"The hardest part was picking the cherries last night with Mother," Hildy persisted. "Lots a' mud out there at the lake. Her cane sank—"

"No more talking about the Betty Hildy," established Harriet.

Marge moved on. "What about other potluck dishes? What'd you bring?"

"Mine's spinach salad with bacon grease," called out nervous Minnie, raising a steel bowl high enough that her blouse lifted to reveal a champagne-colored underwear waistband.

Neighbors cheered for the salad, perhaps with relief, too, after the puzzlement of the Betty.

"It's a pretty dish Minnie. Look at those beautiful green leaves. I bet you could win a contest," complimented Sheila.

"Oh I would *not* win it! Would I?" Minnie blushed, eyes locking to Sheila for extended moments with hope, and Sheila looked away.

Cissy stepped in, eyeing the salad, stating, "A bowl like this must be assembled quickly and at the very last moment."

"The last moment *of what*?" jollied Brahms.

"I'm only mentioning for everyone's benefit that this salad has mistakes," Cissy said. "First of all it's wet."

"It's not wet!" cried Minnie.

"The leaves are absolute hulks," Cissy added, "if you don't mind my saying so. You couldn't be bothered to chop them. And all that oil! I tell you this salad will fall."

For the third time that day Minnie looked near tears. "Salads don't fall!" she rebutted.

"I say they do."

"You're nothing but a bully Cissy!"

The elder laughed to the sky. "Oh everyone says that! You're no different."

"Anybody bring liver?" coughed Lance, wreathed in smoke.

Suddenly I glimpsed Jody, still and solitary, in profile near the bakery door, and my heart ratcheted. Posture rigid and tense, she nevertheless seemed to have come to herself after the short spell of helplessness attended by Marge and Sheila. As the sister caught my glance, I withdrew into the leaves.

But suddenly she was in the little alleyway beside me, a sky-vine trailer dragging over her shoulders, flowers catching in her brown hair.

"Girtle where have you been?"

All nerves, I jabbered in an open, breezy manner, not unlike Marge, "Jody! Flowers look good on your head. Did you see the wasps' nests?" I pointed to the paper nests like small, stylish purses adhered to the passageway's wall. "They make their homes of mud and saliva." But at this moment I realized the nests were long-abandoned husks.

"That's disgusting Girtle. Now listen. You were supposed to bring Mice to the party then leave. Well why are you still here? Where is she? And why are you *creeping around* where you're not wanted?"

"Oh Jody I've never been wanted. I—"

"Let's not get into all your catastrophes." In the sky vine's upper branches, a knot of sparrows had landed and now jabbered busily overhead. "She absolutely must check with Florence about that job. If she fails I'd have to do it *myself* and I don't want to. But the first order of business is to *find* her. Oh Girtle—I'm *tired*."

"Yes Jody."

She was very down. Yet her pained, velvety eyes focused on the rear wall of the dank passageway as if searching for solutions, her smooth forehead a dazzling prow on the move.

"If the bookmobile doesn't work out," she mused, "maybe she could find employment at The Sea Gull."

"That supper place with the blue roof?"

"Of course that's The Sea Gull," Jody snapped. "I'd like to tell people that my sister works there. I'd be so proud! Oh Girtle—does everyone have so much weight to push? So much effort to make?"

"Some do Jo. I know a bit about that."

"Tell me. Out with it," she said, looking through the thick vines to the sidewalk where neighbors swarmed, laughed, and continued to debate the spinach salad's merits versus disadvantages.

I couldn't look her in the eye, but I spoke. "I haven't mentioned this before Jo. But to be honest? When I was born I was not kept." Shame instantly heated my face. "Before my eyes were even open I was handed out to some other family but that family did not want me after all. So they brought me to a big place with three dormitory buildings—"

"Girtle I *just said* this isn't the time for your *entire* life story. When was the last you saw Mice?"

"Oh. I happen to know she's lying low somewhere," I said. "It's not clear when she'll get here but I'm expecting her."

"You're *expecting* her? Oh that takes it all. Listen Miss Uppity Girtle . . . she's not *your* sister. She's mine." Jody lifted her hand only very slightly, to what intention I was not sure, but it was enough. I shrank back.

"About an hour ago she went underneath the sidewalk," I said, head down.

"*She what*?"

"Near the bank. Not Piccolo Bank," I detailed, to show Jody that I hid nothing. "And not Guardian Bank either—there's no Guardian on Reef Way of course but downtown there's—"

"Girtle quiet!"

"Settler's Bank. She went under the sidewalk by Settler's."

"Just down the road? Girtle you *dud*. Why didn't you come *tell* me *right away*?"

Through the vines I saw Minnie on the sidewalk, flushed among neighbors and smiling with high emotion, calling to Harriet: "Maybe someday I'll open a restaurant!" as the high schoolers guffawed.

"*Girtle*! I said why didn't you come for me?" Jody breathed, inches from my face.

"It happened fast," I said, sweating. "And you swore me to watch Mice today. She jumped into the cement well when the kids said she looked like the boy with eight legs."

"Damn them!" Jody looked away, the breeze lifting strands of her chestnut hair. "I *told* you never leave her alone with the kids!"

"I didn't."

"And now those teen beasts're running around here at the party? They'll badger her all night. I must make

Florence hire my sister. If Mice had a job those kids would leave her alone. Oh Girtle I could just *beat* you!"

"Don't!" I raised my hands over my head briefly, my throat producing sour flavors, and retreated to the passageway's mushroomy back wall, not understanding that the alley was a dead end. On the sidewalk, neighbors again spoke and laughed about something I didn't understand.

Then it occurred to me that since I'd begun to live with the sisters, I'd never once been struck—not even close. Warmth rose in me, and I retraced my steps down the alleyway to Jody, happy and appreciative. "I'll wash the woodwork and windows with soap as soon as I get home Jo. Remember the butterfly eggs we found on the blinds?"

She softened. "Oh. The soldier butterfly eggs? I remember. They're orange. Leave them be."

"Yes Jody." I felt a bursting pride and sensed this was a good time to ask again. "Oh Jody? Since Mice's away and things're uncertain . . . may I stay with you sisters a few more days or months—may I Jo?" I held my breath on the sun-warmed narrow stone ledge on which I lived with the sisters and hoped not to fall.

"Well . . ." She sighed directionlessly and looked at her shoes.

I was sure this meant *yes.* "Oh Jody," I breathed, immensely relieved, falling against her in a hug she did not return, and then somehow Jody lowered herself softly to the stony, mossy floor of the passageway and was asleep.

I would stay. Happiness snugged beneath my skin.

* * *

Then, as if it were not a sudden, small accident but seamlessly part of everything, I tangled myself into the sky vine, grasping shoots and trailers, then falling over the sidewalk, clinging to the vine, and finally lowering myself to the cement.

Marge called out for more displays of potluck, her gaze falling on Joyce, who stood alone, carrying a large stone crock. "How about you?" asked the hostess.

Looking vulnerable without the other high schoolers beside her, Joyce pivoted away. "I'll pass," she offered.

I extracted myself from the sky-vine area and went to sit cross-legged against the bakery's front wall. Did neighbors see me? Of course not.

"Aw. Tell us what's in your bucket," Moates addressed Joyce from the crowd, humor in his eyes.

"It's not a bucket. It's a crock," answered Joyce, meeting no one's eyes.

"Go on Joyce! Tell us about your dish," partygoers cooed to her, curious-looking, so Joyce announced faintly and somewhat tremulously over the lidded vessel, eyes closed, "Well you see . . . I discovered that when I briefly heated blueberries . . . this released a delicious juice. And do you know I spooned some of that juice into a glass and added cold water? Oh it was so blue and icy that I was excited to drink it!"

The high schooler opened her eyes as neighbors bent closer now, faces interested, serious, investigating the stone container as Joyce finished, "And that's how I got the idea for the blue water." She set the weighty crock on the bench.

Cissy spoke up. "Joyce—you're telling us that for potluck tonight you brought . . . *water*?"

Slowly scanning neighbors' perplexed faces, Joyce's expression dropped, and she blinked against the blaze of their scrutiny. "But it's not *just* water! I *told* you it's a mixture. What's wrong with that?" She turned to the serious-faced hostess. "Marge?"

"Nothing's wrong Joyce. You did wonderfully," Marge said.

"Hell. Not even fruit juice but fruit *water*," the veteran Lance shook his head.

"Jack—it's all right," Marge asserted.

"Water isn't a *dish*," Cissy said, with her penchant for arguing small points. "No."

"Why didn't you hear what I said? It's not *plain* water. It's *blue* water," pushed teary Joyce. "What's wrong with everybody? Laurette?" she wailed.

"No—your school friends cannot help you now," insisted the widow-notary. "Laurette's inside. She's busy. So you will have to explain it to us."

"It has flavor!"

"Look," Moates reasoned with the young woman. "If it's ninety percent water then you're scrimping on juice."

Joyce answered swiftly: "I didn't scrimp on juice—I was *generous* with water."

"Water is lesser than juice," theorized Cindy.

"No it isn't," said Millie. "Water is higher."

"Patent nonsense," said the dentist, and Cindy giggled.

"Milk is significant," broached Riley, and Remnick nodded like an insider. After this, many leapt into animated conversation.

"Is that your toe?" came someone's voice.

Eddleston raised a toy kaleidoscope to his eye.

Then from down the street, Solly ran to them happily, returning from his errand to Slaughter High, pulling the school custodian Gerry Sage by the hand. "Here's Gerry everyone!" he cried. Yet the party's tenor had changed since Bianchi had sent Solly on the errand, so neighbors now displayed no interest in Sage, as if he were little but blown sand.

Joyce swiped sweat dots from her forehead, clearly relieved that the questioning was over. She hoisted the crock as if to take it indoors, but stumbled, and the vessel's lid fell to the ground as a blue ellipse of water slipped from its mouth, breaking on the cement with a splash that wetted Joyce's feet.

"Oof," Joyce emitted, almost a sound of pleasure.

Laurette ran outside to see what had occurred. "What a disorganized mess she is," breathed the leader.

"A mess by definition *is* disorganized," Moates returned.

Joyce began to cry.

"Oh now," said Harriet, going to her. "As a high school student you're brand new to cooking. You'll learn."

"I'm not actually in high school," Joyce sniffed in her upset.

"You're *not*?" said Laurette.

The others looked, faces surprised.

"Of course you're in high school Joyce," Laurette said. "We have assembly together."

"Well I already graduated from a high school—in the Keys. It's called Key High."

Neighbors exclaimed to each other, dart-like questions now arising, such as "Which Key?" and "Did Joyce lie?" Finally Harriet clapped for attention and asked the next logical question: "Joyce. If you already graduated then why are you attending Slaughter with these kids?"

Joyce stammered, "It's hard to say."

Laurette moved close and wedged Harriet away. "Let's get the facts Joyce. We thought you were a senior. Now you say you've already graduated. Tell the truth. *When* did you graduate?"

"Oh—some years back," Joyce jittered.

All appeared dumbstruck, vocalizing and remarking, except for Laurette, who breathed hard, anger on her face, noting, "And is *that* a made-up story too?" while Helen-Dale said at once: "I knew it all along. I know the signs of deception."

Yet perhaps from the relief of airing her secret and its bloat, Joyce grinned slightly while pressing a little handkerchief to her mouth and teeth.

"Joyce you better come clean," said Eddleston. "Why d'you spend all your time at the high school with the kids? Tell us!"

Folding the handkerchief, Joyce nodded before all neighbors, as if acknowledging her deceit would disintegrate it. Then she said: "After I came here to live with Great-Aunt Phenice I met the teenagers and *liked* them." She glanced at the group and Laurette, who had tucked herself into the high schoolers' fold. "The kids never minded me tagging along. So I got in on their fun. I became part of them! I like you Laurette!" she called to the leader, who blew out a steamy, incensed breath.

"You see at Key High I had no friends. That's because I was separate. I wanted to go back to high school all over again."

Harriet asked: "But dear I don't understand. Why did everybody think you were enrolled at Slaughter High School in the first place?"

"Because I made up a story that I was enrolled!"

Now Solly appeared enraged and therefore more dimensional than before. "But we were in the same *math* class Joyce! Didn't you do the *home*work?"

Joyce's mouth trembled. "No."

"Just a minute. How old *are* you Joyce?" It was Cissy, pushing through the crowd.

"Twenty-eight," confessed Joyce.

Everyone gasped.

Then old Lance struck his leg and laughed hard. "Hell! Near-thirty years old and she can't even tell th' difference between a potluck dish an' a pail a' water!"

"I told you it's not *water*! And it's not a *pail*!" J oyce cried, face sweaty, perhaps in humiliation, but with these words her habitual uncertainty seemed to vanish, as if maturity had arrived like a sudden ship, sharpening her on the spot. She continued firmly, "It's a good blue drink that everybody'll enjoy."

"Not me," vowed Helen-Dale. "I won't touch that drink."

"Heck," said Eddleston. "I'll try it. Why not?"

"I want some!" said Minnie.

Then in a fresh tone, Harriet encouraged, "Everyone now—don't let's dwell on the blue water. We need to start the party. Right Marge?" She sought the hostess's eyes.

"I thought this *was* the party!" laughed corny Brahms.

*　*　*

After Joyce's confession, neighbors took time to cool off, eventually conceding to return to the patio when Bianchi propped open the green-glass door and Marge stood there too, waving guests in. As if subdued, guests trooped through the doorway in a column, rounding the pastry case and proceeding to the patio. Certain that no one in the crowd saw me, despite my being among them, I felt safe.

Ahead of me, Moates groused at Remnick: "Move along Mike. I'm hungry! Why're you in front of me?"

"I'm in front of you because you're behind me."

Then the stream of moving partygoers stopped due to heavy volume, and I veered from the crowd, going behind the bakery counter, close to the kitchen where sweet steam, raisins, yeast, and faraway coffee were one scent saturating the air. I noted the hallway's assortment of antique flour bins, upside-down bicycles and chairs, sacks of flour, the recently delivered yeast drum, and a few loose carrots that the library branch head Florence soon kicked aside.

Moose Riley stood near the counter, staring unblinkingly ahead, the tied-up shoeboxes of potluck food still under his arm. Honey looked at him from across the crowd, then leaned to Joyce, whispering warmly, "Moose seems so gentle doesn't he?"

"I wouldn't know," Joyce thudded.

"He works at the Student Prince. What a nice boy!"

"I suppose."

"Charlene's his steady. She works patrol on Cocoa Beach. Know her Joyce?"

"Kind of. Charlene's all right," Joyce answered. "Except for that white bump on her chin."

"Oh that blemish is terrible," said Honey feelingly. "What will she do for it?"

"I wouldn't want that bump on me," said Hildy behind them.

"No," Laurette posited, also nearby.

165

Joyce looked at the leader, face worried. "But Charlene's overall normal—isn't she?"

None answered this question. As the surfer heard his girlfriend's name, he maneuvered through the crowd, cheery-faced, though. "Charlene's just fine," he offered. "She's like you or me. Sure she has a bump but I don't think about it."

"That's because you know her," analyzed Helen-Dale.

Solly called baitingly to Riley: "Charlene's a Commie. I heard that."

"Nope," the surfer breezed over his shoulder.

"Charlene the Communist!" Eddleston bent over laughing. "Sounds like the name of a storybook!"

"I said no!" The surfer stamped. "She's no Red I tell you. She only joined th' Party 'causa her mother was in it. You hafta understand: Charlene loves to sing. An' you know how Communists sing day and night. Oh all their parties an' picnics. All their parades—Char and her ma go to sing. They enjoy themselves. Look." Riley pulled a billfold from his trousers, opening it, raising the photo window for all to see. "Here's her picture. See—Char's no Commie! She's blonde."

"Moose!" scolded Honey. "What's hair color to do with Communists?"

"Aw Honey if y'really look into Reds there's patterns," the surfer carried on. "First of all they're dumber than a pack a' dogs. Second thing is they have dark hair."

Eddleston was outside again, playing with the cup and ball again, the wooden toy's components clinking together. "I know a Red when I see one!" he cried into the bakery.

"Burt don't talk dumb!" Sheila called from the front of

the crowd. "What about Harriet? She has dark hair and never joined the Communists."

"Sure," the surfer made known. "Not all dark-haireds are Reds. But all Reds're dark-haired."

"Oh *Moose*!" Sheila raved, and Remnick called over to the surfer: "The Party's mostly dead Moose. It's going out of style see. No one joins the chapters anymore."

Amid the crowd, Solly gulped from an upended soda bottle, smiling around its glass neck. "Good."

The surfer looked angry and headed out the door. No one stopped him.

Neighbors continued slowly down the hallway toward the patio, the high schoolers first, followed by the others. Through the window I saw Minnie outside with her salad, about to enter, and Eddleston in front of her, reaching for the door with one hand, the cup and ball toy in the other.

Yet the ball on its string somehow flung back and struck Minnie or her bowl, and the small woman startled such that the salad flew from her, arcing through the air and landing on the pavement with a resonant crash. Rolling on its lip down the sidewalk, the bowl flung spinach leaves plus crescents of egg in a wheel formation, and neighbors turned, exclaiming as the container wobbled far down the sidewalk before coming to rest.

Minnie clutched her head and screamed "*No!*" a few times hoarsely, whereupon Marge and Sheila ran outside to calm her. Neighbors still inside the bakery's storefront and hallway came pouring back outside to the sidewalk, eager to see the melee. I went too and sat on the far verge of the bench, there spotting Jody who stared at the lacquer-shiny salad components on the ground.

Eddleston apologized to the upset woman: "I didn't mean to spill Minnie. Boy was that dumb." He swung his arms in the manner of a comedian onstage, then brushed a few oily onion sickles from his jacket and tried unsuccessfully to wipe salad oil from the bakery's glass door with his sleeve.

"All these things happening," remarked the dentist Warm in the relative quiet after the salad spill, and Cindy nodded.

"First the blue water and now the spinach," Florence specified.

Cissy looked at the spinach leaves on the sidewalk. "You see?" she told Joyce. "The salad was soggy from the start and this proves it. Why on earth dress a salad to the moon and back?"

Minnie's face crumpled and she briefly raised her fists to the sky as if beseeching gods. "I ruined it not once but twice!"

The high schoolers laughed and put together a spontaneous chant: "Minnie ruined it once! Minnie ruined it twice!" They mimicked each other, falling forward, laughing and pushing as the library-clerk hopeful wept, her chin gleaming with moisture.

"Aw Minnie don't cry," Eddleston told her uncomfortably, smoothing his tie. He went down the sidewalk to retrieve the slippery bowl, which again dropped to the ground with a bang, rolling farther, the lanky man chasing it in long, dreamlike strides.

Raising both hands for attention, Harriet called, "Please everyone—that's enough today in terms of spinach. Let's go inside."

"Yes please come back to the patio!" Marge begged,

tired-looking, as the buzzing crowd seemed to ignore her all over again. "There'll be music!"

"Do what Marge says everybody," Harriet underscored. "And don't touch the salad in the gutter. Filthy!"

Standing beside the salad detritus, The Artist with the Scarf asked, "What is 'the gutter' exactly and why is it considered so vile? Isn't the gutter part of the curb? Neither is any dirtier than the street."

"Oh you tedious thing!" Cissy carped at him.

From the bench, I watched her. Another question came to mind, different, yet related to The Artist's question: Could the definitions of "up" and "down" ever change or be reversed? It was years before I understood that the answer is *yes*.

*   *   *

Then cheerful Bianchi poked his head through the doorway once again, Vinnegar's glum face behind his shoulder as he entreated, "Come *on* people. Party's already started!"

But a wailing cry from down the sidewalk caused everyone to turn. A young flustered woman rushed toward the doorway, calling: "Miss Stroke! Oh Miss Stroke! I have a question!"

It was Sherrie Gagel, the younger of the two look-alike sisters in their twenties, and she pushed through the throng, going straight for Florence, who, about to enter the bakery, turned around, startled. Reaching the older woman, Sherrie declared with a patchy pant: "May I ask you something Miss Stroke? I've wanted to for ages."

Florence looked at the young woman heavily, then scanned the crowd. "Can't it wait a moment Sherrie? We're going into the party."

The mass of neighbors listened.

"Oh *please* Miss Stroke."

"Come on. Let's hear it Sherrie!" hollered Eddleston.

The well-known branch head sighed and looked to the ground. "What kind of question?"

Sherrie bent to scratch her leg with the fidgety energy of a student. "It's just a small question in my mind."

Florence glared, her mouth a line. I wondered: Was the branch head beginning to revert to the earlier, less tolerant and more rule-bound version of herself, as she had been before the book-mold incident? I hoped not.

"What kind of a question? Is it a 'why' question?"

Sherrie giggled with nerves. "Not really."

"I am not a walking encyclopedia for you to open as you wish Sherrie. I do not exist to answer your spur-of-the-moment questions. Is that how you think of me?"

"No Miss Stroke! I respect you!" The young woman looked dumbstruck, ashamed, hand on her cheek. "I think you're knowledgeable."

"Is that so."

"Yes! Remember when I was in your finals cram session at Slaughter High? You impressed me a lot Miss Stroke. Because you know things."

"That was years ago," said the fed-up librarian through her teeth. "I'm tired of people using me to get information! Yes my role is to be the librarian but can't you think how I might *feel*?"

"I *will* think how you feel!" Sherrie cried.

Suddenly Honey poked her head out from the cluster of high schoolers. "Sherrie! You look so nice today—did you make up your face?"

Sherrie turned and conveyed nasally, "Honey hi! I used

some eyebrow pencil but I washed it off with soap."

Then Cissy, behind Honey, waved for attention. "Sherrie! Listen to me. Never wash off your makeup. That's the worst thing to do. Makeup boosts a girl. It made your brows lovely today."

"But like I said I scrubbed my brows Mrs. Lax."

The widow-notary continued with loud, clear enjoyment, eyeing the crowd: "The *truth* is Sherrie you and your sister're so young and pale that neither of you understands what it *means* to have eyebrows!"

The branch library head alone laughed deeply at this, the shirring on her flowered dress trembling as Sherrie corrected Cissy: "We *do so* understand what it means to have eyebrows Mrs. Lax. Me an' Trudie pencil our eyebrows dark when we *want* to and sometimes we *don't* at all!"

"All right now," said Florence, an expression she used at the library to shift from one patron's question to another's.

"Let Sherrie ask her question so the party can begin," said strained Marge, squeezed in the doorway by Florence and silent Vinnegar.

"Ask your question pretty Sherrie!" urged Moates from the sidewalk swarm.

In that moment, Sherrie seemed to fully realize that two dozen or more closely packed neighbors had been listening to the entire exchange keenly. She bowed her head; the yellow hair fell across her eyes as she reddened.

"Never mind it Miss Stroke," she told the branch head quietly. "You were right. This isn't the time to ask questions. It's time for the party." Sherrie pulled a tight smile and began moving toward the crowd. But with a quick, extended, dark-shoed foot, Florence stopped her.

"Just a minute. You wanted to ask me something. Ask it."

Shamefaced, Sherrie looked to the ground. "I don't want to bother you."

Florence's face showed a hint of rich, cross enjoyment. "You didn't mind bothering me a minute ago. Ask your question Sherrie."

"Um . . ."

"Answer the child's question Florence!" called old Phenice from the rocking chair now placed under the awning, gripping cloth and a seam ripper.

"I *will* answer her question when she *asks* a question," the branch head shot back at the elder.

"You can do it Sherrie!" encouraged Marge from the side.

"Yeah!" neighbors called, faces patient and mild.

Still looking to bow out, Sherrie smiled miserably, scanning the crowd.

"Maybe she'll faint!" whispered someone.

"Shh," stifled another.

Red as wine, Sherrie began to cry. "I'd rather not."

"*Ask—the—question*!" Florence steamed out a breath, regripping her purse strap, seeming ready to explode.

"All right! All right! It's not a—it pertains to—" Sherrie emitted a series of coughs.

Meanwhile, newly arrived partygoers with potluck dishes jumbled along the sidewalk near the edge of the crowd, among them a few clerks from Keely's Brink drugstore, each toting a slim french bread loaf over their shoulder.

But why bring bread to a bakery?

Then Sherrie, perhaps motivated to end this episode, began to ask the question, closing her eyes as if against the unknown. "Miss Stroke?" she began. "Is it possible to freeze . . ." She angled her face to the vivid evening sky over the rooftops, as if longing to go there. ". . . cheese?"

Whispers, buzzings, and knuckled-under chuckles arose among neighbors, while Eddleston sent a short hook punch overhead, smiling open-mouthed with pride, it seemed, for young Sherrie, and the newcomers with the bread began to laugh in high spirits, despite not knowing what had led up to this moment.

The librarian hewed out an unhappy laugh. "For the love of all that is human and good Sherrie. Freeze *cheese*? Are you trying to make a fool of me?"

"No Miss Stroke! Nothing like that!" Sherrie seemed appalled at herself or the scene at large, yet ground on-ward. "Why are you angry? It's not such a bad question is it? So many questions are worse . . . aren't they?" She began crying anew, long bangs, lashes, and eyes a wet mess.

Florence looked furious. "Don't make me out to be a bully. You're the one making a fuss."

"But Miss Stroke!"

"Now Sherrie. When we develop a research question we should never trumpet it in public for we can't know early on if it's viable. And research is quiet. It is private."

"Take it easy Florence," urged Moates softly from the crowd. Hushed comments rippled far back into the crowd, and Lance remarked, "Kinda tough bird—Florence."

Sherrie tried again. "It all happened so fast Miss Stroke. The question got bigger than I meant it to get. Haven't you ever made that mistake?"

"Girl's embarrassed," said someone in the crowd.

"Hmpfhh," the librarian blew out. "I don't like those who want a *garish* amount of attention when others need and get none."

At the front of the crowd, Sheila asked, "Did *you* ever want some attention Miss Stroke?"

The librarian glared. As neighbors in front of the bakery murmured, I suddenly wondered what Florence *was*. How could a person's conglomeration of traits exist stably through all the days? Was the senior-most branch librarian happy-go-lucky, a wearer of bright dresses and headwear and a joker, or was she a quiet, order-minded, impassible researcher? Why did I dislike believing that Florence contained contradictions? As I surveyed her, she seemed implausible, and then her seeming unrealness applied not to her, but me.

"Aw who wants attention Florence? Tell us. We'll go throw tomatoes at 'em!" cried Bianchi through the doorway, and everyone laughed.

Sherrie laughed too, nose dripping as she wiped her eyes, face blazing scarlet, scalp glowing pink through her yellow hair, and suddenly from her throat came a thick, duck-like sound.

Sherrie's sister Trudie had arrived to the party. She saw Sherrie in the doorway immediately and instantly pushed through the crowd. "Sherrie!" she called, and heads turned. "Why're you crying?"

"Trudie!" Sherrie answered, chin quivering as she set eyes on her sister. "I'm all right. Florence got mad at me."

The two sisters, staring at each other, appeared so similar that a third presence like the hieroglyphics of heredity itself or the steamy exertions of the girls' tired ancestors seemed to vibrate over them. "It's fine Sherrie," said Trudie. "You just got overexcited like you get." She eyed Florence. "You lay off my sister!"

Several neighbors chimed in, "Yeah!"

Sherrie swallowed and looked at the library branch head. "You could've said: 'Of course you can freeze cheese Sherrie darling!' Or 'No darling Sherrie you can never freeze cheese and don't you ever forget it.' But you didn't say those things did you?"

"Of course she didn't!" said Trudie.

Sherrie, now dark red as a match tip, glanced at her sister. "Miss Stroke why'd you get so angry when I asked you the cheese question?"

The branch head's fingers wiggled within the beige arm sling and she shrugged, a little rising grin on her face.

"Ha! See?" Eddleston cried out, raising his hand, pointing. "Florence isn't mad anymore!"

"Hooray!" neighbors exulted, laughing, the drugstore clerks waving the french bread as Sherrie fell against the librarian's shoulder, rolling her forehead to and fro as Florence looked away with distaste.

"Good lord," said Laurette to the high schoolers.

Then Bianchi in the doorway took a corn broom, laughing and raising it along his arm's length as if a rifle. "Now everybody get inside to th' party or I'll shoot every last one of you!"

High-spirited laughter and shouting broke out, with Moates punching his fist three times in the air, and the dense crowd of neighbors, some yelping, began to amble once again through the bakery's doorway and down the hall, with the exception of Florence, who seemed to want some quiet, and Millie and Minnie, who stayed beside her.

The baker taped a pastry doily to the glass door, words scribbled crookedly there in orange grease pencil: OPEN HOUSE PATIO. SPRING POTLUCK & MUSICAL ACT. JAROUSE BROS FOUR. TONITE!

At last almost everyone had gone in. I remained on the bench. The librarians and Minnie stood nearby, murmuring together for quiet moments on the near-deserted sidewalk before joining hands, gathering themselves, then bursting into a simultaneous run—flying indoors past the counter and down the long hallway as one.

III

The spring party had begun. I wandered to the patio's center garden, the guests' noise careening around me. Mike Vinnegar bristled at the sawhorse juice bar. "Too many orders Sal!"

The baker smiled, passing overfilled tumblers of juice to guests.

I glanced down the hallway with its little side rooms, observing neighbors standing, cradling tumblers and small plates, calling out to each other with pleasure, laughing. How do they do it? I wondered, regarding their easy conversations, the way they experienced one another lightly, without dread.

Then a voice, maybe Eddleston's, sounded through the hallway crowd: "There's the rich lady!"

It was Mrs. Lou Fox, an offhand philanthropist from the neighborhood who generally bought and sold painted plates. Mrs. Fox was known for wearing furs even in the sun and for dashing into stores from a white car she perpetually left idling at curbs during her errands.

From the kitchen, Bianchi pushed two bags into the pass-through window. Mrs. Fox took them in her arms. Across the woman's shoulders lay a flowing taxidermied stole with a snout, paws, and tail. She told the baker: "I can't stay dear heart but you know I love you and every crumb you bake."

"Sure Mrs. Fox."

She floated into the Pink Room where The Artist with the Scarf sat on the salmon-hued couch, focusing on a sheet of paper, pen in hand. I parked myself against the doorway's molding. Mrs. Fox sat on the sofa's arm. "What are you doing dear?"

"Oh hello Gabby." The Artist removed small eyeglasses. "I'm finishing a poem. Free-form."

"Marvelous!"

"I'll read it aloud tonight for the poetry circle."

"What's the title?" Mrs. Fox peered at the oversized page.

"'Lilacs and Gym Shorts.'"

"You're terribly artistic."

Eyebrows shifting with feeling, The Artist read the first line: "In that we are growing . . ." But Mrs. Fox had already left, sailing down the hallway with her pastry bags, past the counter and out the front door. I ran to the window, glimpsing in the passenger seat a plump, motionless husband in shadow as the car spun away.

The bakery felt empty without Mrs. Fox. Yet the place was more crowded than ever. Large clusters of guests continued flowing in past the green-glass door, through the hallway, and into the jewel box-like rooms or the patio.

Ribbons of statements like sprung confetti scattered upward.

"The schoolteacher's not a bit pretty," said a voice outside the Pink Room.

"I belong to the wild fruits movement," said someone—Millie.

"Tornado Ruth hit Kansas awfully."

"Hurricane wind's much easier," came a reply. "You just walk away."

Cousin Harriet's voice arose from a doorway: "We had burglars last week but they didn't steal anything."

"Can you believe the gall of Russia?" It was Cissy, in the hallway, holding a glass of pink juice.

"But that's what an enemy *is*: gall," Remnick told her.

"I like my home. I don't go to other homes," said someone.

Then, to my surprise, I spotted Mice at the end of the hallway. She looked small as a baby. Crouched against the baseboard beside an old brass lamp, she tickled her hand along the wall, giving the impression that she'd been exploring the corner for hours.

"Mice!" I whispered, but she did not turn. Could Jody still be asleep in the narrow passageway between the buildings? If so, how could I wake her and bring the sisters together despite the party's noise, untold faces, and pairs of eyes that seemed to hem me in? I recognized that Mice might remain where she was, so I made my way past the screen door and onto the patio, thinking to ask Harriet for help. Then, to my right, I saw the long aluminum potluck table.

It was a tumult of a meal. Sprawled over the table's near end lay a sheaf of rainbow-stained hyacinths, beside it the huge fruit horn I'd seen that morning, overspilling with hands of bananas, melon, split pineapples, mangoes, and the black grapes I'd watched rolling across the sidewalk hours before.

Beside the fruit lay a salver of hot spaghetti coated with powdered cheese and next to that sat the chicken legs and chicken flips in bowls, then mushroom stew in a stone vessel near Millie's potato boats. Next came tomato halves, hot oysters and steaming liver, creamed spinach, a tureen of chicken à la king, and a plate of stacked toast. I spied The Blur's bowl of colorless gelatin, a stone pitcher of buttermilk, and three pink bowls containing the macerated ingredients of cherries jubilee. At the table's far end sat a listing, putty-colored cake, butter pillow candies, a can of potato sticks, and gingerbread men.

I moved around the table, flies and midges circling overhead. Weighed down by the sight of the meal, I returned to the garden and sat beside a potted date palm.

Moates and Remnick trooped past with piled-high plates, heading for the patio's low wall, digging into their chicken à la king and toast. The men appeared too hungry to speak. Off the side of Moates's plate, noodles drooped. Remnick knuckled bread into his mouth.

The importer's freckled scalp shone in the tiki lamps' glare. After minutes of eating, he told his friend: "I don't know why you don't like onions Mike. I do."

Remnick shrugged, forking the food.

Nina Remnick joined them.

"Do *you* like onions Nina?" Moates asked through another mouthful.

She ignored him. "Mike," she said to Remnick. "I need to talk to you. About Phyllis."

"Phyllis is fine."

"I know she's fine. I need to talk to you."

"You said that."

"She—"

"I don't like you hungry Nina," intervened Moates. "Go get your dinner."

Nina glared at the importer, absently tugging at her delicate chain necklace, which had caught on a mole. "Mike—"

The Blur raced into the patio's center, bellowing, "Who brought mushroom stew?"

"Florence did!" someone answered.

The Blur seldom seemed to eat, though he was known to ask about food. Occasionally, I'd heard neighbors remark that the quick-footed man worried incessantly without real cause that he would be poisoned. In moments The Blur was gone.

I lingered by the potluck table, my urgent wish to find Jody mostly forgotten. Florence and Eddleston arrived for the mushroom stew, plates in hand. The branch head reached for one sauced mushroom, which she raised toward Eddleston's face. Seeing the morsel, the lanky man opened his mouth slightly—a reflex.

"Taste it," the librarian told him, shaking quietly with a laugh, but the tree salesman refused.

"Tell me," Florence asked the man. "Have you ever seared mushrooms on the stove?"

Eddleston shook his head.

"*Try* it. Sear them Burt."

"Miss Stroke I don't cook."

"They *squeal* when you press them. Whistle too. Sometimes almost scream. Oh yes. It's an experience none of us should miss," said the branch head. "All those changes they go through in the pan."

"Aw," Eddleston laughed uncomfortably, wiping his forehead with a napkin. "You're teasin' me Miss Stroke."

"No."

"But . . ." the salesman gulped. "What's the big deal in getting cooked if yer a mushroom?"

Then I heard Nina's voice. "You said you'd put Phyllis to bed Mike! You *promised*. She's so tired she can barely stand and she hasn't had a BM all day. Take her upstairs. Sal left some blankets on the guest bed."

Now I watched Remnick swallow his food and tell his spouse, "Okay."

Nina sighed rattlingly and went to the fruit juice bar, jabbing her long-nailed fingers into the ice bowl, exhaling, closing her eyes as if with relish or tension.

Marge reappeared on the patio with a broiled rumaki tray, passing the Remnicks, going to shake the appetizers onto other guests' plates.

Still within his storm of hunger, Moates gobbled his portion. "Mm. In ancient history this stuff would've been called the food of gods."

"Sure Larry." Marge moved on with the tray.

"This tastes good," Remnick mumbled beside his friend, more toast in hand.

"Oh daddy!" Moates chewed. "You can't get something like this anywhere. Lotsa vitamins."

"Health was not a factor for the caveman," Remnick remarked, swallowing, jostling a leg.

"He had the sanctity of his cave to think of," gnawed Moates.

"He had a greatly beneficial life you see—the caveman. Fresh air. Philistine advertising? None. American conformism? None of that either," Remnick added.

"Freedom," Moates concurred, chomping.

"Exactly. Well. Except freedom from getting his skull bashed in."

"I resent your constant quibbling Mike," Moates went back at his friend cheerfully.

They set their empty plates aside.

"By the way. You know what's wrong with this whole place?"

"No. What?" Remnick dabbed his mouth with a napkin.

"The women," said Moates. "They're driving me crazy."

"Oh not again. Larry you're a walking cliché."

"Well I shouldn't be walking. I should be running. Lookit over there," the businessman gestured to the high schoolers. "Don't tell me you're not thinking the same."

"I'm married Larry."

"'I'm married Larry,'" Moates mimicked, high-pitched. "So you've got everything you dream of at home. I see."

"Look. I never discuss my wife with anyone."

"I never discuss her either! Oh we have so much in common." The smiling round-faced man wiped fingers across his brow. "Okay Mike. I understand—you made a vow. Blah-blah. And then there's life itself." He surveyed the patio. "Lookit over there. Those little knees."

"Knees come on. Meaningless."

"You'd jump at the chance."

"I wouldn't."

"Square," accused Moates.

Remnick stared. "*Me*? *You're* the square."

"You are." Moates's eyes crinkled. "Lookit the dresses."

"Stop that. Those girls over there Lar? They're children."

"And don't act the pastor with me. Okay—you want older? Try her," Moates nodded toward Florence, seated alone for the moment with her plate, spooning dinner into her mouth.

"Her?" Remnick nodded.

Florence glanced at the men.

"That one's an utter Valkyrie I tell you. *Wild*," Moates whispered.

"You're nuts Larry," Remnick grinned. "I feel like buying you a new tie."

The two friends laughed together, Moates holding the other's arm.

"Hey," said the importer. "You think I don't know something's eating you lately?"

Remnick's eyelid jumped—a tic. "To be honest," he said quietly, "Nina could care less about the hanky-panky lately. Might be interested in that with somebody else."

Moates's eyebrows lifted. "Oh. There's someone else?"

"No."

Moates smoked. "Then this is the perfect moment for you to explore our world."

At that point, Honey strode to the patio in her yellow party dress, beckoning and hugging Marge, laughing, twirling a white evening handbag as small and integumental as an animal's pouch. Embracing, the two women seemed less to converse than conspire, laughing with pleasure, each word delicious-seeming to them.

But I couldn't hear the words. The nearby men's voices blared.

"Women always have this notion of a best friend who's similar to a beau but not," said Remnick.

"That's brilliant!" Moates snapped his fingers. "You could start that way. Be her confidant and move on from there. If you don't . . . another guy will."

"Then I'd worry about her. The guy'd be a creep no doubt."

"But he'd be *her* creep."

They smiled again together.

Then Remnick looked down helplessly at his feet. "Truth is Lar . . . I never feel that way about anyone. I never have."

"Felt what way?"

Remnick motioned Moates to speak quietly. "Look. I know it's almost deviant. But what can I do?"

"What're you talking about Mike?"

"Women and men. Hell queers too. Everybody. Love in general. It never clicked for me."

"But Mike you're *married*. You and Nina must've fallen in love."

"Me an' Nina were the best of friends. Less so now. At some point she wanted a baby. I thought why not."

"What about crushes? On actresses? Lola Falana?"

"*Who*? Anyway—I'm not like the rest of you louses. I'm *empty*," Remnick gestured. "Deeper feelings? No. Not me."

"Son. You need a doctor."

Now steamy-pink and warm-appearing as shrimp, the architect's face looked almost proud. "I thought the marriage'd make us real together. But no."

I didn't really understand what sort of problem Remnick was talking about—I was that young. More concerning for me was that partygoers might see me at the base of the date palm and begin to ask me questions. So I ran deeper into the garden, finding a thick plot of starflowers, hibiscus, and a spread of dwarf palms I could not begin to name. Well concealed now, I abandoned myself again to the torrid watching and listening.

Nina returned from the potluck table with a plate of spaghetti and cheese, eyes on her husband, as if trying to gauge him. Then she tripped on a little foot rug. The spaghetti flew, landing on the patio's concrete with a small clicking sound, lying in a tidy heap. Red sauce spattered her shoe.

"This is the last straw!" she cried, slowly bending, reaching for the fallen fork, her expression as low and lost as I'd ever seen it. Now as Sheila and Marge ran to her, rags in hands, Nina looked up to them. "I'm sorry. I hate spills," she said helplessly. "It's been a horrible day and now *this*."

As the women worked to calm her, Lance strolled past, glancing at the spilled sauce, rolling his cigar ash against a tree trunk. "World's fulla horrors Nina. Don't fuss over spilled food."

The women swabbed up the mess together, running to the kitchen with the sauce-laden rags and back again until it was done.

* * *

Then Eddleston played chase with Phyllis, lurching out from the garden to pinch her bottom when she ran by. With each pinch, the child screeched loudly, laughing with surprise. Meanwhile, the baker circulated with slices of mango cake wetted with rum or caramel, offering this special dessert to neighbors, including the Remnicks, who spoke little together but glanced up to wave and smile at Phyllis as she darted away from Eddleston.

After circling the patio with the cake, Bianchi returned to Remnick, nudging the tray's edge into the architect's flank. "Hey. You know those two don't you?" The baker nodded across the space to a little rock enclosure beneath the trellis. "Kinda look like movie stars."

The waxy-looking pair, newly arrived, stood together, stiff and near-identical with their fashionable eyewear and short, blunt-cut bangs.

"Gruelin's their name," Remnick, listless, told him. "Hal and Eve. Brother and sister."

Bianchi nodded. "They moved onto Bird Road a few weeks ago. Family owns a business."

"Oh? What business?" The architect's eyelid jumped: the tic again.

"Cat food factory."

"Ah. Lucrative?"

"Do I know? Ask him." Bianchi shifted the tray.

"Sounds like a dumb setup," said Remnick.

"Look—cats eat."

"I thought cats ate other cats."

"That's how dogs think." Bianchi went off with the tray.

Then nearby Moates returned to the architect. "You jealous of th' new neighbor Mike? Go dream up your own business. I know you could do it." Moates sipped from a foam-topped tumbler.

Remnick shrugged.

"Dream a little Mike," said Moates. "Now me? I'm the type I need people t'think *for* me. I take their ideas and improve 'em. That's how civilization progresses."

"Which civilization?"

Moates chewed ice. "Hey Smolt," he called to the beatnik behind the hi-fi. "Your avocation is music. So lemme ask—don't musicians borrow musical ideas for new songs? They've got to—right?"

The beatnik, rifling through a stack of albums, gave the importer a dry, chalky look.

"Answer the question delinquent!"

"What's your *deal* man?"

Observing nearby, the librarian Millie now displayed her professional penchant for categorizing, saying, "The younger Larry collects musical records. The older Larry sells umbrellas," as Minnie nodded.

"I don't *have* a deal Smolt," jeered Moates at the younger man. "You do though. I see right through it. And this beatnik thing? Pfft. It's an act. Phony."

Remnick tapped Moates. "Lar. Their generation asks to be let alone."

The reedy, angry-looking Beatnik Larry returned the albums to the gray shelf, then lifted the record player's arm over a polished black disc, announcing to neighbors gathered near the patio dance floor: "Ladies. Gentlemen. You're in for a treat. You're about t' hear a sound like no other. This is . . . Mingus."

Bianchi looked up. "Who?"

"Never heard of him," said Vinnegar, unwrapping a lollipop.

"*Mingus?*" Moates cried loudly, with amusement. "Is he a . . . *dingus?*"

Neighbors laughed.

"Will you shut *up*?" the beatnik told the importer hotly. "Some of these compositions were written for a *film*."

"Well. In *that* case a thousand pardons." The importer bowed, laughing, encouraging neighbors to cheer him on.

The song rose up—a cadre of horns flying in, followed by fuggy bass notes entering a forest of their own creation. The beatnik turned up the volume. Chatting neighbors raised their voices. The noise was tremendous. Cissy stepped to the front of the group, the trellis's warm blue lights over her body's contours, and she faced the beatnik. "I was looking forward to dancing tonight," she told him, strong feelings in the front of her voice. "This tune has no melody!"

Moates's juice sloshed. "Cis—I'm with you. What I hear? Are the sounds of a dying toucan."

A few neighbors tittered.

"Calm down folks," Florence told the two, hiking her foot up on a chair, leaning in. "Didn't you hear Sal say we'll hear much musical variety tonight? Well we will."

Remnick smiled meekly at the branch head. "I tell myself to be open-minded Miss Stroke. I'll even listen to music as far-out as Brubeck. But I draw the line there ma'am."

The branch head smiled. Then, voice catching, the beatnik called out to them all: "Mingus is a man people are talking about!"

Moates, Cissy, and Eddleston shook with laughter over this, falling against one another as the beatnik stamped his foot, face furious.

"We believe you Larry," said Cissy, trying to recover from her convulsions. "We really do. But . . ." She looked for the baker. "But the fact is there's a place and time for everything and we want dancing music tonight. Real music. What about some good ol' swing?"

"*Geez!*" the frustrated beatnik vented. "Can't any of you just listen? Stop talking and take the time for once. Listen."

Saxophone notes gusted in, then moved in separate directions.

Eddleston called to Smolt: "Hey Larry. If this is such a great song? How come a buncha people're *talking* in the background of th' recording?"

Cindy cut in, hand on the silent dentist's shoulder: "To me this tune has a foreign flair. Where's it from?"

"Earth Miss House! Where else?" Smolt beefed as the dental secretary touched her chest questioningly.

Upon further less-cacophonous questions from the dance-floor group, the beatnik abruptly removed the Mingus record from the hi-fi. After wiping the phonograph needle with a fingertip, he reached for another record. "*Fine,*" he mocked. "Have it your way. We'll listen to another one. Here—I've something good."

The sound of a lone piccolo, like water on rocks, ran through the amplifier, helpless with gravity. A trumpet arose, blurring. A singer's voice emerged.

"Hey," said Sheila, looking up. "This's Abbey Lincoln. She's new."

"She's not *new,*" the beatnik snarled.

The group listened. A cymbal rang, then rose the singer's voice: torpor.

"I hear off-notes!" Millie cried, hand cupping an ear.

"This song's about our times," Sheila told them.

"Sad music. Who needs it?" swiped Vinnegar.

"I hear a clacking sound!" said unhappy Cissy.

"Calm yourself Mrs. Lax," Remnick told her. "It's a drum."

"All I want is to dance," the older woman repeated, seeking others' glances. "Oh Sal?"

Bianchi strode to the hi-fi with the towel. "Larry," he told the beatnik. "C'mon. My guests want to dance. You gonna stand in their way?"

"Sal give me a minute," said the beatnik, pacing beside the gray shelf. "This record really blew up the scene a couple years ago. It—"

Moates stepped in, jeering tone drawing the crowd's attention. "Hey Mister Big. Didn't y'hear Sal? Lemme make a point in case you're deaf or somethin'. *This*? Is *not* music. It is an abstraction of real music which requires no formal training. That's why abstraction is always boring. And I've got more t'say about it too."

"Shut yer piehole!" the beatnik fired at the importer, all temper.

"Make me."

Immediately the beatnik hopped from behind the console and feint-lunged at the older, rounder Moates, who used a half moment's hesitation on the beatnik's part to advance into the younger man with a fist. The beatnik flailed in return. In their tangling, Moates lost his balance, falling backward, grabbing the younger man's sleeve for balance, hollering in Smolt's face: "You're nothing! You pinprick!"

Marge rushed in, plying the two men apart with her hands as if well accustomed to this peacemaking activity. Moates went on the offensive again until Bianchi stepped in, scolding the Larrys: "Get outta the diaper stage. Both of you!"

"I wanted to dance," moaned Cissy.

Then the high schoolers repeated a chant at the dance floor's perimeter, which stifled all other talk: "We want Fabian! We want Fabian!"

Lumbering to the screen door, opening it, the angry baker turned back. "Smolt! The music! I'm warning you."

"All *right*! Have it your way!" The threadbare young man yanked the Lincoln album from the phonograph and swapped it for a Fabian disc from the gray shelf. Instantly, quick-prickling guitar scales ascended above a to-and-fro beat as the beatnik dutifully announced: "This is 'String Along' by you-know-who. And what a *magnificent work of art* it is." An ecstatic cheer swept over the patio, drowning out his voice as neighbors flocked to the hi-fi area, seeming to drink in the quick, bubbly music, exploding into jolting dance.

Near the potluck table, Marge clapped in time with the tune, laughing, then went to pull her fiancé's floury wrist. "Sal I gotta dance to this!" So they, along with streams of other neighbors, went to dance too. In the center of it all, the widow-notary churned her arms wildly, smiling mouth open, eyes closed, relishing it all. The Remnicks danced with Phyllis nearby as well, looking to enjoy themselves if only mildly, and the surfer Riley hopped to the song's lockstep rhythm, short hair quivering as he hollered lyrics. Jumping Brahms did the Twist, crying out, "I heard this number on the *Beech-Nut Show*!"

Only the beatnik and Vinnegar did not dance. Beside the hi-fi console, the defeated beatnik nudged the barman. "They're not sophisticated enough to notice the awful singing."

Vinnegar grinned. "I'll take Puccini any day."

Smolt nodded. "Popular music for the masses is going downhill. Let's see if any good music at all comes out in the next few years."

"I doubt it," snorted the barman.

When the Fabian song wound down, the beatnik played another of the crooner's hits. Its insolent, slumbery drumbeat led gangly Eddleston to run across the dance floor as if in slow motion, laughing, beating his arms as wings. Soon the dance-floor group formed a pulsating conga line wholly out of step with the song's rhythm, guests laying hands on the shoulders of those in front of them as neighbors at the sidelines sang along, brush-clapping to the music.

After the line broke up, Eddleston, Sheila, the clerks with the breadsticks, and others crowded the bar, thirsty for juice. Then The Blur returned, barging to the front of the line, grabbing a juice out of turn.

"Be courteous!" cried Eddleston and Sheila.

Downing the juice instantly, The Blur ran the dance floor's perimeter, singing Fabian's lyric "If you want me come and get me" to himself before exiting the patio through the back gate. By then the evening was fully dark. The Blur pelted down Reef Way alone.

*   *   *

Not long after, I left the garden and returned to the Pink Room. Moates and Remnick stood beside the bookcase, so I went to the other side of the shelves, laying the side of my head against the dark glazed wood as I listened.

"She's coming this way now," Moates told Remnick. "The red-haired one."

He was talking about Honey, who, swinging her purse, crossed the floor, heading unawares toward a small off-to-the-side pyramid of fallen spaghetti that the women had missed in their cleanup. Moates and Remnick signaled wildly to her, but Honey did not understand and trod on the sticky sauced heap with her sandal. Bare in her ruched party dress, her shoulders lifted at the cold surprise.

"Oh shoot! I stepped on . . . what is it? Noodles?"

The two men rushed to her, taking her elbows. "Don't worry Honey," they cooed.

"I'm not *wor*ried," she laughed, bending with a napkin to wipe the paste from her shoe.

"I'll help you clean it," said Moates, crouching.

"It's really all right," Honey said.

"Spaghetti," he pronounced. "It falls constantly. All over the nation. Doesn't it Mike?"

"Oh yes. Understandably. Because it's slippery."

"Don't be embarrassed Honey," Moates said, passing napkins.

"I'm not," she laughed, wrist to her mouth.

Then Nina led Phyllis by the hand silently past them all, perhaps toward the bathroom, and she glanced at her husband, whose eyes were on Honey.

"The last time I saw you Honey," said Remnick, "was a New Year's Day picnic at Dezertland Park. You were probably thirteen. You were with your father."

"Now I'm twenty-one," Honey told them proudly. "Sure. I remember you old guys."

Their faces fell a little.

"Well—thanks for saving me from the spaghetti," she faltered, stepping away, shoe more or less clean.

"Wait," Moates called, fingers raised. "Just one question for you . . ."

"What?"

"I mean as a young person . . . well what d'you think of the world situation?"

Honey laughed. "What do I think of . . . what? The whole world?" She shook her head, wrinkled her nose at the two men.

Remnick pitched in, "You see Larry and I've been talking about the A-bomb. How it could be the start of humanity's end. Or will we step up as a species and learn to get along?" In smallish steps, he and Moates moved closer to the young woman.

"Aw geez Mike," Moates told Remnick. "Why not just ask her to discuss th' Stalingrad bloodbath?"

"*You* were the one to bring up world problems," Remnick charged his friend.

Easygoing Honey shrugged. "The news says th' A-bomb's a bright flash and then you're baked." She smiled beatifically at the two men. "The world's still beautiful though."

Moates laughed, eyes to the ceiling near-tearily. He took Remnick's arm. "Isn't she wonderful Mike?"

"Oh yes. She is."

They beamed at Honey.

"C'mon outside for a walk," Moates told her, taking her arm, pulling hard. "I'll listen to your troubles."

"Not now Pops."

Moates's eyes flickered. "Then let Mikey come along too." He tipped his head at Remnick. "He's closer to your age. You can walk with him. I'll follow behind as chaperone. Sound okay?"

"No thanks." She strode off.

They watched her go. "That was just the start," Moates told his friend quietly. "I'll find her later. Then she'll cave in."

*　*　*

Still holding the wet cigar, Lance sidled up to Moates and Remnick. "Speakin' a' the Bomb," he told them, "I saw one a' them things explode."

Moates looked away, into the hallway.

"It was a dozen or more years ago in th' desert," Lance said. "Witnessed a test shot. Big bright thing," Lance coughed. "Blinded a couple men for a while. Good weapon."

Picking up words from the conversation, several neighbors drifted closer, gathering to listen.

"Oh th' Bomb can't be used again Jack," the architect told Lance. "It's somewhat immoral."

Florence approached and braced one foot on a chair's rung. She leaned an elbow onto her leg, allowing the slinged arm to hang. "Mother called a little while ago. She was at the market in Riverside today. Said everyone was talking about some kind of raid on the country to the south—Cuba. An attack authored by our country. It was in the newspapers."

"Riverside?" Eddleston exclaimed, going toward the branch head. "That area's gone to the dogs these days. It's all Spanish!"

"Riverside people are not from Spain Burt. They're Cuban," said Florence.

"What was in the paper? I didn't see anything," said Moates.

"That we could use an attack to put Cuba in its place. Send a message to the Russian Reds," the librarian answered.

"Oh that's all speculation," Remnick shrugged.

More neighbors drew around them, listening.

Lance went in: "See all the folks that moved here from Cuba hate Cuba."

"Well why shouldn't they? Their country went nuts," declared Cissy, resting nearby in a chair after her bouts of dancing.

"Everyone—let me finish. Mother said the Riverside women formed a committee against Dr. Castro. You see Mother understands almost all languages including Spanish," the librarian added, tender-faced.

"I'll tell you right now," Lance pushed at her. "Attackin' Cuba's been a rumor for months. An' it won't happen. Too dangerous."

"I saw it in the Sunday paper," said Millie. "*I* say it's worrying!"

"The only question's whether to invade out in the open or in secret," said Remnick. "I advocate for secrecy. That keeps it clean."

"Mike!" said Nina to her husband, face astounded.

"Son of a gun. You war hawk Mike!" the baker grinned, clapping Remnick on the back.

"I second that Mike!" cried Eddleston, jumping, face eager. "Th' Cuban invasion's absolutely gotta be secret."

"I don't like this talk," said the dentist among them, nervous-sounding, and Cindy touched his arm. "Why think how an attack could steam up the Russians."

"Yeah. Worrisome," Moates said, placing a butter pillow candy in his mouth.

"Mother was frightened over it," Florence admitted. "Hate to say it but if we attacked that country . . ."

"War'd break out," supplied Eddleston.

"Yeah. Russia'd roll us into the ground," said the branch head. "We could die."

"Mommy!" cried Phyllis, reaching for her mother.

"Look—you upset my daughter," Nina scolded Florence, picking up the child. "I mean really."

"No one believes their life will end," Sheila said, dreamy-sounding.

"And *you* stop it too!" Nina spun around to Sheila before hurrying Phyllis from the room.

"Beyond th' blast radius plenty a' folks'll survive," Moates told onlookers, leaning comfortably at the wall.

"Russians? Aggressive creatures," said The Blur, suddenly tearing past, a butterhorn in hand.

"But some of them are *nice*," called The Artist after him. "That I know from the laundromat."

*   *   *

For some time then, neighbors flowed in and out of the Pink Room, hallway, and patio, swapping places repeatedly. Night surrounded us; the lamplight grew more golden. I remained beside the Pink Room's bookcase, my face on the warm wood, sleepy until Cissy, from her spot in the room's easy chair, rallied partygoers by calling shrilly: "How's about Trudie Gagel's fame?"

Trudie's sister Sherrie, on the salmon-hued couch, looked startled. "My sister has fame? What do you mean?"

"Didn't you know that Trudie's writing was published in a magazine?" asked the older woman, slowly lifting a hand to her mouth, tongue flashing to her knuckle to swipe away drops of yellow juice.

"Goodness is it true?" asked Harriet, overhearing, coming closer.

"That's wonderful news!" came the astonished voice of the dentist.

Under the far wall's high window, Sheila, Harriet, Marge, Florence, Millie, Minnie, and others exchanged glances, then headed to the sofa as well, the closer to listen.

"It's a fact. Trudie is a published writer," Cissy told them.

"I think I heard the same from somebody's mother," peeped Joyce.

Marge asked Sherrie: "Your family always preserves fruit in the summer—right?"

"Yes but what has that to do with writing and magazines?" Sherrie cried, face blotched.

Marge shrugged tiredly. "Sugar is famous for memorializing the past—you know. The preserves of the summer yard and that sort of thing."

"Photographs preserve food too!" cried out Moates. "My old piano teacher taught me that."

"Marge is right. Because Trudie—if she writes expressively—preserves life in a way. So it must be a family trait," Harriet reasoned, ignoring Moates. "I wonder if she wrote about you in the magazine Sherrie?"

Sherrie paled. "Oh I hope not!"

"Ask her," said the poet Kulp, brittle-voiced, kneeling on a cushion, holding a Tinkertoy.

"I never even knew that my sister was an author of writing."

Cissy gestured to the sister with an upturned palm. "People change."

"No Cissy," insisted Harriet, coming along. "I believe this firmly. People and things don't change. They really *don't*. People are as they are."

Entering the room, Eddleston offered: "Potato chips changed the snack world."

"Are potatoes people?" Harriet challenged.

"Are you sure it was our Trudie wrote in the magazine?" asked Millie, leaning in.

"Didn't I say so?" snapped Cissy.

A raft of further neighbors—Solly, Honey, Laurette, Helen-Dale, Brahms, the dentist and Cindy, and The Woman Who Didn't Speak—all pushed through the doorway. "What happened?" they asked, squeezing around the sofa.

Old Cissy held the center. "Trudie's gotten into some kind of writing career," she re-established. "I even have the proof in my purse." She leaned down for her pocketbook, stretching its leather mouth widely. "Here's the magazine—the most recent issue of *Teenagers Weekly*. Should I read it aloud?"

"Yes!" neighbors cried.

"Why Sherrie—what's wrong?" asked Honey from behind many others, palm upon a small drinks table. "Why're you so red in the face?"

"I know why," Solly said, sidling close. "Because Yum-Yum's on the loose."

"To lose a dog is terrible," said Florence. "Sherrie get a horse."

"No—here's the problem," Cissy kept on, relishing it. "Sherrie craves attention. I can feel it. Don't you Sherrie? Oh we know that Trudie's won more blue ribbons at school than Sherrie ever did. Each girl's jealous of the other's accomplishments. Oh they've squabbled for years about who's best. Hildy herself said she can't tell which of her daughters is better. Doesn't your mother have trouble deciding about that dear?"

Sherrie sat tightly to herself on the couch, glaring at the high window. "Yes."

Cissy upended the purse and the thick magazine slid out, its bright color cover photo depicting smiling, open-mouthed young people holding milkshakes. The crowd of partygoers cooed.

Marge cried: "Trudie's out on the patio. Go bring her here the little intellectual! We should congratulate her." So Eddleston and Marge ran to find her.

Cissy flipped through the pages. "Here," she pointed, and everyone wedged in to see. "Believe me now?"

Joyce breathed over Cissy's shoulder, "There's Trudie's name in print!"

"Yes indeed. She wrote a letter to the magazine," said Cissy proudly.

"Let me see!" cried Moates.

"Could that be some other Trudie Gagel?" asked Solly.

"I wondered that too," said Helen-Dale.

"Course not!" admonished Cissy. "It's our Trudie. I always knew she was a good girl."

"Frankly," Moates opined, "Trudie's an attractive enough young lady and with a trim enough waistline that she actually *could* succeed as a writer in the public eye."

Everyone nodded, considering.

"I'll read it out loud," said Cissy, flattening the page, crackling the binding.

"Gosh Mrs. Lax. Don't you see?" Sherrie broke out from the couch, terribly uncomfortable-looking. "It's nothing. *Thousands* of people write letters to the magazines every day."

"And yet," Moates faced them, raising a finger, "how many letters are selected to appear in the pages of *Teenagers Weekly*? So very few. Case closed."

"Now Sherrie: don't steal Trudie's thunder," warned Cissy.

Sherrie brought quaky hands to cap her knees.

"What does it take to be accomplished these days?" idly wondered a Gagel family uncle or cousin who'd wandered in late, Bell.

"Hurry—let's hear the letter!" said Minnie. "Read it!"

"Oh look. There she is the famous author!" called out Cissy.

"Hooray!" cried the group.

Eddleston and Marge pulled scarlet-faced Trudie into the room while a raft of further curious, smiling neighbors and guests jammed into the doorway behind them. One of the last, Bianchi bared his rough grin and hollered, "I hear you've got a new career as a poet Trudie!"

The rest of them cheered as Trudie tripped to Cissy's chair, explaining: "All I did was write a letter."

Millie shrugged loosely. "I'm with Larry. Trudie's writing was chosen. Maybe that's nature's way of showing that she should continue to develop her art."

Sherrie visored a hand to her damp forehead.

"Go on. Read the story!" cried Eddleston.

Cissy reached for her eyeglasses.

"No! I'll read it," said Moates, jumping forward and grabbing the magazine, standing before the group aglow.

"Goodness!" breathed Cissy.

"'Dear Editor,'" Moates read. "'I don't often write

letters but your magazine is terrific.'" He glanced up and smiled, drinking in the group's interest. "'I found your story "Copper Angels" by Mrs. Gretchen Bullis extremely enjoyable. In fact it was romantic.'"

Giggles arose from the group.

"'I especially liked the part about the hair. This is what I expect from a good romance story. To be entertained and enchanted,'" he continued. "'Others may have their opinions but "Copper Angels" made this girl happy the whole day after I read it.'"

"You—wrote—that?" asked Helen-Dale with dull awe.

Trudie shrugged.

"You're modest!" called someone.

"It was just a letter," Trudie said.

"Wonderful!" called out Cindy, her hand on the dentist's hand, while at the rear, Bianchi pounded his fist against the doorjamb, underscoring this view.

"Why'd you write a letter to the magazine Trudie?" asked Marge.

"I dunno."

"Girls like reading romances," Eddleston informed all, jiggling his foot.

"I don't wanna *read* romances," laughed Moates. "I wanna *live* 'em warts n' all!"

"Trudie always was the go-getter," said Bell, with a defeated air that made him seem more an uncle than a cousin.

By then, Trudie's blush was so acute that her thin yellow hair alongside her face appeared near-green, and Sherrie, who'd slid to the far end of the couch, leaned over its arm as if about to be sick.

"Heavens finish reading it!" cried Cissy.

"Oh okay," said Moates. "There isn't much left. 'Please print more stories like that. Yours sincerely, Trudie Gagel, Reef Way, Miami.'"

The group clapped patteringly. Moates turned the magazine out to show the page and print.

"Yep—smack-dab in the magazine," Cissy confirmed.

"Remarkable," said Honey softly, pouring water.

Suddenly Sherrie jumped from the couch and moved toward the crowd, extending her wrist, on which hung a slim gold chain. "Did everyone see my new bracelet?" she cried.

Cissy turned to Trudie, telling her, "Your writing career has gotten off to a good start dear." With an enormous final pulse, a high blush then overcame not only Trudie's face, but her jaw, neck, shoulders, arms, and the backs of her hands, and she began to wheeze.

Meanwhile, Moates told her slowly, advisingly, hand slicing through the air, "Trudie look. You're young. Your life's just starting. So I'm gonna tell you something. Through life you're gonna do some smart things and you're gonna do some dumb things. But if you don't keep writing articles for the magazines? That'll be a very dumb thing indeed. Do you understand?"

"Yeah," said Trudie rotely.

"Don't say 'yeah.' It's very rude," the man told her.

"Trudie could move to New York City," whispered Millie in the crowd.

"Chicago?" gestured the uncle.

Bianchi boomed over the others: "Sherrie! Congratulate your sister Trudie. Go on—go hug her!"

Slowly, painfully, like an old woman, yet taking care

to exhibit the bracelet for guests, Sherrie approached the sister, each girl harried- and sapped-looking.

From my place beside the bookcase, I saw Jody in the crowd. What could she be thinking? Had her fears ebbed? Her eyes rose to the Pink Room's high window with its frosted glazing and dark frame, trued by builders decades before.

"Go ahead girls. Do what Sal says. Hug each other!" Cissy prodded.

The Gagel sisters embraced stiffly, avoiding each other's eyes until Sherrie dropped her head and sobbed into Trudie's blouse, her voice thick with saliva, "You do everything better. You win everything and I always lose. Every morning as soon as I wake up I've already lost!"

"Sherrie don't say that! No!" cried alarmed Trudie.

"But you—" Sherrie began.

Cissy frowned. "Simmer down you two. You'll sort all this out when you have husbands. Where's you girls' mother by the way?"

"She went home to watch television," said Trudie.

Cissy leaned back into the couch, sighing with near-contentment. "Oh me. Trudie's doing awfully well. And you Sherrie? If having a smarter and better older sister's the worst thing ever happens to you . . . then I say you're doing just fine."

Sherrie's eyes glowed with a difficult mist.

*   *   *

Soon the Pink Room's crowd thinned out. I tried following Jody, who'd lit out for the patio, and dodged around guests, realizing that Mice might still be at the base of the brass lamp, concealed by the heavy crowd, and that Jody might've passed her by.

The hallway and patio were congested. I spied Jody leaning beneath the trellis upon one of the large garden boulders. "Jody!" I waved, my arm slow to rise, as if in water. She did not hear me. She faced the police detective who stood beside the potluck table, pushing mushrooms onto a plate with a two-tined fork; then with the utensil he beckoned her.

My hairline burned with anger as she went to him. *I* needed to speak to Jody and let her know that her sister was mere steps away. *I* had the important news for her. Mice was worth hundreds of Dennys, I thought, and then I heard a voice behind me: *This night will keep you honest.*

I turned but saw no one. Who had spoken?

Denny led the elder sister to the corner of the patio where piled boulders formed a small grotto-like space topped by the overhead trellis. I went to the grotto's far side, squidging myself to the boulders, finding a crevice through which to watch both of them as the stone pleasantly cooled my face.

Denny extended his plate. "You should try this stew."

"I'll taste it when I eat."

"Now don't take this wrong Jo. But I like how you came in here with me while I eat my meal."

She spoke quickly. "Don't *sidetrack* me Denny. Have you seen Mice or not?"

"I was out on the road so no," he said. "Did she show up?"

"You know she hasn't. Oh could my life be any more ridiculous? Do you know that today Mice ate *string*?"

"Sounds like Phenice's cat. Smathers ate string. Got sick."

"Did you hear what I just said? My sister's *missing*. She's been acting strange and rebellious for some time. Have you or the chief done a thing about it? Oh Denny Mother warned me that someday Mice'd disappear completely—like it was her destiny. But I worry she could be lost or even trapped in a culvert. Can't we go now? Get a team to start looking?"

The detective swallowed. "What's a culvert anyway? I'm not sure I ever knew."

"*Please*. She's the only thing I have," the sister whimpered. "Don't make me suffer."

The detective set the plate aside. "Maybe she's on The Way."

"The *what*?"

At this point the voice behind me sounded again. *So Jody's lived on Reef Way for almost a year and isn't aware of the little grass path, the yellow one, that everyone else knows about but that almost no one uses? Well, she'll have to get wind of it.*

Without much pitch or expression, the voice nevertheless resembled the voices of the few people I'd known best in my life, just as the youngest, most adored child looks like everyone in a family all at once.

Jody was too jittery to listen closely to the man. "Another thing Denny. Those teenagers! I've got to give them a talking-to but I just don't have the stomach for it."

He nodded. "Try Jo. They could use a warning."

With a nervous jolt, I wondered suddenly if Denny White, in fact, was the story's helper. What if he was the one? All nerves, I gripped the rocks, sensing the very likely possibility that the story could go completely upside down and turn on me.

But my curiosity about both sisters kept me, in the moments of my most extreme worry, afloat. Jody's eyes squinched shut and as if in a dream, she raised her arms out before her. What was wrong with her?

"See these arms Denny?"

"Sure."

"My arms have changed over time. At this point they look just like my legs."

"You sure about that?"

"It's been happening for months though I haven't spoken of it." The sister bent forward, laying an arm alongside her leg, explaining, "See? This arm's nearly identical to my leg. It's just an impossible situation."

"Not ex—"

"Are all *your* limbs alike Denny?"

"Well my legs are pretty veiny," said the man, brow wrinkled in seriousness, implying a confidence, drawing closer. "So they probably don't count."

". . . count?"

"Gee it's—"

Without warning, a storm of a kiss blew in. It stunned me. I leapt closer to the boulders, placing my face to the rock crevice in order to see everything.

Below the detective's shadowed face, Jody's face rotated as if under water, strands of her hair appearing to float. She worked on him avidly. Jody could really let herself go. My surprised body tightened as coils. *Why?* the voice behind me asked softly, though I couldn't be bothered to understand the question. When I closed my eyes, yellow sunshine appeared.

Surely the two of them, working so hard, felt my hands squeezing the rocks as their kissing continued, draining off some of the story's excess. If only Mice, I thought, or even Jody could sit beside me, watching this through the crevice as well! I would describe for Mice all the details she was unable to see.

Jody abruptly asked Denny: "Remember when this happened before?"

"Yeah."

"That was different than this."

"It's a little different each time—isn't it?" the man grinned. "Jo? I need to tell you something. About an hour ago Chief sent me to check the kitchen in your apartment."

"*What*?" She stepped back from him.

"Yes. I drove over there. A neighbor called in to report a small kitchen fire with no one home."

"Which neighbor?"

"I'm not tellin'. When I got there sure enough the range was turned on but it wasn't like a regular stove flame. The fire was small and jumped—I didn't like it. There was a can of vegetable oil nearby so it all could've been bad. I turned off the range of course."

"Oh did you."

"Yes. You mentioned earlier that the stove once lit up all on its own. Mind telling me what's been going on Jo?"

Her face was rigid. "Denny. How did you get into my apartment?"

"Walked. Who turned it on?"

"My sister maybe."

"Mice can cook?"

"Boils water."

"Hm." The man wrote in the notepad. "And your housewoman—what's her name?"

"Girtle."

The sound of my name filled me once again with a sea-sickness as I held the boulders, noticing the stone coated with a thin, pinkish mud that now smeared my arms and blouse. The substance was delightfully cooling.

"Her last name?"

"Uh? Ross."

"All right. And does this Girtle Ross cook?"

"Course not Denny. She'd ruin the kitchen."

"Well how's this Girtle supposed to get up a meal at your place?"

"Denny she only eats dough! Look—forget about Girtle. She's not important."

"Jody? I've been sleuthing on Reef Way for quite a spell. In other words I'm experienced. And—"

"I know all that already!"

". . . I believe it was Girtle who tampered with the stove. Not Mice."

Like nitrogen, which freezes as it boils, my veins and their life began to go cold. How could Denny have known that I switched on the stove?

"I told you Girtle doesn't *cook*. If she did I'd punish her."

"I think Girtle lit that stove as a signal."

Jody looked stunned. "A signal for *what*?"

"I think Mice and Girtle have a plan."

Jody turned white as a sock.

* * *

A minute later as Jody left the grotto, concerned-looking Denny followed her. Closing my eyes, I lay back on the rocks, replaying the kiss in my mind, scraping the wet pink slip from my arms. Then near the dance floor, I heard several neighbors exclaiming—Eddleston, Remnick, Marge, Cissy, and more—"Look at that fancy pair!"

They were referring to the neighborhood's newcomers, brother and sister Hal and Eve Gruelin. I went to the low stone wall to watch the new residents stroll onto the patio arm in arm, each wearing stylish, dark-framed eyeglasses and tailored clothing.

Neither sibling seemed older or younger than the other. Eve wore a small blue box hat, its surface smooth as a cake's. Hal tipped his fingers at the baker and otherwise avoided looking at neighbors. Marge ran in to make introductions as Florence leaned to the library workers with words difficult but not impossible to hear: "The *Herald* wrote about those two. They're tycoons. Or *from* tycoons. Just moved to town."

Marge greeted the new neighbors squarely. "I heard that you two hail from New York! Why of all places did you travel here to little West Miami?"

"Girls. Sunsets," the brother answered, turning away to cough, hand to mouth.

"Liar," Eve sniped at the brother.

Neighbors glanced at each other. Gruelin's face: disklike, impassive. "Fact is we're remounting one of our father's businesses here. Fact is things're coming together nicely."

"My brother loves money you see," the sister added with a skewered-looking smile. "However. *I* appreciate life's higher aspects. Hal—he mixes in with the ruck. You should see where he—"

"Shut up," Gruelin told her meanly.

Vibrant Eve seemed no worse for this rebuke. "Oh isn't

it funny that I'm telling all about us right out of the gate? In a word—well I'm the pure opposite of my brother. Everywhere we go people ask why we stick together. I simply remind them that we stick together because we're stuck!" She laughed. "And you see I do get along with Hal. It's he who doesn't get along with me!"

"What is she talking about?" whispered Sheila within the enveloping crowd.

"Why—she's foreign!" exclaimed Millie from the front of the group while neighbors stared at Eve in wonder, a few murmuring to each other.

Cissy edged through the assemblage of guests. "Miss? May I ask what kind of accent do you have?"

Eve regarded them all with a charged smile. "I'm a Swiss mutt!" She punctuated the final words with two quick nods and performed a microscopic curtsy.

"Mutt's about right," mumbled Gruelin, hands in pockets.

"We like your accent Eve," Sherrie blushed.

"Oh—do you mean it?" the woman asked them, noticeably pleased.

"Yes we do!" cried the group as Eve's head dropped back and she gave a deep open-mouthed laugh, clearly relishing the attention.

More neighbors drifted their way through the hallway and to the patio, getting an eyeful of the new neighbors. Now sitting against the low stone wall as if a lump of rock myself, I wasn't about to wander away and look for Jody. I wanted to go on floating on the buoy of their voices, listening.

"Talk more," Millie and others pleaded to Eve, pressing in. "Say something!"

Eve beamed again. "Something!"

They all laughed. As Eve glanced at her brother, who leaned against the wall and rolled his eyes at the fanfare, her smile waned. Numbers of guests asked the woman near-simultaneously: "What kind of accent *do* you have?"

"Oh I'm from the Continent and just about everywhere else," Eve replied as everyone laughed again, unaccountably.

Cissy approached the Gruelin pair. "Oh you wonderful blue bloods!" she cried, reaching, then swept up the new neighbors' four hands in her own, struggling somewhat to maintain a hold on this fleshy mass. The widownotary's eyes shone. "You two are incomparable!"

"Yes darling," Eve purred over the hands as Gruelin gave an irritable grunt.

The Artist with the Scarf spoke up. "Her accent isn't from Europe. Eve talks like they do in Rochester."

"No!" Millie insisted. "Eve said she was European and so she is!"

"I agree!" Cissy added, angry-sounding, releasing all the hands. "It doesn't matter where Eve comes from. She speaks wonderfully and I like her awfully. I'm a fan of the rich you see."

"Me too!" shrieked Minnie from the crowd.

Eve told The Artist and everyone else: "I've never set foot in horrible Rochester. Of course Daddy's office is in Wisconsin but you see we lost our father last year—to death that is. So Hal and I now need to concentrate our energies on the business and Mother. She's a great horsewoman by the way."

"We're sorry about your father Eve," Marge said, lowering the bread tray.

"Where were you born?" Minnie blurted out to the socialite from the crowd.

"In a field hospital," sighed the new woman as if with a sharp, indescribable burden. "Of course last month we visited Manhattan New York and it practically killed us—didn't it Hal?"

"More or less." The brother, now farther off at the patio's rear gate, coughed.

"You see in New York everyone's expected to have a specialty," said Eve. "And not only that. They seem to adore New York. Can you imagine getting giddy over a city? That is so sad. Their lives are empty I suppose. Plus one is expected to be witty in New York. Of course I am a natural wit but I refuse to be so on demand.

"New York made me sleepy you see," she continued, "and Hal got a stomachache. So I said, 'Hal, let's go.' Well he drove me straight back to Moose Lake Wisconsin where I still might be if he hadn't dragged me here to Miami! Didn't you drive me Hal?" She laughed again with a scraping intensity that seemed to forbid commentary or questions.

"Oh did I," the brother said.

"But you see none of you have any idea of the *romance* to be found in Wisconsin," she went on. "The summer of '58? It was Bob Drithers. Of course the summer of '59 it was Burr Rolt," she ticked off on a finger, "and summer of '60 it was . . ." She raised her dark eyebrows meaningfully. "Luigi Contouri."

"Stop the nonsense Eve," the brother rasped, but she continued.

"Luigi was from the island of *Italy* you see."

Upon hearing this, Harriet, Millie, Minnie, Eddleston,

Laurette, Solly, and others from the group squeezed even closer to Eve, a few of them touching her sleeve, and Hildy, now returned from her TV program, noted, "Italy?! How elegant!"

Harriet asked: "Do you carry a snapshot of Luigi Contouri? If so—oh please show us!"

With a slow, gravid nod, Eve pulled open her small purse, extracting a Polaroid photo, holding it alight, with neighbors oohing and remarking over the image, though moments later, Florence stepped in to peer closely at the photo's grayish and white-streaked surface, concluding flatly: "That's a picture of a rabbit."

Hastily, Eve stuffed the photo into the purse, glaring at the library branch head. "You're a terrible spoilsport whoever you are. It so happens that Luigi is long-haired in the style of a count from a more distinguished past. There's no rabbit. Now I must go for water because Hal must be thirsty," she told them, the Continental accent vanished, and she squeezed past the group, en route to the potluck table.

Marge ran to the sawhorse bar for water as Florence chuckled and others, following Eve, still reaching for her sleeves and hands, called out: "It doesn't matter! We love your stories Eve."

"Tell us about Switzerland Eve!" called out Millie, altogether fascinated with the socialite.

"Oh it's really nothing. Just clocks and cheese," the woman pshawed, gulping down water from the glass Marge offered her, pressing it back on the hostess.

"Are all the women in Switzerland as dressy and beautiful as you Eve?" Millie persevered.

The sophisticate laughed, looking Millie up and down,

chuffing, "How immature," her upper lip rearing back.

Millie's eyes filmed instantly with tears.

Eve seemed to recognize Millie's hurt and worry it. "You just reminded me of something very wise that Daddy used to say long ago: 'Most adults are ugly.' And you know—it's true! Just look around. Of course Daddy didn't mean *me*. He meant everyone else."

Helen-Dale called out, "What's your favorite perfume Eve?"

"Hartnell's of course," the socialite replied immediately, to murmurs, though Laurette, arms crossed, seemed to smirk within the group's folds. Then Hildy asked loudly, "Where exactly *were* you born?"

Eve touched her blue hat. "Gee. I'll have to ask Daddy. You see we always moved around like moths and Daddy was at the helm. He always said—oh—*no!*" she cried loudly, upper lip flexing again in a slightly new formation of displeasure. "I forgot that Daddy *died*! I *can't* ask him! Isn't it strange that for a moment I for*got*?" As neighbors gawked, Eve began to laugh and cry at the same time; a few stepped back from the new neighbor's outsized intensity and loud pangs. Soon she took herself toward the rear gate, wiping tears, telling them all, "Go back to your silly party!" Then Eve hiccupped.

Gruelin went to the baker. "Listen. What goes on in this neighborhood? I mean what *really* goes on?"

Bianchi pondered the question. Standing beside the suave socialite, towel in his fist, he owned up, "Well let's see. On Fridays I make th' turnovers. Uh an' pretty soon Dog Derby Day's comin' up. An' every summer we have gator races . . ."

Gruelin looked annoyed. "That's for babies. What about real races?"

The baker shook his head. "Every spring we have a rose-growin' contest an' . . ." The man seemed at a loss to describe the life he knew and lived.

"Hmph," said Gruelin. "Read in a magazine about Indian Creek. Good fishing there. I'll go Sunday. Bring Eve."

Cissy approached the new neighbor, wiggling her fingers in a wave.

"So Mr. Grueling. How do you like our corner of the world?"

"Didn't you or somebody else already ask that question?" Gruelin wiped his forehead with a handkerchief, looking at the widow-notary with some distaste. "Haven't seen much of Reef Way. Thing is . . . I'll be working long hours this month. Busy," he pinpointed. "I'll need help. Need to find a day companion for Eve. A woman. Someone to keep my sister out of trouble while I work. Take her on walks and so forth. Of course I pay well."

Overhearing this from the rear gate, Eve's face pinkened quickly and she turned on her small, black-shoed foot, returning to him. "Oh Hal don't! We've barely met them. I *don't* need a minder. It's humiliating."

"It's not humiliating," the brother let her know. He turned back to the partygoers. "I can't leave her on her own you see," he explained. "Trouble finds her."

"It *does not!*" Eve cried.

Moates smoked deeply, studying the brother-sister pair as Cousin Harriet had.

"We'll help you both in any way we can. Won't we everyone?" said Cissy.

"Yes," a few faltered.

Millie suggested: "What about Cindy? She could keep Eve company."

The dentist Warm raised his hand from the crowd, appearing nervous to speak before them all. "No-no. Not my Cindy. She works for me. Besides every day at four she goes to The Sea Gull to cook the corncob broth for the dinner rush. Then she goes home. So she won't have time to take care of Eve. Besides—Cindy's husband has gout you see," Warm finished, clearly miscalculating the breath he needed required for these words and gasping savagely for air in a high pitch.

"Well. Then she won't work out for the position," Gruelin determined, throwing down a matchbook, irritated-seeming, looking at Warm.

"*My* husband has gout too," Harriet told everyone quickly. "He acquired it little by little. Still I blame myself for his illness. But then I think: I *couldn't*'ve given him gout because I don't have it!"

"It's good to remind yourself," Marge told her reassuringly.

"Why remind yourself of something you *already know*?" asked Florence, sounding crabby as well.

Then Minnie approached Gruelin, taking small steps. "Sir could *I* be Eve's companion while you're working? I think she's wonderful."

Gruelin looked Minnie over. "No—I don't think so. Not you."

"Gee!" Sheila flared at Gruelin on behalf of the library-clerk hopeful.

"Then what about Marge? Let Marge do it," said Millie. The patio crowd seemed enthused by this idea, remarking overall about Marge's suitable fit for the job.

"Eve could sit on the wooden bench while Marge bakes the bread in the morning so that would be perfect!" Millie went on. "They'd keep each other company and Eve could drink coffee."

Neighbors enjoyed this scenario and began discussing its picturesqueness, but Gruelin raised his hand and said: "No. I don't want my Eve sitting on a plain wooden bench. That's not my notion of a good life for her." He paced near the screen door, clearing his throat, telling Millie and Harriet, "But I'm eager to find someone else and settle this. Tomorrow I'll—" His face dropped. "What is *that*?"

He had seen Mice.

*　　*　　*

The girl squatted alone beside a pallet of flour sacks. Louche Gruelin threw his cigarette down and strode purposefully indoors toward the girl; I ran from the low stone wall and in through the screen door behind him, planting myself in the hallway, leaning to the wall. Going to Mice, Gruelin murmured to himself: "But this is astounding. Never seen one of those. Heard about them though."

He leaned over the girl, seeming to examine her, and tapped lightly on the brass lamp pole beside her. "Hello," he overenunciated. "May I speak to you?"

Sheila ran up behind him. "Mr. Gruelin? Oh no need to raise your voice. She's not—"

"I speak the way I need to so get out of the way," the businessman puffed at Sheila, who backed away. Then he turned to the girl. "Pardon the intrusion Miss but I've a few things to ask. First of all I find you fascinating. And also—this is an interesting question—given your . . . uh condition . . . why do you live here in the land of sunshine? Wouldn't a northern clime be better for your ilk?"

The girl answered in a wry, adult tone I'd never heard before in Mice: "I was born in Florida. I've never been out of Florida. Doesn't that prove that things just tend to work out for the worst?"

Gruelin laughed appreciatively.

Eve joined them. "Look at her hair Hal."

"Miss I have another question. First—"

His sister broke in, "Really Hal. You're pushing the poor thing to the wall! Give her some room."

"Butt out Eve."

Marge stepped through the hallway, loudly calling past her hand up the staircase as neighbors milled around, making remarks to each other. "Jody Marrow-wherever-you-are! Come downstairs—it's your sister! Mice's here!"

"Jody!" other neighbors cried up the staircase.

"You go to school Miss?" Gruelin asked the girl.

"I make radios."

"Ah. Had a set when I was a boy," he said. "Tinkered with it."

"I build crystal sets," the girl told him. "I'll build a midget crystal soon. Every night I listen to the airwaves and every afternoon I tell Mr. Lance what was on Radio Swan the night before."

"Swan? Ah. Pirate station. Heard of it. Cubans," the businessman nodded, hand in his pocket. "Of course most of the decent folk're unhappy with the state of affairs down there lately. I would be too."

"Radio Swan said a revolt's coming," the girl told him.

"In Cuba? Oh yes. Of course a revolt. It'll happen.

They'll start killing each other down there but don't you worry. We in this nation are safe and always will be."

"Nations can change over time Mr. Gruelin."

Eve drifted back to the girl, cupping her angular chin. "*Oh,*" the socialite told Mice, "*you* are div*in*ity. Where did you pick up your philosophies?"

"Encyclopedia," Mice told her.

The woman turned to her brother. "Hal look at this little seer! Couldn't *she* be my companion?"

"I don't mind the thought of it frankly," said Gruelin, smoking again with masculine gestures.

"Wonderful! Oh Hal!" Eve burst forth, jumping to kiss the brother's cheek in what seemed a familiar routine.

Marge exhaled, looking to Millie, Cissy, and others with relief for the outcome of the companion search. "Whew!" they said.

"It's settled then," Gruelin established, pulling Mice by her thin arm down the hall and toward the patio. "Now. I'd like to ask you some questions little dear."

"No Hal—it's *my* turn!" Eve put her arms around the girl, grabbing her away from the brother. "*I* was talking to her."

"You weren't. And I need to interview her."

"You *always* think that *you're* in charge—oh Hal don't *yank* her so! Can't you see she's skittish?" Eve pulled back on Mice's arm, leaning with the effort, while urging the girl, "Come! I'd like to get to know you. Let's talk as we walk."

"Hmph," the mogul grunted, releasing his grip on Mice such that Eve and the girl hurtled backward, both skidding across the hallway floor, and Eve's skirt flared up. Laughing, tugging down the skirt, the woman then crept her hand along the floor to retrieve Mice's sunglasses.

Not seeming to notice that his sister and Mice had tumbled to the ground, Gruelin strode around and lit another cigarette, waving it in small flourishes, perhaps speaking softly to himself.

From the screen-door area, Harriet stood looking at the new neighbors with disapproval as the high schoolers stood clustered together. My eye caught a movement: Laurette turning to Solly, beckoning him. "Are you thinking about something?"

"Yeah," said the boy.

"Me too. Mice's going to work for the Gruelins. That means she'll be close with them. She'll get rich!"

"Yes," the boy averred.

"Solly . . . do you think if Mice were dressed in a blue gown and tiara . . . that she actually might be pretty?"

"Gosh. She'll be beautiful," the boy admitted, mouth open, staring far away, and the high schoolers who now collected around the two seemed to agree.

Still on the floor and holding the fallen sunglasses, Eve kneeled and asked Mice, "Why *do* you wear these Staten Island-sized glasses anyway dear? You'd look nicer if you showed off your—" In that moment, the socialite appeared to notice the movement of the girl's eyes. "Well goodness. Let's just wear the glasses after all," she said, sliding the frames onto the girl's face. "There. It is *best* that you wear them."

Now on her feet, the socialite groped a pocket for cigarettes. "Let me tell you something Mice," she continued. "For years I thought the world was a sad and dingy place. But then I realized it was *me*. Do you ever mistake the world for yourself? Oh I don't mind telling you that

I've done it many times," she finished, blowing mauve smoke. Quiet neighbors watched as Mice returned to the wall and brass lamp—suddenly I could not tell what she was experiencing or who she was at all.

Then the school custodian Gerry Sage wandered past me and through the hallway, snacking on fruit, still wearing his janitor's work shirt with gloves hanging from his tool belt. Energetic Solly ran to him, pulling him toward neighbors, calling out just as he had previously: "Look everybody! Gerry's still here! Marge? Sal?"

Marge and the crowd hurrahed and cheered Sage, raising hands and tumblers, and Vinnegar fetched a glass of gold juice for the young custodian, who waved to everyone, laughing over all the attention.

Eve Gruelin looked him over. "A *jan*itor?" she exclaimed, horrified-looking.

*   *   *

Every day, we are so small.

From the gritty thick of it, I heard Jody's distressed voice and her footsteps pounding down the stairs; though I remained leaning in the hallway among the crowd, my pulse jumped. From the storefront, she called loudly for Mice. Then, passing the Pink Room's doorway, she shoved the brass lamp aside, grabbed her younger sister's hands, and pulled her upright. "Where *were* you? Oh Mice I might've *died*!" She touched the girl's cheek, kneaded it hard, then tugged the wiry white hair with her other hand.

Eve stood by. "I adore that child," she said, exhaling smoke.

Gruelin went to Jody. "You're the older sister?" he asked, taking out a memo pad. "I've got a question or two. Want to know about this girl. And who knows—I can't say that someday she won't have a future in our enterprise. Now what's her actual name? I'll make a note."

Jody's face grew brightly furious. "Who *are* you? What do you want with my sister? And by the way you won't write a word about us."

"Oh come on Miss. Taking applicants for a position here. Now let's hear it. Her name."

Jody seemed to crumple slightly. She grew soft-looking. "Actually sir. Nobody around here's ever asked about my sister. Not what she's interested in or what she does—nothing. No one's spoken the least real thing to her either unless you count old Jack Lance. Can you hire Mice?"

"Ah. Well. It could be. A position of a sort—yes," Gruelin told the elder sister. "Down the line she could make a good mascot for us but in the immediate present we'll consider this other appointment. Let's hear what you have on her."

Neighbors waited, listening. With a great exhalation like a released balloon, Jody spoke in a rushing welter almost too rapid to hear.

"When we were tiny children my sister Ivy's name baffled my mouth. I couldn't pronounce it," Jody told Gruelin as neighbors listened and more came near. "All I could say was 'Ice' and that became 'Mice.' Mother thought the nickname was just hilarious. She'd joke on the telephone with her friends about it and said there couldn't be a better name for the baby. Mother was ashamed of Mice you see . . . but I think also she was ashamed *of being ashamed*. Still she decided everyone should start calling my little sister 'Mice' and said if people were amused by the name they wouldn't so much pity the baby. The nickname stuck. The baby grew and Ivy . . . disappeared. She became Mice." Behind Jody's eyes a surprise seemed to register as she stared at the wall.

Eve turned to her brother, shrugging. "Well nicknames usually *do* have some kind of pathetic story behind them. But—oh Hal! Wouldn't it be funny if she'd never had a name at all?"

"Nonsense," said the brother. "There's always a name."

"But I'm sure waifs and all kinds of useless creatures go around unnamed or even undiscovered—right Hal?"

Gruelin told her no.

*　*　*

Why? said the same blank-sounding voice that seemed to arise behind me. And then this voice seemed right up against me. I knew its gist.

As Marge circulated with a little saucer of potato sticks, the beatnik now played an album with ROACH printed in large letters on the cover. Some neighbors went to inquire with Smolt about the music; meanwhile, the Gruelins, arm in arm, moved to the patio's back gate, speaking together with intensity, and my sisters leaned together against the stone wall just inches from me, not seeing me. Jody's face was open and she smiled, again reaching for the younger one's hand.

"You won't believe it," she said. "I spoke to Florence and everything's all right! To be honest I almost got on my knees."

"Knees?" the girl said.

"I pleaded."

Then Cissy passed with a very small glass of juice, turning to the sisters with a slow, laden smile. She squatted beside Mice. "Want an egg?"

"Will you go away?" cried Jody with shooing, irritated motions, driving off the widow-notary, then turning back to her sister. "And Florence agreed."

"Agreed to what?"

"Mice don't you see? You *have* the bookmobile job! I clinched it for you. Not only that—these Gruelins want you too as a hire." Jody looked upward through the trellis, smiling. "Oh you see? Tonight has been life-giving."

"But Jody?"

"Not now Mice. We did it! You have not one job but two. Now. Go onto the dance floor and dance with someone—anyone! You must begin. Otherwise . . ."

"Otherwise what?"

"Spring—"

"*Spring*? Jody stop it."

"—spring and summer will pass you by."

"If—"

"Don't change the *sub*ject!"

"But Jody I've been thinking."

"About what?"

"I wonder if you and I . . . if someday we'll both die at the same moment? I've—"

"*Oh be quiet!*"

"But Jo? Do people ever die with their arms raised up in the air?"

"I said stop it. Now listen. We've achieved something today. Let's be thankful and not ruin it."

"I don't want to. I—" The younger one threw herself against Jody, thin arms encircling the sister's waist, pushing her head into Jody's blouse, rushing out a single syllable like "can't!" while pulling and scrunching the older one's skirt and its cotton sash.

Face it, some fabrics like these can be reassuring, crisp and soft both.

Jody gave the appearance of tolerating this, and she bent to Mice's ear. "By the way. What's the big secret between you and Girtle?"

As ever, I jumped at the sound of my name. And I leapt up before anyone could start gaping at me and ran into the garden of palms to sit on the loam, my spine against the cool trunk of a palm, and I listened from there.

"There's no secret," said Mice into the skirt. "Girtle and I are going to sit in a cabin and listen to nothingness. What of it?" She dragged her hand across Jody's skirt pocket.

In the garden I closed my eyes with sudden contentment, my cheeks filling with a rare smile as well: I was elated. The girl had remembered our plan.

"Oh there'll be no time for a cabin Mice. You'll be working in the bookmobile," Jody brisked as the girl's hand continued wriggling on the skirt, then fumbled at the pocket; Jody shoved the sister's hand away.

"What's in there Jo? Did you bring me a yo-yo like Burt's?"

"There's no yo-yo!"

Then they began to grapple outright in the pocket with their hands, the younger one pushing and Jody resisting, their feet shuffling in a slow, to-all-appearances-harmonious rotation: a circle dance.

"Look at those sweet girls sway!" called Harriet from the sidelines, smile tender.

"Is it a *bread* roll in here?" Mice grunted, trying to grasp the object in the pocket.

"There's no roll!" Jody tried sweeping her leg against the girl's foot to bring the sister to the ground, but Mice was quicker, now the winner. She plucked the thing out of her sister's pocket and jumped back, hand overhead. "Jody! Is this . . . ?!"

A lump of beige plastic. Yes, it was the radio knob.

*   *   *

The girl was crestfallen. "Why was it in your pocket?! You knew I was looking for it. Jody? You hid it from me? Whyn't you say something?"

"I didn't hide it." Jody did not look at Mice.

"But you *took* it! Stole it from my worktable didn't you? You made me think it was lost. *Why?*"

The beatnik stopped the music, looking on. Dancers broke apart. All looked at the sisters, listening.

"Mice if you'd had that knob . . . you wouldn't've come to the party. You'd've stayed home with those dumb radios and *Girtle*." Jody's voice made a smear of my name.

With the strongest, least-childish words I'd heard from Mice since the story had begun, she said to her sister: "You *lied* to me. You *stole*. You stole from your mother's *daughter*."

"I didn't steal it. Not really. I *moved* it."

"Oh Jody Marrow!" It was Minnie, suddenly fiery as if part of the sisters' clash herself, leaning over the low wall at them, quivering like Mice. "Could you be fibbing? I say *somebody* here is fibbing!"

Jody turned to the library-clerk hopeful with aversion. "Keep out of it biddy!"

Minnie shrank back and began to cry.

"Look everyone—it's the times," Remnick said beside the wall, pliant-toned. "People *like* to lie. Even government leaders lie. I heard that."

The circle of neighbors fixed their glances on Jody, who took the girl by the shoulders and pressed her face close to her sister's. "Let's talk about something much more important Mice—who turned on the range this morning? You did."

"I didn't!"

Brahms spoke up from the group. "Sisters have troubles between them. That's how they are. Me?" the guard gestured to himself with a confident air. "I was delighted to be the only boy."

Florence turned to the security guard with an open, curious smile. "You Ron—an only child? How unusual. Was it very lonely?"

"But I wasn't an only child," the guard disclosed.

"Mice!" Jody went on. "You could've burned down the whole apartment with that stunt. Don't play with stoves."

"And I was never lonely," Brahms told the librarian, fingers playing at his mustache.

"I didn't do it Jody. I *told* you that."

"You didn't?"

"No."

She looked to the group. "Mice can't lie," Jody told neighbors. "It's something in her brain. Impossible—she wouldn't even understand how to lie. That means *Girtle* turned on the range. Girtle!" she hollered, running to check the small grotto, which was empty, and then the garden of palms where I crouched.

Jody brushed tree fronds aside. Neighbors amassed

behind her. "Was it you Girtle?"

"Uh—" I grunted.

"Leave Girtle *out* of it!" I heard Mice cry from the wall, and these words gave me more happiness than almost anything else in the story.

But the elder sister leaned through the trees, porcupining me. "The range Girtle! Did you turn it on? Just say it."

So I had to confess.

*   *   *

"I asked Mice to turn on the range for *me*," I said, hating neighbors' peeking at me from behind Jody through the branches and leaves. I hated their breaths scudding into the garden I felt was mine. "The stove burner was our signal to meet at the cabin."

"Oh not this cabin phooey again!" Jody cried.

"The cabin would've been perfect for me and Mice to sit in chairs."

"No!" the elder one stormed.

"But Mice didn't agree to go. In the afternoon she left the apartment. I waited," I said, panting with the stress. "Don't you know how it is—waiting for someone not all day but *every day*?"

"That's really enough from you Girtle—" Jody began.

"—so *I* turned on the range. And that was *close enough* to Mice turning on the range for *me*."

I was not only horrified by the outright horde of neighbors looking dull-eyed at me through the green leaves, but by my own lighting of the stove that morning. I should not have done it. Now neighbors' various-sized hands began pulling and tugging at fronds, the better to see me, until I couldn't stand it and screamed: "Stop!"

They stared at me even more. Then the sisters looked at each other, something tough between them. Mice had begun to emerge from her present life, a somber wet snail, foot half out of the shell, near-unrecognizable. Now she told Jody with everything in her confused heart, "You *accuse others*. You complain and harass and boss and herd people—you did that to Mother. You told her she was a failure even when she was *sick*. I felt *sorry* for Mother."

Jody said: "*You* were too young and wrapped up in your nonsense to understand. Mother *forced* me to take care of you *all the time*. She left you with me for days. She was *horrible*. Do you know the chores and cleaning up I did for you? Even so it was *you* who practically broke Mother in two with all those—" Her voice lowered then, furiously quiet: "with your *stupid questions and your terrible whiteness*. Didn't you notice that you mostly *killed* her?"

The patio fell to absolute silence.

❊   ❊   ❊

"Listen up," said the baker finally, moving about the patio to unclear purpose. "At Th' Crescent we don't talk bad of the dead. We never do that. You hear me?"

Lance hemmed and hacked, then tapped the cigar on a tree. "Ah! I remember ol' Candy. Knew her from dances at Electrician's Hall. Sometimes she was funny. Sense of humor."

"I remember her too!" Minnie cried.

Hildy stood near the center garden with a pan. "I heard Candy had a big ol' personality. Lands—always sounded like she was a busy one."

"No Hildy. She wasn't *busy*," said Harriet. "She was in bed most of the time."

"What'd I just say?" the baker warned her.

"And Candy was generous," Eddleston said. "She gave me three green Life Savers."

Cissy said, "Candy was stuck on some notion that this world must be morally perfect twenty-four hours a day. And I told her: 'Now that's too fussy Candy!'"

"But it was more than that," said Jody. "Mother believed in dignity for all. She loved workers and wanted them to have rights. She admired peasants all over the world. She loved the Five-Year Plan and anything that was good for the garbageman or maid in the kitchen. The street sweepers and dishwashers too. And she was proud of any nurse." Tears rolled down Jody's face. "How can she be gone?"

Florence went to the sister, then set a foot on a small boulder at the garden's perimeter. "We miss her too Jo."

Both sisters cried silently, neither bothering to wipe her face, and Marge emerged with a tray of flan.

Then Mice restarted it, voice stunningly harsh. "*You lied* to me when Mother was dying!"

Jody's face fell.

"You told me, 'She's sleeping. Go outside and play,'" continued the girl, as if releasing this detail caused her body, rid of the oily memory, to shake slightly with the clarity of emptiness. "And so I went outside where I was hardly ever allowed to go. You wanted to get *rid* of me so you could hog the last of Mother's life—be with her alone. Without *me*. You wanted me *out* because that's how you are and—" The girl seethed. "I *hate* you!"

"I hate *you*!"

The heat in their voices!

*　*　*

Who hasn't said "I hate you," fiery and raw, when she means "See me"?

Jody bolted from her sister and everyone up the honey-colored stairs. I heard a door slam above. Twilight was long finished and the patio poorly lit, neighbors' faces appearing dark-lipsticked in night's mire. The high schoolers on the mostly empty dance floor looked above, pointing to the Pleiades. The beatnik put on a gentle jazz number and I climbed from the garden, fresh dirt on my shoes, going to the screen door. The steel mesh's scent of petrichor. I saw, all the way down the hallway and out the front door, a figure across the boulevard standing beside a smallish station wagon.

It was the helper. He'd arrived to the story ridiculously late.

IV

He'd parked in one of the diagonal parking slots. I saw him pocket the car keys and cross the street. Surely he'd heard the beatnik's music purling over the rooftops and parked in order to find the source of that music, wanting to hear more. Now he skimmed past the sidewalk planters, going to the bakery's glass door.

I nearly leaned into the hallway to beckon him in, so great was my wish to get his intrusion over with and find a way to oust him from the story if I could.

Somehow even his ridiculous sheeny-blue jacket had been imprinted onto my mind at some point in the past to form a precognizance. Then I heard the unknown voice coming from behind me again, taunting: *Now there'll be no more waiting.* I cracked a sad smile.

The helper's entrance makes the tale curl a little closer to the haven of its ending.

At the door, he studied the grease-penciled note that Bianchi had posted with transparent tape and lifted the doily's thin lace, checking its reverse side, as Cissy's voice rose with her repeated complaint: "This tune has no melody!"

As he entered the bakery, trumpet notes from the hi-fi's music slid down a scale one by one, pearls on a nylon line. It was possible that the helper had never heard such spare, careful music. I hadn't.

He is your antagonist, the voice reminded me as I shooed the words away with my hand.

His face was absolutely new to me. Moving down the hallway while I watched through the screen door, he did not appear as dangerous as he was. His hair at the temples short as sand. Shoes long as keels. I anticipated the grief of losing the sisters to him. To ward him away, I considered leafing the story back to its beginning so as to luxuriate in its pages there. But that wish is shopworn—haven't billions dreamed of dialing back time?

I moved out of the way as he sailed past me onto the patio. I noted the repellently deep chambers of his ears. He leaned against the bakery's rear wall, ignoring Vinnegar's half-friendly offer of a fruit juice, and a few partygoers glanced. Then Bianchi saw the newcomer and approached, grinning, extending his hand.

"Welcome!"

I felt the unknown.

The helper took the floury handshake. "Say fella. What's this place about?"

"Friends. Bread. Welcome!" Bianchi clapped him on the shoulder. As the baker turned to look elsewhere on the patio in his usual way, the tray tilted and warm rolls rained down to his soft, grimy shoes and the concrete.

"Doggone it. Marge!"

But the helper with the brush-cut hair swooped in, smiling, hands flashing out to collect the rolls, returning them instantly to the tray.

Eddleston stood nearby, ropy wrists in pockets. "Hah! What a stunt! Sal—new fella here's a gent."

The baker laughed, urging the newcomer toward the food table. "Here's potluck son. Eat. We gotta band comin'. Jarouse Brothers—know 'em? They sing. Guitars and such so stick around! Now—what brings you to Reef Way?"

"Traveling for work," the stranger told him.

It was no lie. Within two weeks or so, I would understand the newcomer's situation in full.

Bianchi sailed off with the tray. Had he stared at the purplish-black bruises along the newcomer's hand and wrist, or was that me?

I took my place beside the low wall, squatting. A crescendo of laughs and further chat across the patio. "Lookit that handsome devil!" Helen-Dale cried to her friends, who turned to see the newcomer with his brilliant blue jacket.

"I can't *stop* looking at him!" whispered someone.

But with his buzz cut and callow face, how could he possibly have been the linchpin of the story with the power to knock me away from the sisters? What was he?

As he approached the girl, I began to loathe him and the story itself all over again. I hated that not even a mote could escape a story's incontrovertible structure. The narrowness of it was stunning. And now, I thought, the helper would step to her, begin helping her, change her life as if he really belonged.

In typical fashion, Mice stood beside the low wall, crawling her hand along the texture of its stone. *Leave Mice alone*, I heard the voice say behind me as though it were my own. *If she went to sit in the cottage chair in stillness, she'd shimmer out of sight like a coin spun into a pond. Is that what you want?*

"Be quiet," I said.

Now he stood near the dance floor beside the girl, withdrawing what seemed a small silver strip of paper from his jacket pocket.

"Chewin' gum Miss?"

*   *   *

The beatnik put on an orchestral-sounding tune, homey and slow-warm. Dark smudges of dancers faced one another on the dance floor like big upright fingerprints. At the sidelines, knots of neighbors continued to chat.

Why don't you leave? The voice directed itself either to me or the stranger, who spoke to Mice shyly: "Urh. Hello Miss. I'm Kenny Anther from Dularacette Alabama."

Fresh from her most recent clash with Jody, strained-looking, the girl did not seem to hear him.

"Sure you don't wanta sticka chewin' gum? It's awful healthful fer th' digestion," he lathered. "See I chew mine 'til the flavor's gone. Then I have another stick'r two. You ever do that?"

Beneath the patio's trellis lights, neighbor groups began buzzing over the stranger and his one-sided conversation with Mice.

"I always keepa packa gum on me see. Now you lemme know if y'change yer mind Miss. You ever chew two flavors at once? I do," he grinned.

Helpers in stories often talk too much.

"Miss may I ask why yer eyes're covered with those dark glasses? I got a quarter says yer eyes're awful beautiful."

And this fraud believed he would get to know Mice better than I?

The old, innocent tune on the hi-fi was "Whispering," its two slowest bars almost devastating for their surge of sudden passion. Dancers tipped against each other, eyes averted with shyness or faint shame.

"You dance Miss?"

No reply.

Girls in stories must always refuse the stranger, at least at first. Past the patio's trellis, glowing orange light from the tiki lamps revealed ledger-like lines around the helper's eyes. Strange—even he had done a bit of living.

"You waitin' on some other fella honey?"

Mice: silence.

"Aw yer lovely Miss," he jawed on. "Kinda unique. Why I might just be over th' moon."

In those days I was far too reticent to scoff aloud. But the helper so appalled me by insinuating himself cluelessly into the story that I scoffed inside myself.

"Whispering" and its spell had ended. The dancers stood, waiting for more music. Near the low wall, Moates regarded the newcomer in the blue jacket as a person looks at pond scum—or was that me looking at him so?

"New guy over there," Moates called to the dentist, Cindy, and a few others. "Who is that?"

"No idea. He's not my type at all," the dental secretary declared, one hand absently patting the dentist, who in that moment bent to the wall to examine an extension cord, grimacing.

"Miss? Yer jus' . . ." the stranger said, vowels boomeranging. "Why yer sweet as pie. I could look atchoo day an' night. What's yer name honey?"

"Mice Huberman," honked the girl.

The helper's face opened in surprise. "Now where'd y'getta name like that?"

Solly shrieked amid the high schoolers from the dance floor, "Guy'll be lucky if he scores a couple radio parts off her!"

As neighbors' laughter bounded across the patio's concrete, the boy dashed to the screen door, nearly shearing it away to get inside, then hurtled through the hallway. At the Pink Room's doorway he flipped his hands to friends within, calling: "Kids c'mon! Y'gotta see—man's goin' after Mice!"

So Joyce, Laurette, and Millie, too, faces eager, jostled in a bunch back to the patio behind Solly, hands companionably on friends' shoulders as all gasped with laughs while the stranger, oblivious to them, continued: "An' darlin' . . . you must be one a' God's special . . ."

If he would just shut up.

"How 'bout takin' off those dark glasses honey? I'd like t'see yer eyes."

Instantly she pushed the sunglasses against her face as if to seal them to her skin. This clearly caused an itch, for Mice then began scratching intensely at her nose, and the glasses dropped to the ground.

As the helper squatted to retrieve them, he glanced at her: "Why Miss—yer eyes're dancin' around! Looky— they're *wobblin'*! *What in—*"

"Oh they do that all day long."

"But Missy . . . is that *natural*?"

Now there was a stupid question.

"Say honey. You blind?"

"Nope."

But what about the cottage? the voice behind me said again in my ears.

Then Cissy came running in small steps, tossing dried flowers, smiling open-mouthed at bystanding neighbors, addressing Mice: "Darling girl! Men are dogs. Fight through it. Fight! And good luck." The notary danced before the girl, bulky leather purse bumping her hip as she raised both arms in nevertheless lovely, limber arcs before twirling, dress pleats spinning and lifting as blades.

Ravels of dried blue flowers lay at Mice's feet.

＊　　＊　　＊

He continued at her ear: "Honey you like dancin'? I sure do. Oh—an' I love big suppers an' summer beans. D'you? An' lyin' down under the stars."

She faced the stranger quizzically. "Are you in high school?"

He laughed. "Course not honey. I'm a man."

The screen door opened. Three gnomish figures in black suits trooped through silently, each carrying a black case and a folding chair under his arm. "Jarouses!" the baker cried out, nervous-seeming, giddy. "Let 'em through. Mike!" called Bianchi to Vinnegar. "Get 'em juice."

The brothers lay their cases on the ground and together withdrew guitar, cornet, and flute. Then Merv Jarouse held a small set of bongos. Tuning and tending to the instruments, the brothers converged, heads close together as if planning their performance without speaking.

*   *   *

"Mister?" Mice asked Anther. "A minute ago you said my eyes are 'awful beautiful.' Did you say that because you think my eyes're awful? I don't care if you think that but . . . people usually say what they mean even if they don't want to. Sir did you say 'awful' because—"

I smiled to myself and the voice said: *Now she'll start in with all her questions and confuse him right out of the story.*

"Did I say . . . *what* honey?"

Near the low wall, Helen-Dale called out in a state of grump, "Of all people why's he talking to *Mice*? I want t'talk to him too!"

Laurette leaned close to the high schoolers. "Just you watch—he's going to run away from her fast as he can. Any second now . . ." She counted with sipping breaths, "One thousand one . . . one thousand two . . ."

Too many people. I dashed from the low wall and into the garden of palms' safety.

"Mister," Mice told the helper, "people say the words that come to them. That's how the human mind works. It works loosely but strictly. Did you say 'awful beautiful' because you actually think *I'm* awful?"

Neighbors' voices rose: laughs and shrieks. I glimpsed Laurette falling gently against squashed-looking Joyce, the back of her beautiful peach-hued hand over her laughing mouth.

"Someone go get Jody and bring her here! Please!" Harriet shouted.

At the border of the garden, Remnick gave old man Lance a tap and pointed with his chin. "Who's the new guy?"

"No idea," the veteran coughed. "But—lookit his stance. He's standing at ease. See that? Military. Good man."

"Oh *Jack!*" Now Harriet joined the men, hands on their shoulders. "I was *just thinking* that stranger over there *must* be a good man—y'know taking all that time and effort to talk to Mice . . ."

Beside them, the dentist, now having dropped a crushed napkin beside Remnick's foot, reached for it, whispering, "Excuse me," with integral shame.

The girl asked the helper, "Sir? You said hello to me."

"Sure I did honey."

"No one else told me hello today. Not even Jody."

"Aw." The man squinted. "Who's Jody?"

"She's . . ." The girl flung out a throwaway gesture, an adult-like movement I'd never seen in Mice before. "She stole the radio knob."

"Oh did she now."

"Yes. You see me an' my sister fight every day—"

Why? asked the voice behind me—but did it mean why did the sisters fight, why did the story exist in this way, or why hadn't I done anything to change it?

"That's too bad Miss. Whatcha-all fight about?"

"Well one time she threw a radio toward my head so I went to her room and chewed and broke her favorite compact mirror which twinkled."

"Why yer as funny as a top Miss. Would y'wanna—"

"But you see Jody is *fair* to me when I am not pleasant."

"Oh. Is she now."

"Yes."

He is treating her so real, the voice told me as ice began to seep up my legs. Now a cruel angle became evident: the helper was almost likable.

Merv Jarouse had now finished his instrument tuning and strummed a strong guitar chord as neighbors turned, faces brightened, though a few appeared wary, as if the band must prove itself to them.

"'Go to the Store'! Play 'Go to the Store'!" hollered Millie brutishly from the sidelines, and Merv Jarouse, a strand of dark hair curled with sweat over his forehead, gave her a stoic look, setting the bongos at his feet.

"Everybody?" the beatnik called in general to the big crowd, stepping to the front. "Everybody! The Jarouse Four'll play for us now. Copacetic band-about-town. These boys deserve our respect. I know 'em well. They have a lady singer in their group sometimes if you didn't know — Mina. But she has a cough. Most recently Jarouses played Th' Tangier Room where suffice it to say a ball was had by all." Neighbors halooed and cheered at this.

"And last night they played Watkins House in Memphis and I heard it was swell! Now I'll ask Merv a few interview questions. Ready Merv?"

The band leader stared at Beatnik Larry as if incredulous.

"I know we didn't plan it but it won't take long — c'mon Merv. Just tell us how you an' the guys get that wild sound of yours?"

Jarouse rubbed his throat skin, pinched it a moment. "You askin' me for musical advice?"

"Well. Not really but — "

"Play fast and hard and loud as you can," said the band leader. "Round up a few friends whose voices're all equally loud. Make everyone sing all at once. Don't let up. Repeat the choruses constantly. If there's a piano, keep your foot hard down on the sustain pedal at all times." Then the musician turned aside to confer with his brothers, who picked up their instruments.

Someone counted, "One-two."

The musicians instantly found a syncopated rhythm, as if it had already been going and they grabbed it from the air. The silken number caught neighbors' attention. The instruments seemed to play themselves. The brothers began singing then, continuing their composition as I wondered from the low wall how I might demolish the helper before he did the same to me.

Minnie called faintly from the brink of the dance floor, hands clasped: "Ooh—the notes you choose!"

*　*　*

As the crowd clustered around the band, I watched Mice closely, realizing that fraternizing with this complete stranger had suddenly become easy as breathing for her. This too must've been due to the string and seeds.

As I watched the helper touch Mice's baby finger, I realized the story itself had produced all the good things that Mice had eaten. "Shut up!" I cried into the trees.

With the tree's skin against mine, I felt the story's inevitability, my decision to get off the bus at Reef Way attached to it. The voice returned. *But once, long ago, you were the central girl. And you gave it up—you left. Remember?*

I remembered.

I remembered that during the rainiest month I left the iron-dark dormitory, the site of slaps hard enough to knock out children's teeth. I decided to run away. My heart, barely weatherproofed motor, bumped as I tucked my belongings into a sack and ran down the stairs to the front door.

And the friend who helped me flee the Kendall Children's Home? The kind ally who'd walked alongside me in strength as we passed the ghastly slab-faced night attendant, then ran with me across the rain-filled yard, the confidant who boosted me up the wall and watched as I jumped down the other side and ran in the dark to the road ahead? There was none.

I was sixteen and still a child. As friends, I counted only tiny children and the lunch cook. A few of the orphans had run away together, a feat that grew legendary among dormitory inmates for a week or so before the escapees were caught. But I planned an escape on my own and met grim success. Racing from the three hulking buildings, doling out no goodbyes, I climbed the riprap hand over hand, slow as death, the sack roped to my waist. The bricks cut me—it felt right. Once atop and seven feet up in the dark, I was disappointed to understand that I'd have to climb down the wall's other side and walk for perhaps the rest of my life to find a place where I could rest.

The children's home had bent me up. So I didn't climb down the wall's other side carefully, but jumped instead, more like toppled, into the loose soil and burnweed below, the unplanted garden plot where my life began.

*   *   *

Even with the Jarouses' rousing singing, I did not lose focus on Mice and the man.

"You see Jody was always my leader," the girl explained to him. "She kisses me hello when she comes home. I *like* her."

Chewing his gum, Anther nodded comfortably. "Course y'do honey. That's sisters."

"Even so mister. I'll have to leave soon."

"Leave? Ah. Where to?"

"Far away."

He smiled easily. "Oh Miss I don't *doubt* you'll go far."

He listens to her, the voice observed, coinciding with my own thoughts while I stared at the helper's softly moving Adam's apple and vegetal-appearing ears. In all those stories, the central girl never thinks twice about accepting the helper into her concealed and painful world.

Why? repeated the voice.

"I'll leave soon," Mice told him. "I'll wait for the right time."

The stranger's glance lingered all over her. "Well Miss I figure everybody's waitin' for somethin'. See those folks over there?" He gestured to the hi-fi area where Marge, Sheila, Eddleston, The Artist with the Scarf, a few high schoolers, and others chatted and bobbed their heads to the Jarouses' music. "Why they're probl'y waitin' to dance. An' that funny-lookin' guy over there by the record player? He might be waitin' for a compliment on his musical taste. Oh—an' that gal up in th' window there?" He pointed to the bakery's office on the second floor overlooking the patio. "Why she could be waitin' for you Miss. She's starin' atchoo."

As Mice looked up, so did I. Leaning out the window, her strong back stretched forward, was Jody, looking at her sister and the man with abhorrence, her face a stewed green.

"Gal up there's kinda upset," the helper discerned.

* * *

If the sisters had previously been close, now they were poles apart. I hated that. I wanted them close again, lying on the carpet runner together, talking and watching TV. But the unity had broken and I felt myself diminishing.

"Mice!" moaned Jody from the window, mouth open and in some kind of fugue. "Don't go anywhere—please. Did you take your vitamin Mice? Vitamins are like fruit. You need a new skirt for your job. Haven't you danced yet? Next week we'll get you a lunch box—"

Florence turned to the sound of Jody's high-up voice, moving toward that open window, as much surprise on her face as if she'd seen a plush comet scouring the sky.

"Jody Marrow!" called the branch head in her rich voice. "Why are you up there alone?" In spite of the Jarouses' music, neighbors turned to listen to her. "Now come down here and talk to me. Would you like to dance with your sister?" She gestured across the patio toward the singing Jarouses.

"I'm not one for dancing Florence," Jody called down, much drama in her voice. "Besides my sister will probably never dance with me again."

The branch head set her foot on a small patio bench. "I know a little of what's happening Jody," she called up. "We try to make life go a certain way. Then it doesn't happen how we want it and we keep living."

As if surprised to hear such bald facts, Jody stared at Florence.

"And time's like a saddle confining you," the librarian offered. "By its rule you can only go forward. And such time goes by! So much of it. Then one day you see that your parents have died and you're alone in the world. Your hair turns gray as a train and memories are nothing but flimsy scraps and you feel you've lost some kind of game. Jody," said Florence feelingly, "you're so young. And yet so much of that has *already happened* to you! It's not fair."

Jody leaned heavily on the window frame, head dropped, hand extended to Florence as she cried silently.

"Come down here with me Jody Marrow," Florence called to her again.

* * *

The girl looked closely at the helper's wrist with its purple and bluish bruises. "Sir what happened to your hand?"

"Aw," grinned the man, clearly enchanted by Mice. "Y'care about my hand darlin'?"

"No. I only care about my questions and the answers to them."

The helper's grin fell. "Well. You certainly have yer social graces dontcha Miss?"

"Mother said I should learn my social graces."

"Bet she did."

"Sir? Did you smash your hand in a car door? Or did you hammer your hand by mistake? Are you a carpenter?"

The helper looked around with discomfort, eyeing the screen door as if he would go there. "Heh."

"And your watch sir."

"Eh?"

"It has three dials. That's a pilot's watch. Why do you wear it?"

"Eh—you're a real wedge kid. Keep yer voice down. Okay?"

I strained to see the watch too.

Then from the second-story window Jody hollered like a wraith, voice cracking like a split platen. "Mice! Don't leave with him! You'll never come back!"

It was a question.

"Of course she'll be *back*," Harriet called up to Jody cheerfully from the dance floor's edge. "And I say it'll be nice if that young man took Mice on a little walk down the boulevard."

"No!" Jody called in her frenzy as suddenly Sheila, Marge, and Florence ran up the honey-colored staircase, the six feet battering the wood, presumably to locate Jody in the office and care for her.

The girl continued her rash of questions.

"How fast does a plane fly sir?"

"Ah. Depends on th' wind speed," he murmured, again looking at the screen door.

Why? the voice drilled.

V

"But sir. Why did you decide to be a pilot and fly?"

"Mice please don't harangue him," Harriet called to her.

"Well I'll tell you Miss. I love birds. Always have. Always wanted t'fly. An' here's somethin' else: When somebody comes up an' offers you a lotta money to fly . . . well that's just good fortune. It's just what a guy needs."

"Oh? But how do you get *into* a plane sir? Does it have a front door?"

"Eh? Go up through th' aft cargo. Or trapdoor," he motioned absentmindedly.

The girl's face lit up in wonder. "A trapdoor on a plane?!" She seemed giddy.

Elsewhere on the patio, Lance told the men: "Hear that? Trapdoor. No such thing as a trapdoor on commercial craft. Trapdoor's military. Sounds like a bomber."

"Jack was right. Kid's military," intoned Moates.

"Yippee!" Beside them, Eddleston kicked his heels.

Remnick and Moates whispered together.

"Hey guy!" Eddleston broke out, jogging up to the helper, arms swinging to and fro. "You flyin' south soon? Gonna bomb those Reds away for us? Haha!"

The stranger looked at the group of men, fingers encircling his bruised wrist, bending as close to Mice as possible—she would've felt the warmth of his face on her face. I had to strain, yet I heard him. "Missie no more questions. No more talkin' about planes."

"Why not?"

"Shh."

It dawned on me then that helpers in stories are not usually pilots. Nor does a helper usually walk into a story with an overwhelming hand bruise, nor does he command a story's central girl to stop speaking about airplanes. Something was wrong, I thought, and in the garden of palms I stood.

Who was he?

Cousin Harriet's smiling face, illuminated now by the tiki flames like a white gouache, seemed to murmur to no one specific, "We don't pester guests dear!"

Mice called out, eyes squeezed shut, mouth illuminated inside by the tiki flame, "I'm not pesting Harriet! He's a pilot. He got paid a lot!"

"Oh how wonderful!" the cousin cried in reply and turned to discuss it with Millie.

Kenny Anther closed his hand, clawlike, over the girl's milk-thin upper arm; he pulled her to him and push-walked her toward the screen door. "Y'damn well know I *tol'* you keep your trap shut. *Move*," he said, voice harsh. "Yer goin' in here with me."

His goofy-boy act had fallen away.

"Do you get questions in your mind too sir?" Mice asked, moving alongside him readily.

"No."

"Why not?" she asked. By the time he opened the screen door and pushed her into the hallway, I'd already leapt from the garden, earth cool on my feet as I rushed inside to keep Mice in my sight. When had my shoes disappeared?

Jody's head rose up once more in the upstairs office window, voice desperate: "Mice don't *go* with him!"

The party grew more chaotic, Moates, Remnick, Eddleston, Cissy, Lance, Parrott, and Harriet in animated discussion about the pilot while the librarians and others knotted together for talk, and at the dance floor's edges, the Jarouses launched into a sad, sharp number about workers and lovers. And the Gruelins, arm in arm, re-entered the party through the rear gate.

As my eyes struggled to see in the hallway's dimness, I made out the helper standing beside the girl, locking her against the wall, still grasping her arm. I went to crouch beside the large drum of yeast.

"You smashed your hand in an airplane's door—didn't you mister? Why'd you do that?" she whimpered.

"Because I got careless and smashed it!" the stranger burst out. "Now thing is Miss—you shouldn'ta talked about planes. All those folks out there listenin' t'what we said?"

"Oh they always listen."

"No Miss. That isn't gonna happen. They can't know—"

From somewhere on the patio, Cissy horse-laughed.

"It's important Miss. Nobody can know about th' job. I was wrong t'tell you about it."

Then it dropped on me like a load of sand. I'd been wrong the whole time. Kenny Anther was not the story's helper. He was just someone who'd wandered into the party. The state of the story went blurry to me. What was this?

He hadn't shown up to change the story. Anther was just a young man—a pilot—driving around on his night off, looking for music and fun. And if there was a helper, I didn't know who it was. In my eyes, the story had fallen open, spinning me.

✳   ✳   ✳

"What you need t'do Miss is get back inta that party now," Anther told her heatedly, "an' you tell those folks that the fella you talked to—that he's notta pilot. You go on an' tell 'em he went on home."

"Tell them that you went home? Why?" she asked.

"They can't know anything about this."

"But you *are* a pilot sir. You have a pilot's watch. So what?"

Anther sweated, whispering, "You hear that fella said I'm out t'kill Reds?"

"But lots of people say that sir."

"Nobody can know 'bout th' job."

"My job's at the bookmobile sir but I haven't started it yet. I never will. Where's your job sir?"

"Shh Miss! I'm sworn. Know what I mean?"

"No."

"See if all those fellas out there tell their friends an' so on—you know the trouble I'll catch?" His hand went to his damp hair. "Why'd you ask me all those questions?"

"Mister I listen to the crystal set every night. I listen to Radio Swan and Corridos Texas. And every night they talk about bringing down the Cuban Reds. It's nothing unusual."

From the patio I heard the batting of a lone rhythm stick, and the band began "Go to the Store." With the swirling flute notes, a huge fanfare arose from the partiers; I heard the cornet enter, lush. The guitar came up behind and neighbors skipped to the dance floor. Now it seemed more musicians were playing than the three that I'd seen— I heard tender-sounding notes: a bassoon.

"You don't know about th' operation Miss."

". . . No."

"So you gotta tell those fellas I'm notta pilot. That I *never said it*. Get back out there. Tell 'em there's no pilot. It was all a joke."

"No."

*　*　*

Kenny Anther, a government hireling, looked at Mice. He was not the story's helper. I looked at Mice and the necessity of her stubbornness, along with the sweetness, which no one had the power to erase. Something in me reached for her. Anther was angry and pushed at her slightly.

"Who are you?" he asked, eyes cold, hands on her shoulders, then at her neck. Slowly he raised her, clearly out to scare her. She tried shaking her head, a small noise burgeoning from her throat. Her feet left the ground— from behind the yeast I saw it.

Hanging silently from his hands, she looked at him, eyes utterly neutral. The stranger panted: "Whatever you

254

are—you're not gonna spill about th' hit." My entire blood stopped short, yet I stood and shoved the yeast barrel hard. It went over, brown granules rivering across the hall, over the tops of the man's long shoes. Startled, Anther dropped Mice—landing easily on her feet, she was already down the dim passage and out the bakery's front door.

*　　*　　*

Looking at me, hollering that I was dead and insane and a traitor besides, Anther slipped and skidded on yeast, stumbling toward the door. I followed; on the sidewalk he ran after Mice but wouldn't catch her, I knew.

She was gone. The partygoers were already draining from the patio and down the hallway or out the back gate, slow-moving as lake water, making as one for the sidewalk where they gathered, some calling out in the dark for Mice, and a few for the stranger, not knowing his name. I saw them: Eddleston, Bianchi, Moates, Brahms the guard, the Remnicks and Phyllis, who'd never managed to go upstairs to sleep; Hildy and her girls; Minnie and Millie, hand in hand; Denny; Harriet; The Woman Who Didn't Speak and her calfskin purse; Parrott; Vinnegar; The Artist with the Scarf raising a cigarette in a fluted holder; the chittering high schoolers; Moose Riley, hand in hand with Charlene, who must've arrived to the party outside my awareness; Cissy arm in arm with the Gruelins; Cindy and the dentist; the shuffling beatnik and the poet Kulp; the West Horn custodian and namesake Flora Horn, her dark, full hair flowing; the home nurse, Gerry Sage, and more.

"Moose you must eat better," Charlene advised the surfer, as if capping a one-sided conversation.

Perhaps only Jody, her women-carers, and the Jarouse band remained inside. The spirited music kept flowing around us, and in the alleyway a full-grown alligator muscled along, surely having scented the patio's abounding table of food. But the creature continued and crossed the empty boulevard. He scaled a low fence, then seemed to dive down the slope adjacent to the Stevens cornfield, gliding as if swimming atop the grass.

Harriet pointed to the edge of the boulevard. "There she is! There's Mice!" I saw my last flash of Mice as she furrowed into the corn.

VI

Sitting here, having pulled the blue blanket with its bright red threads to my chin, I still feel the cold evening air biting through the window. I'm waiting for that memory, a moving photograph of Mice, to arise again in my mind's eye.

She plunged down the slope to the cornfield—everyone knew that bits of wild sugarcane grew there. Then deep in the rows, all those leaves concealed her.

I'm ready to be brought to my room and doze through the night.

Winded and weak, I'm reminded of oxygen and how it, and light, both bring us to life at the start, then damage and erode us so we can get to the end and finish living.

I remember how Marge and Sheila came to stand near me at the boulevard's edge, diminished-looking Jody between them.

"Such a strong girl is Mice," said Marge, with an expression of wonder, and Sheila, serious as ever, called through cupped hands to the field, "Best of luck!"

A big feeling for neighbors washed over me. Invisible Mice still ran in the cornfield, I knew. Now the library's branch head appeared at the side of the boulevard with the others, yam-colored dress whipping in the breeze.

At the road's edge I spotted Kenny Anther as well, hands on hips, eyes on the field.

Now a pack of dogs in an arrow-like formation moved up the boulevard toward us all. Lost Yum-Yum was not among them. Those neighbors who knew Yum-Yum best—Joyce, Sherrie, Trudie, and Hildy—noticed this, looking to each other across the distances, faces heavy with the questions of those who have no choice but to wait.

Among the dog pack ran the black-and-tawny Boatsmann. A shared striving in the dogs had pushed them to find us.

One means everyone, I told the story, or the story told me.

"Boatsmann! I thought you were dead!" I hollered insensibly from the raw crux of my throat, a little stunned to realize that the story was not separate from life or living, but instead just another side of it. The richness of this spread through my belly, and my body impelled me toward the black-golden dog, no longer missing, who recognized me as part of things, running to me as well, and I embraced him.

From the mouth of the alleyway, the high schoolers and others called with relief to Boatsmann, who was finally home. The Woman Who Didn't Speak joined too, in her way, raising a hand and crying aloud in plain delight,

"Aiyoo!" as The Blur raced to and fro behind her.

Then Jody was next to me. "Get her Girtle—please? If anyone can find her it's you. Go scoop up Mice and bring her back—it's not too late. Hurry! *Go!*"

But I hung on to Boatsmann, the dog's broad muscles beneath my fingers, my nose pressed into his fur so musky after all his travels.

When I looked down into the field again, it seemed that a white daub moved along, though it might not have been so. A thousand silk filaments lined each corn ear. Each thread linked one kernel to the plant's stalk. The white daub might've veered onto the trail of yellow matted grass that continued west. Short and long, narrow and wide all at once, the path coiled and corkscrewed ahead of Mice in more ways than I could believe. The voice asked: *Is that really The Way?* But I knew it was.

ABOUT THE AUTHOR

Stacey Levine is the author of two previous novels, *Dra—* and *Frances Johnson*, and two story collections, *My Horse and Other Stories* and *The Girl with Brown Fur*. Her fiction has appeared in *The Brooklyn Rail*, *Tin House*, *The Iowa Review*, *Yeti*, *The Santa Monica Review*, and other magazines. For her fiction she has received a PEN Award, a Genius Award from Seattle's news weekly *The Stranger*, and numerous prize nominations, grants, and fellowships. She lives and teaches in Seattle.